The year is 1969 . . .

As Sly and the Family Stone sing "I Want To Take You Higher," Americans are aiming higher than ever before. They're raising their consciousness with sit-ins and peace marches. Expanding their minds with transcendental meditation and watching in awe as Neil Armstrong takes man's first steps on the moon.

Hippies are wearing hip-huggers jeans, sandals and patchouli oil. Men have exchanged their suits for turtlenecks, bell-bottoms and desert boots, while women don microminis, maxicoats and thigh-high patent-leather boots.

Laugh-In is the rage on television. Hollywood pairs heartthrobs Paul Newman and Robert Redford in *Butch Cassidy and the Sundance Kid*. And lovers everywhere are dancing to the Beatles' "Something."

It is a time of idealism, as people power forges new dreams of freedom and equality.

It is a time of ambition, as those dreams galvanize a generation to change its world.

It is the time of Jennifer Wright and Lij Branigan.

Dear Reader,

We're sure you are enjoying A Century of American Romance, a nostalgic look back at the twentieth century. These stories give us all a chance to relive the memories of a time gone by and sneak a peek at romance in an exciting future.

We've traveled all the way from the turn-of-the-century immigrant experience through the decades to the free-spirited fifties, where Barbara Bretton recreated the postwar baby boom.

In the months ahead watch for all the titles—one per month—in A Century of American Romance, including next month's book by Elise Title, who tells the poignant story of a group of friends whose lives are interrupted by the Vietnam War.

We hope you continue to enjoy these special stories of nostalgia, written by some of your favorite novelists. As always, we welcome your comments. Please take the time to write to us at the address below.

Here's hoping A Century of American Romance will become part of your most cherished memories....

Sincerely,

Debra Matteucci
Senior Editor & Editorial Coordinator
Harlequin Books
300 East 42nd St.
New York, NY 10017

LIBBY HALL

1960s
**H E A R T S
A T
R I S K**

Harlequin Books

TORONTO • NEW YORK • LONDON
AMSTERDAM • PARIS • SYDNEY • HAMBURG
STOCKHOLM • ATHENS • TOKYO • MILAN

For Alison and Colleen,
who had to read every word,
and the ''Pleasanton'' bunch,
who got bits and pieces

With grateful thanks to the following:

Lt. Col. Martin ''The Big Kahuna'' Kahao III, U.S.A.F., for advice
on the flying sequences and for recognizing and giving
me the name of the Immelman turn.

Ray Neilsen, Chief Scientist, Lockheed Corporation, for letting
me observe his building of an airplane and for opening his
library to me for research on the B-49.

Howard Dewitt, educator, Ohlone Community College, for
information and the use of his library on Woodstock and
the music of the sixties.

Truman Clark, Ph.D., Historian, Edwards Air Force Base, for
answering all my questions about the base, the area, the
test programs . . . by phone.

The Public Relations Offices at the various space centers, for
packets and brochures and photographs and referrals to
the right people with the ''right stuff.''

Published January 1991

ISBN 0-373-16373-8

HEARTS AT RISK

Chapter One

"...Five...four...three...two...one...we have ignition...lift-off..."

The Saturn V rocket lifted from its pad at Cape Kennedy, Florida, like the mighty chariot of a god ascending, with all required dignity and splendor, toward the heavens. The Apollo 11 Mission was on the way to the moon.

Jennifer Wright watched the spectacle from a safe distance—a thousand miles away at the Manned Spacecraft Center in Houston. The viewing room, located behind the Flight Control Room, erupted in cheers as smoke and steam filled the screens of the many TV monitors. A camera inside the spacecraft focused on the three astronauts, Armstrong, Aldrin and Collins, lying side by side in the tight space, their faces invisible behind their visors.

Within milliseconds after lift-off, data on the flight began flowing into banks of computers. A map of the world glowed on a giant screen in the Flight Control Room. On the map, a blip shaped like a rocket indicated the position of the manned spacecraft, already far downrange on its first lap of the earth.

Jennifer mentally ticked off the tracking stations that were monitoring the flight through radio signals sent back to earth by the Apollo transmitters. Grand Bahama, Grand Turk, Antigua, Ascension, Africa, Australia. Faraway places with romantic names, but none so far as the Sea of Tranquility.

Several Australian bushmen had performed a special ceremony to ensure a safe return, she'd read. She wondered what they thought of this strange endeavor. Men often put their hearts and souls into goals that were mad . . . *mad*.

With the capriciousness of the human mind, Jennifer was catapulted back in time to another day when a rocket engine spewed out flame and smoke . . . and death on the Bonneville Salt Flats. . . .

THE DESERT WIND FLATTENED her cotton bellbottoms and long-sleeved shirt against her body. Jeffrey Theodore Morrison, her fiancé, dressed in his fireproof suit, reached for her and took her into his arms. His grin expressed everything he was—fun-loving, cocky with the confidence of his own indestructibility, daring and bold.

Today he was going for the land speed record with the new engine he and his crew had developed.

He kissed her, quickly, lovingly, then pulled on his fireproof hood. The crew chief snapped the helmet into place. Jeff gave her a thumbs-up sign and climbed into the car.

Jennifer moved behind the safety barrier while the engineers and mechanics made their final checks.

"All systems go," the crew chief said. The men joined her behind the barrier and the countdown began.

On ignition, the rocket motor roared; the ground shook. In less than five seconds, the engine had attained maximum thrust and the car had leapt to more than two hundred miles per hour . . . three hundred . . . three hundred fifty . . . the front end tried to rise, to become airborne as if the rocket knew its fate was in the heavens.

"Three ninety . . . three ninety-five . . . four hundred . . . God, he's done it!" the man monitoring the telemetry equipment shouted.

The nose of the vehicle settled down as if resigned to its earthbound status but yawed to the right. Jeff brought it back on course. It stubbornly yawed to the left. In her mind she could hear Jeff curse as he forced it back to the marked line of the straightway.

Slow motion—that's the way Jennifer remembered it later—a slow swerve to one side, then the other, then another and another, each one longer, more uncontrolled than the last, as if the driver couldn't decide on the path he should take.

Next, the vehicle pitched up and down.

Only one movement was left—a total roll of the rocket car—to complete motion along all three axes of rotation. It happened even as she thought of it—a long, spiraling roll.

The fuel exploded into a sheet of flame in which no solid object was visible. One second there had been a car on the salt flat, the next there was nothing but an inferno.

A second explosion followed the initial one. Parts spewed out of a central ball of fire; a flaming tire, whirling like a tiny sun gone mad, spun off across the desert.

Jeff, she tried to cry out but couldn't. Only silent screams issued from her lips....

"ARE YOU ALL RIGHT?" The man next to her in the Mission Control Center's viewing room peered at her in concern.

She nodded and managed a smile. "Too much excitement, I think." With an effort, she unclenched her hands and focused once more on the activities connected with the space shot.

The excitement of the lift-off had settled into a tense, busy checking of data. Inside the control room, she saw Chris Kraft talk to his second-in-command, Gene Krantz. Over the speakers, Neil Armstrong advised, "All onboard systems are go."

Jason and the golden fleece, she thought. Men and their quests. And once they had a dream in hand, they wanted the next one, and the next.

Glancing briefly at the simulated picture of the spacecraft atop the rocket, circling the earth like an inverted candle, she rose and went to the women's lounge.

It was deserted. She slumped onto the sofa and clasped her hands in her lap as memories again claimed her. Six years ago. She had been twenty-two, just out of college...one month before her wedding...1963...John F. Kennedy running for reelection...

"Ask not what your country can do for you, but what you can do for your country," he had said two years earlier.

The idealism of the New Frontier. She smiled, remembering how young and sincere she and her fellow students had been at the time. They had believed so earnestly in Camelot. And Jeffrey...he'd thought the world had been his for the taking. He had lived his life at a reckless pace. Jeffrey, beloved...

Drawing a deep breath, she wrapped her personal dreams in the misty haze of yesterday and put them away. Some dreams, she had learned, never came true. Her life had taken a different direction after her fiancé's death. She had reached her personal goals and was content. Breathing deeply, she rubbed the tight nerves in her neck until they relaxed.

She returned to the viewing room. A couple of hours later, the astronauts left earth orbit.

"They're off!" the man next to her exclaimed, nearly spilling his coffee. "My God, the moon! Kennedy said we would land a man on the moon before the decade was out. He was right."

Jennifer gazed at the TV monitor. Since there was no camera in outer space to record the flight, a simulation indicated where the spacecraft was in relation to the earth and its satellite. The moon was still a long way off.

"JENNY, ARE YOU ALL RIGHT?" Elaine McLeod placed her tray on the table and slipped into the chair opposite Jennifer in the noisy cafeteria. Nearly every table was taken.

"Yes, I'm fine," Jennifer assured her friend. "A-OK, as you space folks like to say."

She and Elaine went back a long way. Both were navy brats. They had met on a base in Greece when they were twelve, just entering puberty and noticing boys. Over the years, they had kept in touch. Their fathers had been sent to the same base near San Francisco during their daughters' last year in high school, and the friendship had grown. They had shared an apartment, along with Tissy, while attending college at Berkeley.

Jennifer and Elaine and Tissy. J-E-T. They had called themselves the Jetters.

"I saw you leave, but I couldn't abandon the VIPs. I had two senators and several other wheels in tow."

Elaine was in public relations. It was she who had urged Jennifer to try for the job of writing educational brochures for NASA for use as teaching aids in schools.

"I just needed to...get away for a minute," she explained.

Elaine pulled a pack of cigarettes from her purse. "Here, have one."

"No, thanks. I've quit."

Elaine's dark shapely eyebrows rose. "Since when?"

"About three months ago. I'm hurt you haven't noticed." Jennifer was glad of the change in subject.

"With this place like a madhouse, I wouldn't notice if my own mother signed up as an astronaut."

"Unless she was on one of your lists."

"Right. I misplaced the list of dignitaries who were to speak to the press right after the shot. I thought Dillon would have a heart attack before I found it."

Dillon was Elaine's boss. "Did you get them lined up according to protocol, or did you wing it?"

Elaine grinned at the teasing tone. "By order of importance. They're speaking their little minds now. CBS wants to interview Chris Kraft as soon as he's free via a hookup with Walter Cronkite, who's down at the Cape." She picked up her fork. "I've got to eat on the run."

Jennifer nodded and finished her meal. Elaine could do more in an hour than most people could in a day. She was tall, slender and had the most graceful walk Jennifer had ever seen. With her thick dark hair and wide-spaced hazel eyes teamed with a quiet, organized determination, she could have succeeded in the fashion world. She had chosen public relations and had landed a job with NASA right after graduation. Three years ago, she had married an astronaut, "Mac" McLeod.

Elaine was independent, goal-oriented and conservative. A cool customer.

Jennifer had been the bridge between Elaine and Tissy when they had roomed together. Banter had sometimes escalated into sparks of disagreement over life and life-style. Elaine had been the practical one. She had reminded the other two when it was time to clean the apartment, when they were out of milk and whose turn it was to go to the grocery. She had kept lists even then.

Tissy was... well, Tissy was Tissy. Theresa Irene Smith, social reformer. She was small and intense, a gypsy waif with her black hair and large brown eyes, her thin body. She took up causes, such as the Youth International Party. "Yippies," they were called by the press, supplanting the beatniks and hippies of earlier years.

What would happen to the YIP now that its leading spokesman, Abbie Hoffman, had been arrested on conspiracy charges, one of the Chicago Eight, who had been accused of a planned disruption of the Democratic Convention?

"Berkeley Radicals" was another term applied to the more vocal of the anti-establishment groups. Tissy and her live-in friend, Bradford, rented an apartment from Jennifer in her old Victorian house in Berkeley. They published an underground newspaper—a minor miracle considering their constant lack of funds and equipment—using her basement as headquarters.

Elaine and Tissy. Her best friends, the first a career-oriented conservative, the other a crusading liberal. She liked and admired them both, although her personal sentiments aligned more with Tissy's. She thought of herself as liberal, but more tolerant than radical.

Elaine pushed back her tray and reached for her cigarettes. She lit one. "When you left earlier, were you thinking of Jeff?"

Jennifer inhaled deeply, let it out slowly. She looked away from the temptation of the smoke that streamed from Elaine's pursed lips. "Yes. For a minute, when the flames shot out, it was like I was back there, standing on the salt flats, watching him die."

"Oh, Jenny."

The compassion in Elaine's voice brought back the burn of tears behind Jennifer's eyes. She managed a thin smile. "It's gone now. I'm all right. Really."

"Are you coming to my get-together this weekend?"

Jennifer wasn't fooled by the apparently new direction of Elaine's thoughts. "Will you be pushing astronauts at me?"

"Of course."

"You know how I feel about the military, or NASA, which is quasi-military."

"Don't bite the hand that feeds you," Elaine said, reminding her of the contract she had with the space agency.

Jennifer accepted the reprimand with good humor. "I'll probably get a reputation as a groupie, but, yes, I'll come. I haven't seen Mac this trip." Jennifer didn't miss the flicker of despair in her friend's eyes. "Something you want to share with me?" she invited.

Elaine gazed at Jennifer for a long minute, sighed and shook her head. "Not now. Maybe when we have a lo-o-ong evening and a shaker of margueritas." She stubbed out the cigarette and raised two fingers in mock salute. "Peace." She took her tray and left.

She's becoming cynical, Jennifer thought. Where had all the bright promises of the graduation speeches gone? Their generation was supposed to "reach for the stars," to set their goals high and accomplish great things.

Well, they were on their way to the moon, weren't they? That was a start.

THE WIND BLEW ACROSS the desert in sultry puffs, creating lazy dust devils that swirled away toward the east. An eagle climbed a thermal and kept an eye on another sojourner in the sky. The thin aircraft cast an odd shadow on the sand. It looked like a huge bat skimming over the Joshua trees, heading for Edwards Air Force Base to the west of them.

Elijah "Lij" Branigan tilted the wing and looked at the rows of military housing, all alike, all dreary, that made up most of the base. The streets were named after test pilots who had crashed in flight-test maneuvers. "Augered in," "bought the farm," those were the common terms among the test jocks for pilots who had died pushing the limits of their craft and their skill.

Lij eased back on the controls and shot up like a kite caught on a March wind. Good response.

"Hey, good buddy, you awake in there?"

His friend, Bill "Batman" Davis, who would try anything with wings, spoke to him through the headset in his usual cowboy drawl. Lij knew the closest Bill had ever come to a cow was a half-raw steak on a platter with a side order of fries.

Bill was flying chase today. Together they formed a flying unit, a partnership based on mutual trust. Bill was one of the best pilots in the air force, but not as good as Yeager. Nobody was as good as the colonel. As director of the Aerospace Research Pilot School, Yeager used to take up an F-104 and wax Lij's and Bill's tails regularly in mock dogfights.

Lij liked having Bill along in the chase plane. When things got rough, Bill would be there, observing the experimental plane on the verge of coming unglued and making suggestions that might save the test pilot's hide.

"Say, good buddy," he'd once suggested to Lij, "whyn'tcha let some of that fuel out with the hand valve there behind your head? Lighten up the load some. Hey, you hear me in there? You awake or what? HEY, STUPID, PAY ATTENTION. I'M GONNA ASK QUESTIONS LATER." And he'd saved Lij's neck, bringing him back from the brink of unconsciousness long enough to do the task.

It worked both ways. Lij had talked Bill down more than once.

"Yeah, Bill, I'm awake," Lij answered. He checked the dials. "She looks good. Think I'll make a run at it."

The plane was hardly more than a gigantic wing, a flying delta filled to the brim with fuel that exploded at the most inconvenient times—like when the pilot was trying to get the hell out.

He was pushing the outside of the envelope today, taking the plane a little higher, a little faster than she'd ever gone before. "Be a lady," he admonished, and kicked in the afterburner.

He'd already gone through the sound barrier, the shock wave extending past him in a long triangular cone of sound he couldn't hear. The Wing stuck her nose in the air like a snooty debutante and sailed across the sky, up, up and away.

He hummed a bar from the song by The Fifth Dimension. Only they'd been singing about a balloon, not a rocket plane nosing the edge of space.

He checked the gauge on his oxygen supply. A-OK. He relied solely on his life-support equipment just like ol' Neil up there heading for the moon.

A man on the moon! Hot damn!

The g-suit squeezed Lij's legs and torso, stopping the blood from pooling there and leaving his brain to starve. Fifty thousand feet and he'd left most of the protective blanket of air that seemed to hold him to the earth. Sixty thousand and the sky was indigo. Stars appeared although the sun was still shining.

"Ah, how sweet it is," he crooned to the ship as he eased over for the trip down. He went through a few seconds of zero gravity at the top of the parabola. That was nothing new. He'd flown three of the original Mercury astronauts in training bouts of weightlessness in an old air force cargo plane.

The plane bucked a bit. "Come on, lady, don't let me down." He felt the shudder, faint at first, like the first tremors of a woman reaching climax, and coaxed, "Easy, sweetheart. Let it come slow and easylike."

The tremors escalated into an up-and-down pitch, then the plane yawed from side to side. "Damn," he said to Bill.

"Inertia coupling" was the term for pitching, yawing and rolling violently. The pilots just said she "uncorked." It was like being in a concrete mixer that was falling off a bridge, everything going every which way.

Lij did nothing. The pilots had already learned not to fiddle with the controls during this nasty show of temperament. Nothing helped. If he was lucky, she'd flop out into a nosedive. Hell, he knew how to get out of those. No, it was when she went down—spinning like a pancake, tumbling end over end—that was when things got hairy.

The buffeting grew worse. He was hitting the top, the sides, the front of the plane. Warning lights were flashing on. The panel looked like a Christmas tree. He saw it through a blur. He was losing consciousness.

"Hey, buddy, you awake?" Bill asked on the radio.

"Yeah, barely," Lij answered. He caught a glimpse of something graze by, barely missing the canopy.

"You just blew out part of an engine," Bill informed him. "You'd better do something."

"Tell 'em . . . I don't want a damned . . . street named after me."

The denser atmosphere saved him as he fell out of the sky with less grace than a fractured goose. The craft went into a spiral as if some invisible god held one wing tip and twirled the plane around and around as it fell. Now it might be safe to eject.

"Ol' buddy, I'd get out of there if I was you," Bill advised. "Your tail section's looking scorched."

"Yeah, I noticed," Lij radioed back. "Kinda hot on the backside." He ejected at fifteen thousand feet.

The plane made a new crater in the desert floor when it hit. It exploded and burned.

From his position under the parachute, Lij observed the fire engine and ambulance race the seven miles from Edwards. By the time he was down and they had arrived—the fire engine winning by half a length—there was nothing left of the plane but ashes. He rode the ambulance back to the base.

"You okay?" one of the medics asked.

"Got a sore rib," Lij said.

They stripped him out of his flight suit. "Damn," the first medic said, looking at the bruises. "You have a jack-ass in that plane with you?"

"Naw, just smacked my side when I blew through the roof."

"Well, you don't have more than a dozen cracked ribs, I'd say at a rough guess." He grinned at Lij. "The general's mad as hell about you tearing up his new toy. He's gonna read you your rights, then he's gonna throw the book at you."

"Well," Lij said, wincing as the medic felt his ribs, "that's better than having a street named after me."

AFTER SLEEPING FOR NEARLY two days from the pain-killers the doc gave him, Lij drifted over to the Officer's Club late in the afternoon of the third, thirsty after a five-hour debriefing on the crash. Bill was there.

"Well, you made it back to the land of the free and the home of the brave," he said when Lij sat down. He chuck-led at the grimace on his friend's face as pain accompanied every move. "I coulda told ya to stay away from those wild women." Bill, using two fingers, beat a rapid *tat-tat* on the Formica table top in time with the acid rock blaring from the old jukebox.

"Thanks. Be a sport and get me a cold one. I've an-swered more questions in the last hour than I have in my whole life."

Lij pushed a lock of dark hair off his forehead while Bill went to the bar. His eyes, dark gray like a Montana thun-dercloud, moved restlessly over the occupants of the club. He'd be off work for a month due to the ribs. Maybe he'd hitch a ride over to Houston and visit his old friend and mentor, Dr. Benton. The former CalTech professor was a top gun at NASA and he wanted Lij to join the astronaut program.

"Here ya go." Bill slid a bottle and glass toward Lij and sat back down. He pushed his cowboy hat off his forehead and looked the women over. All were married or with a male friend. "Let's go to town. I feel like dancing." He sang along with the Stones' latest record, "Honky-tonk Woman," with more verve and inflection than Mick Jagger.

Lij gave him an amused glance. "The spirit's willing but the body's a wreck."

"Oh, yeah, I forgot. Sorry."

Lij poured the beer, drank deeply, then wiped his mouth with the back of his hand. "Ah, the elixir of life. I feel better already." He settled deeper into the chair. "Think I'll head over to Houston for a while."

"Give my best to the kid."

"Yeah, I will."

The assumption that Lij's daughter would remember Bill was a myth the two men kept up between them. Amy had been injured in a car accident and had lain comatose for weeks. When she awoke, the doctors found her brain had been damaged. She was irreversibly retarded.

"Gonna see Brenda?"

The question was casual, but Lij wasn't deceived. Brenda was the widow of a good friend. Lij and Bill and a couple of other test pilots had been keeping an eye on her for the past few months. She'd moved back to Houston to be close to her parents, mostly for the sake of her two kids.

An unexpected spasm hit his heart. That happened every once in a while. He'd see a kid that reminded him of his own little girl and the pain would hit, coming in low, hard and fast, before he had time to raise his defenses.

Lij studied his friend, looking for clues to the depths of his feelings about Brenda. Generally, the single men closed ranks around their own. After a decent time, the widow would indicate a preference, nothing overt, but maybe she'd smile brighter for one man or bake him a birthday cake, and the rest would know and back off. Brenda had given Lij the go-ahead by inviting him to her parents' anniversary dinner. He'd had to miss that. It was time for him to make the next move.

What move did he want to make? "I don't know, old son. I suppose so."

Was that disappointment in Bill's eyes?

"Then, how's about I drop you off in Texas," Bill suggested. "I've got a plane to transport to Langley, but I can lay over in Houston for a day or two. Been invited to a moon-landing party. Do you want to come along? We can take Brenda, too."

Lij realized the trip was important to Bill. His friend, a Harvard graduate with a mile-long pedigree who'd never worked on a ranch in his life, forgot to use his good-ol'-boy accent at the last. Lij raised his glass in salute. "You're on."

LIJ GOT OUT OF THE rental car, gift in hand, and walked into the children's convalescent center on the outskirts of Houston, near where the space complex had been laid out. At the desk, he was told his daughter was out on the lawn. He went to find her.

Amy recognized him when he walked across the grass. He was grateful for small miracles, having given up on big ones months ago. "Da," she cried and lifted her arms.

He sat on the grass beside her and let her clamber into his lap with her awkward, coltish movements. She was five, but her mind would always hover in a misty realm somewhere around two. Not even that, really, for at two she had been inquisitive and stubborn and alert. Now she was mostly passive, content to let the world slide past without notice.

She'd been three, the most loving, trusting person he had ever known, when she'd been injured in the automobile crash. Sometimes just looking at her caused an ache inside worse than a cracked rib.

The nurse greeted him with a smile. Mrs. Murrin was a calm, older woman with a comforting manner. He was at ease with her.

"Good morning, Mr. Branigan. We weren't expecting you until the end of the month. Amy's been enjoying the sun. She likes butterflies, I think. She watched one quite a while."

She, too, kept up the myth of Amy's interest in the world. "I got a few days off," he replied, barely suppressing a groan as Amy leaned into his sore body.

"Mine," she said, her fingers busy at the paper on the gift. She took for granted that anything he had in his hands was hers. She had learned that in two years.

Butter mints were her favorites. He helped her open the box before she lost patience and screamed in anger, then watched as she stuffed a candy into her mouth. She grinned at him, and he thought she looked brighter, more alert.

"I'll leave you two to visit while I fill out her lunch choices for the week." Mrs. Murrin rose from the bench.

"Fine," he said, tucking a strand of baby-fine hair out of the way of Amy's sticky mouth.

He let her eat the box of mints. "All gone," he said when she shook it several times, then peered inside.

Her face puckered up in a frown. She had little understanding of limits and less tolerance for frustration. He took the box, opened the other end, and made tooting sounds through it as if it was a musical instrument.

Amy grinned, then laughed. She grabbed the box from him. She stuck it to her mouth and made *ooo-ooo-ooo* sounds, happy with the new toy, the candy already forgotten.

The anger he thought he'd gotten over flamed up in him. He remembered one time when his wife had derided him for getting Amy out of bed at midnight to witness a spectacular meteor shower.

"For heaven's sake, she's only two years old," Rona had complained. "She won't even remember."

"I will," he had answered, wanting the child to experience all the wonder of the world right from the start of her life, feeling it was somehow important. When she was older, he'd tell her about it and she might remember.

He balled his hand into a fist, then opened it to stroke the fine blond hair that curled around his daughter's face. What would she remember now? Her blue eyes stared at him as if she had never seen him before.

"Da?"

"Yeah, that's me. Daddy. Can you say Daddy?"

She grinned. "Da," she said. She tore the flap off the box.

He'd never forgiven Rona. She'd taken Amy to a party with some of her wild friends and gotten stoned. They had decided to go for a ride for some reason. The driver had run through a red light into the path of an oncoming truck. Rona and another woman had been killed instantly. Lij sometimes thought he would have killed her himself if the truck hadn't. Each time he looked at Amy and thought of the person she should have been, he felt the rage swell up inside him and wanted to hit something.

Part of it was his own guilt, he realized. If he hadn't given in to Rona's demands that he leave the air force and take the engineering job with an aerospace company, they'd have stayed at Edwards where he flew in the flight-test program. She wouldn't have fallen in with that wild bunch in Houston. Irresponsible hippies, against everything and in favor of nothing but their own selfish pleasure. If It Feels Good, Do It was their motto.

He sighed and let the anger go. It had happened. It was done. He lifted a blond curl, smoothed it and let it wrap itself around his finger.

For Amy's sake, he'd gone back into test flying, not for the air force, but for the company that built the planes. He'd signed a two-hundred-thousand-dollar contract to fly their experimental planes. Most of that had gone immediately into a trust fund so Amy could continue to live in this special home that had been so good for her. He felt better knowing she'd be safe in case anything happened to him.

Lij was just finishing his second contract and had been offered a third. With the bonuses he had received for flying over Mach two and higher than fifty thousand feet, plus his pay as an air-force reserve officer, he had no money worries.

Still, it was tempting to join the astronaut program. His home base would be here in Houston where he would be close to Amy. So far, he had managed to visit her often with the company jet that was at his disposal one weekend of every month per his contract. But if he lived here, he could see her every weekend, maybe take her to his place for visits once in a while.

"It's time for her therapy," Mrs. Murrin said, apology in her voice as she interrupted his musings. "She's turned into a water baby and loves to swim."

"You're doing a super job with her," he said. He set his daughter on her feet. "Bye, Toots, see you in the funny paper. Can you give me a kiss?"

Amy gave him a solemn smile. She kissed him on the cheek. "Bye," she said. She took her nurse's hand and walked off without a backward glance. Lij knew she'd already forgotten him.

For a moment, he felt the godawful aloneness come over him. It happened each time Amy walked away, unaware of his need for her love, for the way her eyes used to light up when he came home from work, the way she would run to him, arms raised to be swept up and tossed into the air, the way she had reached for the stars when he had showed her the meteor shower. All of life's promises had been in her beautiful blue eyes, his beautiful little girl....

He blinked hard, then picked up the pieces of the candy box and stuffed them into his pocket. No, he wasn't ready for marriage again. He doubted he'd ever be. It had been hell all around for both him and Rona.

As he walked back to the car, he acknowledged they'd wanted different things. He'd been content at Edwards, flying the experimental planes, knocking back a few beers with the other flight-test jocks, then going home to his wife and kid. Rona'd been bored, had hated the desert, the barren ugliness of the base. It hadn't been the glamorous adventure she'd envisioned.

Since the accident, he had lived for two things—Amy and flying. If he needed anything more, well, there were always women glad to offer a bit of companionship without too many demands.

The decision regarding Brenda had been made a long time ago, he realized. He'd tell Bill the field was clear. Lij Branigan wasn't interested in exclusive rights to any woman.

Chapter Two

Four days, six hours, forty-five minutes, fifty-seven seconds after takeoff, the lunar module settled lightly on the surface of the moon.

Armstrong: "Houston, Tranquility Base here. The *Eagle* has landed."
Capcom (Spacecraft Communicator Charles Duke, Houston): "Roger, Tranquility. We copy you on the ground. You got a bunch of guys about to turn blue. We're breathing again. Thanks a lot."

The silence in the living room of the suburban ranch house in Sharpstown also broke as the guests murmured their relief. Elaine passed through with a new pitcher of margueritas and filled glasses that had mysteriously emptied during the past few minutes, no one remembering sipping the icy drink.

Jennifer returned to the kitchen and finished preparing the hot hors d'oeuvres, which were little hot dogs wrapped in biscuits. Neither she nor Elaine was deep into the domestic scene.

"Pigs in a blanket doesn't quite have the proper ring," Elaine complained, following Jennifer into the kitchen. "Couldn't we call them *crêpe de cochon?*"

"You can call them whatever you want, but they're still hot dogs and biscuits," Jennifer answered, giving a final pat to one roll before placing it on the tray.

Elaine poured a can of concentrated limeade into a large bowl along with one can of tequila and a third of Triple Sec. She blended it with a hand mixer, poured the concoction into the pitcher and stirred in shaved ice.

"Presto, Texas margueritas," Jennifer commented after watching the process. She took the glass Elaine poured for her and sipped. "Very refreshing."

"A compliment from a dedicated California hippie?"

"Well, wine is the beverage of choice, but when in Texas—"

"Do as the Texans do," Elaine finished.

They laughed, but Jennifer saw the shadows in Elaine's eyes. "You and Mac have a fight?" she asked casually, turning back to the food preparation.

Elaine rubbed a finger around the edge of her marguerita glass for a moment before answering. Then, "Mac wants a baby," she said. She laughed without humor. "The whole cotton-picking family wants a baby. Mac is the only son, the only grandson, the bearer of the family name. He's thirty-one, I'm twenty-eight. What are we waiting for?"

"What *are* you waiting for?"

"Dillon will be retiring in a few years and I want his job. Someday I'd like to be head of the entire PR department. If I take time off to have a child, I'll be passed over. That's the way the system works."

"Wouldn't they hold your job for you?"

"Yes, but..." She shrugged. "The mentality of the business world is not mother-oriented. Maybe I should have done like you, stayed single." She picked up the pitcher from the table. "Well, this is a party. Let's have fun." She walked out to her guests.

Jennifer thought over Elaine's comments. Hadn't she and Mac talked about their future plans before they married? There was a stiffness between them that bespoke serious disagreement. Mac was in the space program; perhaps that was the root of the problem.

Rumors about the astronauts were as thick as flies around a cattle barn. Some of them were true. The men were idolized; the world lay at their feet—and some of the world's women. One groupie claimed to have slept with all of them but John Glenn. Mac had not been excepted from the group.

Thinking of the rumors reminded her of the article she was planning to write for Tissy and Bradford's underground paper, the *Berkeley Free Press*. Bradford wanted a big exposé, including sex and scandal as well as a comparison of the cost of the space program versus the amount being spent on social services in America. She'd agreed to do only the latter.

Since arriving at the space center and experiencing the excitement of the moon shot, Jennifer was tugged in two directions. On the one hand, she was filled with the shining vision of the future that the space program presented; on the other, she was disturbed about the money expended on a mad dash to the moon while people starved in Biafra.

Shouts and laughter from the back patio turned her thoughts in a different direction. Several of the single astronauts-to-be had brought young women who were very voluptuous, to say the least. There had been a lot of horse-play and flirting among the group, not always confined to the single guys.

Jennifer didn't like it. She wasn't a prude, nor was she generally censorious, but sexual teasing and baiting offended the moral principles she had been raised with. Tissy and Bradford weren't married, but neither were they promiscuous. They were committed to each other as well as to their causes.

She debated with herself about using personal information in her article—sort of a morals-and-money exposé. She'd been to several parties and was a receptive listener. People liked to talk to her. She'd gathered a lot of details and could write a sizzling account of space doings. But should she? Human lives were involved here.

She removed the last pan of snacks from the oven, dumped them into a towel-lined basket and took it out to the picnic table on the lanai next to the pool.

"Jen, here's someone I want you to meet," Mac called out. He wasn't a large man—none of the astronauts were—but the Texan's voice was booming and his gestures were expansive. He waved her over.

She set the basket down and walked across the patio to Elaine and Mac. Two men and a woman waited with them.

"This is our token liberal," Mac joked, indicating Jennifer, then he introduced his friend. "This is my good buddy from jock school, Bill Davis, better known as Batman."

Jennifer knew that Mac referred to the test pilot training school at Edwards and guessed that Batman was the pilot's flying name. Mac had been Texas. What else?

"Glad to meet you," she said. She held her hand out in the straightforward way that men used, which sometimes surprised people.

Bill returned her greeting and introduced his friends, Brenda, a widow who lived in Houston, and his flying buddy from Edwards, Lij Branigan.

"I'm sorry. I didn't get your name," the new man said.

"Jennifer Wright," she replied.

The woman guest was around thirty, very pretty with large blue eyes and a bouffant hairdo held off her face by a blue ribbon. The other pilot stood an inch taller than Mac;

around six feet, Jennifer guessed. He looked like a gymnast with wide shoulders tapering to a trim waist and hips. His hair was dark brown, his eyes charcoal gray. His voice had been nice—deep, quiet, a slight drawl but not Texan.

"Nice meeting you," he said without a flicker of pleasure in his eyes, although his smile appeared sincere.

"Another Connecticut cowboy," Elaine teased.

"No, ma'am," Bill said. "Lij is the gen-u-wine article. A Montana cowpoke, born and bred."

"Bill is from back East, went to Harvard," Mac explained to Jennifer. "Try not to hold it against him."

"We're glad you could join us," Elaine assured the unexpected guests. "But I've got to see about dinner. The steaks are ready to go on," she told Mac.

"The little lady speaks," Bill said solemnly, then ruined it with a big grin across his fair, freckled face.

Quite a contrast, Jennifer thought as she excused herself and followed Elaine into the kitchen. Bill looked and acted like a cowboy, successfully hiding his eastern upbringing behind his incongruous red-blond hair, freckles and fake drawl, while his friend, with his quiet, remote manner, fitted her image of the favorite son of some industrial tycoon.

Military pilots. She put them in the same class with astronauts. All were risk takers, arrogant in their belief of their own immortality. "The chosen of the gods," Jeffrey had once teased her when she voiced her fears. She avoided such men like the plague, or the Asian flu that had gone around a couple of years back and made her sick enough to die for two miserable weeks.

LIJ LOUNGED AGAINST A POST and watched the crowd around the pool. Dinner was over and now a few couples were dancing to some slow music on the stereo.

Everyone in Houston seemed to have a modern ranch house with a pool and fancy stereo. Some of the men, like

Mac, still wore their hair in flat tops or crew cuts, instead of the longer styles that were currently popular. A couple of them were in leisure suits while the younger men all wore low-riding jeans and sports shirts. The women reminded him of Annette Funicello with their fluffy, swept-back hair. He noticed Brenda fitted the same mold.

He had been relieved when she'd accepted Bill's invitation to the party. It had let him off the hook and assured him that the pretty widow had no intense feelings for him.

A movement at the edge of the crowd caught his eye. Jennifer. He remembered her name. She had flitted around the edges of the party, helping Elaine keep the food and drinks supplied.

She was different from the other women. For one thing, her hair was long, halfway down her back and held off her face by two old-fashioned tortoiseshell combs. It flowed in rippling waves of brown-gold and curled up at the ends. A California girl, he thought. This time his smile was in his eyes as well as on his lips.

Where the rest of the women wore slacks or shorts or short dresses, she wore a blue skirt reaching almost to her ankles. Her white blouse was worn outside the skirt with a gold belt at the waist. Love beads bounced between her full breasts. Copper earrings in the form of peace symbols dangled from her ears.

Peacenik, hippie or fashion follower, he wondered. She didn't seem to care for the company, judging by her evasive tactics. He had wanted to talk to her, but hadn't found an opportunity.

Laughter and ribald shouts on the patio claimed his attention. Mac and one of the younger women, her skirt almost to the top of her thighs, were doing the twist to Chubby Checker's old hit.

The young woman shimmied her way around Mac, who was no sloppy dancer himself, Lij saw. He also noticed that his host was feeling no pain due to the margueritas he and several guests had been downing as if they were fruit juice.

Jennifer frowned at the display on the patio. It was just a dance, but it was unlike Mac to make a spectacle of himself. She looked around. Elaine was standing in the shadows, her eyes fixed upon the couple. A flicker of pain mixed with anger crossed her face, then she went inside the house.

On impulse, Jennifer moved forward and stepped into the cleared space just as another person did the same. It was the cowboy test pilot. Lij Branigan from Montana.

With a bantering smile, Jennifer tapped the girl on the shoulder and neatly slid into her place. Lij caught the other woman's hand and twirled her into step with him.

Jennifer swung around beside Mac and gave him a bump with her hip. Everyone laughed and applauded. Together, she and Mac twisted their way down to a low position and back up. At the end of the number, the four dancers bowed and threw kisses to the cheering audience.

There were twenty-four people present, but it seemed a crowd to Jennifer. She was tired of the party. It reminded her of those she had gone to in Berkeley, except here, everyone was very much establishment. At Berkeley, everyone was a dedicated liberal. Here, the conversation revolved around politics, space and fishing in the Gulf; there, it was politics, protests and mantras.

She glanced at Lij. He was obviously career military, and probably supported the government's position on Vietnam without even thinking about it. Robot soldier. Did he even realize the Gulf of Tongkin attacks had been trumped up by Johnson and McNamara so they could send U.S. troops into combat?

She saw him look at his watch as if he, too, were impatient for the evening to be over. Jennifer remembered the purpose of the party. "It's time for the moon walk," she announced, taking charge since Elaine was nowhere in sight.

They trooped into the family room where Walter Cronkite was talking during a replay of the lift-off four days ago. She pushed Mac into an easy chair and perched on the arm of it, holding him captive and keeping the blonde at bay.

The telecast switched to a camera inside the lander. The view from the module window showed a barren rock-strewn plain.

Jennifer felt her heart contract when Neil Armstrong stepped outside the hatch and climbed down the ladder. "That's one small step for man, one giant leap for mankind," he said and made the final step.

"Way to go!"

"All right!"

"Far out!" one of the aspiring astronauts exclaimed, drawing a laugh at his hip expression.

"Groovy," the blonde said, and gave the man next to her a kiss on his jaw.

Jennifer tensed as the man's wife sent a threatening look across the room. Something had to be done. A hand touched Jennifer's shoulder in a reassuring grip and she looked up.

Lij Branigan leaned down to her ear. "Do you know who brought her?" he asked.

Jennifer shook her head.

"Let's circulate and see if we can find out. I think it's time she went home."

"Before she gets a knife in the back?" Jennifer said, giving him a grim smile.

"Right."

They moved separately among the other guests, murmuring questions, but no one claimed the blonde. They met at the kitchen door.

"I'd offer to take her home," Lij said, "but I rode over with Bill."

"I have a car," Jennifer said. They looked at each other.

Her eyes were blue, he noticed, not bright blue, but kind of subdued, like a Montana sky just before twilight. "Shall we go?" he asked.

Resigned to her fate, she nodded.

Lij spoke to Bill while she told Elaine they were leaving.

"You and Lij?" Elaine said, her eyes widening.

"And the blonde. Do you remember if she brought a purse or coat? I doubt if she does. I hope she remembers where she lives."

"She came with somebody..." Elaine tried to think who.

"Well, he's not claiming her now." Jennifer kissed her friend on the cheek. "Talk to Mac. Don't just let things go until you drift apart."

Tears formed in Elaine's eyes, but her face hardened. "We have talked. It doesn't do any good."

Before Jennifer could respond, Lij appeared at her elbow. "Ready?"

"Here, let me get her purse. I think I remember where she put it." Elaine retrieved it from the guest bedroom. "Good night."

Lij, with an arm around the young woman, followed Jennifer out to the rental car. "Jennifer, this is Stacy. Stacy, Jennifer."

"What's she coming for?" Stacy demanded.

"She's driving," he explained as he put Stacy in the back seat and climbed in beside her.

Jennifer got in front and started the engine. "Where to, sir?" she asked. She was unable to keep the cynical amusement from showing through.

He was quick on the uptake. "Home, James," he intoned.

She caught the quick flash of his grin in the rearview mirror. "Which way?" she asked, coming to the stop sign at the end of the street.

"Where do you live?" Lij asked Stacy. She whispered in his ear and he relayed the information to Jennifer. "Turn left, go to the third light. She lives in the building on the corner."

Jennifer drove there. At the apartment, Lij helped Stacy out and up the steps. "Oh, thank you," the girl said politely to Jennifer, surprising them with her manners.

Jennifer remembered the purse. She took it to the couple and dug out the door key. Lij opened it.

She retreated to the car and let Lij handle their goodbyes. He appeared before long. Grinning, he quipped, "Quick. Get me out of here."

Jennifer took off with a squeal of tires. At the stoplight, she glanced at him. Their eyes met and they grinned, then they laughed. He touched her shoulder, sending warmth cascading along her arm.

"You're a good sport," he said.

"You, too..." She hesitated. "Thanks for helping save Mac tonight."

"My...uh...pleasure." He smiled. "How about a cup of coffee and a piece of pie? There's an all-night café at the hotel where I'm staying."

Jennifer considered his invitation. It seemed harmless. "That sounds good."

But she wasn't so sure once they were on their way. The night enclosed them in companionable silence. The air was hot and humid, typical of Gulf Coast towns in the summer.

The two of them had shared an adventure...of sorts. That fact, plus the lateness of the hour, lent a greater intimacy to their journey than it warranted. A faint stirring inside, which she recognized as sexual interest, bothered her.

This isn't a date, she told herself when she pulled into the parking lot of his hotel and stopped. She didn't mention this was her hotel, too. It was a natural choice—closest to the Space Center. Everyone stayed there.

Lij immediately got out and came around to open her door. She opened it herself, but let him take her arm to guide her inside. His touch caused the warm sensation to travel her arm again. She remembered how graceful he had looked when he danced. He had moved easily, his body comfortable with the beat of the music.

His manner was assured. He wasn't a shy cowpoke unused to women. On the contrary, he had all the confidence of a military jock, and Lord knew she had met plenty of those over the years. Her father and grandfather had been career navy men.

A television set up in one corner of the café showed the men reentering the lunar lander after their historic two hours and forty minutes of work. Sixty-five miles above the moon, Collins waited in the orbiting command ship, *Columbia*. Jennifer and Lij watched as the maneuver was accomplished.

"Well, it's done," Lij said. "A man was actually on the moon, two of them, in fact."

Jennifer noted the satisfaction in his voice, the quiet sense of pride in his smile. She felt the same. Maybe it had been a mad scheme, but she couldn't help the feeling of personal fulfillment, as if she had had a hand in the task herself. It warred with her beliefs over the inanity of the goal.

She studied Lij while he watched the newsmen discussing the event. He was a handsome man, with shining dark hair neatly parted on one side and not quite brushing his collar in the back. Hadn't his friend said he was from Edwards?

"Neil Armstrong was a civilian test pilot before joining the astronaut program. He worked at Edwards, too, didn't he?" she asked, curious about Lij.

"Umm-hmm." He related an incident when Neil had gotten an experimental plane stuck in the mud at Rogers Lake. "Colonel Yeager told him the dry lake wasn't dry."

"Didn't Neil believe him?"

Lij chuckled. "Never met a jock yet who didn't think he could assess a situation at a glance and come up with his own decision."

"Including you?"

He studied her as if considering the effect of his answer before saying, "Yeah, including me."

Was there just a tad of challenge in the tilt of his chin? She decided to ignore it. "Are you in flight test?" She remembered that was the way the men referred to aircraft testing.

He nodded.

"In the air force?"

"The reserve. Like Armstrong, I'm a civilian pilot."

Warning lights flashed in her mind. Fighter pilots were known to be supremely confident males who thought they could call all the shots. Those who went on to become test pilots were the worst of the lot, she gathered from her research.

He studied her expression. "You don't approve?"

He wanted to provoke a response in her, he discovered, this straightforward woman who shook hands like a man and looked you in the eye while doing it. She was a master at evasion. He had tried to pin her down several times during the evening, but she was forever on the flit. Now he had her. The thought brought its own response. He grinned at the tightening in his body. He wished.

She shrugged, setting her peace earrings jangling just below her jawline. She had clean features, well-molded and firm. She was a woman who could make decisions, Lij surmised. As soon as he'd seen her head for the patio where Mac and the blonde were dancing earlier, he had known what she had intended to do. He had joined her, deliberately pairing himself with her in her effort to help her friends.

He'd never had to use tactics to get close to a woman before. Her elusiveness interested him. A beautiful woman who wasn't turned on by a roomful of astronauts? That made her different from ninety-nine percent of the other women he'd ever met.

"What about yourself? How do you know so much about Edwards?" he asked, intrigued by this facet of her as much as anything else.

"I'm going to write some educational pamphlets for NASA on the space program—"

"You work for NASA?" he broke in.

"I'm on my own. I do free-lance writing. For this job, I needed to know the history of the rocket planes. I found it very interesting." She paused, then added, "We can't keep sending men up in disposable rockets and having them splash down somewhere in the ocean forever, can we?"

"No," he agreed, "we can't."

"I think it was a mistake to cancel the X-15 program. Don't you?" Jennifer knew that technical or philosophical talk from a woman was guaranteed to put a man to sleep or on the defensive in thirty seconds. She wanted to discourage the growing warmth she saw in his eyes.

"Yes." He couldn't discuss the programs that were going forward; they were top secret. But he sensed in her a kindred spirit who could share his enthusiasm for science and exploration.

To discover something new or prove a hypothesis was an adventure as great as the moon walk to him. He instinctively knew she would understand. Should he mention he had a degree in astrophysics? Would that impress the hell out of her or what?

"Are you free tomorrow afternoon?" he asked. He'd have lunch with Amy, but he was free the rest of the day. "We could go for a drive to the beach. I have a car," he added.

"I'm sorry. I'll be working all day." Actually, she could take the time off. That was one of the advantages of being self-employed. She knew he was cognizant of that fact. "The astronauts will be leaving the moon. I need to take notes."

"How about dinner, then?" he suggested casually, though he didn't feel that way at all. He knew she was going to say no and it was a new experience.

She shook her head. Her smile was apologetic.

On the television, the news was wrapping up. Cronkite said they would be back on the air for the next major event. He gave his signature sign-off: "And that's the way it is."

And so it was, Lij thought. He had asked; she had refused. It was her prerogative, but it irritated the hell out of him.

"I'll walk you to your car," he said. He'd be the perfect gentleman, he decided. He laid out the money for the check.

"I'm staying here." Her grin seemed to mock him. "Everyone does, it seems."

"Yeah."

He escorted her to her room on the second floor, then went to his on the fourth. Restless energy crackled with every step. A shower was what he needed—a cold one.

Later, lying in bed, he thought of her. The way her eyes were always guarded, the way she had sidestepped his attempts to see her. But there had been times when he had seen interest in her eyes, when she had studied him when she thought he wouldn't notice.

He found her intriguing, this lovely woman who was polite, intelligent and reserved without being coy. Not all his reactions to her were mental, he acknowledged. She was damned good-looking.

Going over the events of the evening, he acknowledged he'd made the right decision about Brenda. She was his best friend's widow and he felt a certain responsibility for her, even attraction to her, but it was nothing more. There had never been a—a spark between them, a rush of interest that demanded further exploration.

Yeah, he'd been right. He wasn't in the market for marriage and its tribulations. He had Amy. He had flying. That was all he heeded.

And that's the way it is.

Roger that, Walt.

Chapter Three

Jennifer was back in the viewing room in Mission Control for the start of the return trip to Earth. The range clock read 195:18:35.0, which she knew stood for the hours, minutes and seconds of Mission Elapsed Time, the time since Apollo 11 had been lifted off the launch pad at Cape Kennedy by the mighty Saturn V rocket. The trip home would take about sixty hours. But first they had to get off the moon.

She dutifully made notes while a docent from the public-relations office explained what was happening. There were very few guests now, only reporters and people like herself who were writing specific articles and books on the project.

Stifling a yawn, she scrawled a note to herself in the margin: "Lunch with someone?"

"Yes," a male voice answered.

Deep, quiet, a faint drawl. She'd know it anywhere.

Lij took the chair next to her. "Where would you like to go?"

"I think I'm spoken for, but I don't remember who," she said. She raised and dropped one shoulder. "Elaine is arranging it."

"I know. With Dr. Benton, head of Flight Dynamics. I was in his office when she dropped by."

"Oh."

He radiated power...no, the potential for power, like the Saturn V when it had still been at Complex 39, little trails of vapor steaming off its sides. 7.75 million pounds of thrust. She had felt a shiver down her spine just looking at the rocket and realizing its strength. She felt one now as she looked at Lij.

"Thanks for the information." Her smile was dismissive. Because of her reaction to him, she now tried to be brusque, cool, to view him as just another man and not a very interesting one at that. It didn't work.

She gauged her smile by his reaction and thought it had been just right—not too friendly, not too distant. She saw his eyes narrow. Contrarily, a slight smile appeared at the corners of his mouth While she watched, the smile grew into a grin.

"I'll be joining you. Benton asked me to bring you to the lobby when you were through here."

She had to have an escort to meander around the buildings. Was she being maneuvered? Or out-maneuvered?

Her smile segued into a frown. His became stubborn. With a sudden insight, she realized she was handling him wrong. If she'd been firtatious like that bleached blonde last night, he would have run for cover. Her aloofness intrigued him, she saw. He probably considered her a challenge.

"Don't you have work to do?" she asked. "When do you test the experimental planes?"

"I'm doing my reserve duty." He gingerly took a deep breath, testing his ribs. After half-carrying the blonde into her apartment, he'd expected to be in pain today, but he felt okay. "The air force has assigned me to NASA for three weeks." He laughed wryly. "I suspect at Dr. Benton's request."

"To do what?" she asked, curious in spite of her own caution.

"Look at guidance procedures for Apollo 12, which is coming up in November."

Here was information she could use, and she was tempted to question him. She thought better of it. "Let's go," she said abruptly, edging past him.

He caught her arm when they were outside the viewing room and heading down one of the long corridors in Building 30. "No need to rush. Benton will be late. He always forgets the time."

"I want to go over my notes."

After their camaraderie of the previous night, Lij resented her cool treatment. "Is there some reason we can't be on friendly terms? You have an insanely jealous boyfriend or something?" He managed a wry tone.

"I don't care for your type," she said.

Those subtle blue eyes looked at him without giving away a thing. She was a cool one, sure enough. Except for the telltale tremor of her hands clutching a Bic pen and her notebook.

His eyes swept over her business suit. Dark blue with a white blouse, no frills, no love beads, no peace symbols. The hem of her skirt ended a modest inch above her knees...great legs...plain shoes with sensible heels...demure pearls in her ears...today's businesswoman.

"What type is that?" he drawled, warming to the fray.

Jennifer gave him an oblique appraisal. His light gray pants and white shirt with a gray-and-burgundy tie were impeccable. He wore clothes with the ease of a politician at a fund-raising gala. Like a Kennedy running for office, he ignored personal danger. Oh, yes, she knew the type.

"You take enormous risks with your own life," she said, "but you're very traditional in your relationships."

"Tell me more."

"You expect the little wife to keep the homefires burning while you go out and do brave and wonderful things. She's to have dinner ready and the kids cleaned up when you get home. She should praise you in front of them so they'll know what a hero they have for a daddy."

Jennifer's steps grew faster as she recounted all she'd learned during her years as a military dependent. She hadn't touched on half of it yet.

"She's not to criticize *your* choice of a career, express the least worry over the possibility of your death nor have a life of her own, even though she may be left alone to support herself and any children you might have."

Jennifer glared at Lij, but he said nothing.

"Life revolves around *him*. The family must live by *his* schedule, modify their lives to fit *his* needs. Women's needs are negligible, it seems. Men's are not."

She had done the same, she realized. She'd adjusted her plans to her fiancé's goals. But no more! She'd learned her lessons. Staying away from men like Lij Branigan was one of them. Turning from him, she stalked ahead as they went into the lobby to wait for the scientist.

"That's the message our society sends to its young," she finished hotly. "It's one I intend to change."

Lij guided her to a sofa. "I just asked you to share a meal," he murmured, "not my life."

DR. BENTON WAS ONLY thirty minutes late. He apologized to Jennifer for his tardiness when he rushed into the lobby at half-past noon.

He reminded her of an eccentric scientist—white hair that stood out like a wiry halo around his head, rumpled suit worn with a white lab coat and piercing blue eyes. His smile produced generous lines in his face, she noted as he escorted her outside.

"I hope this young man kept you entertained," he added after the apology.

She ignored the sardonic smile from Lij as she murmured she hadn't minded the wait at all. Actually, she and her escort had sat in a very stiff silence the entire time. Upon reflection, she felt like a fool for her grand speech.

"Good. Then let us go," the scientist said.

Lij drove them to a local restaurant where he'd already made reservations. When they were seated ahead of a long line of customers, she thanked him for his thoughtfulness. He only nodded coolly.

She turned her thoughts from him to the job at hand.

"Dr. Benton, I'm so glad to meet you. I've read a lot about your projects. Tell me, how did NASA lure you away from CalTech?" she asked to put him at ease.

People loved to talk about themselves, she had learned. She gave them ample opportunity, leading them into the areas she wished to explore. Looking at Lij, she exchanged a tension-ridden glance. His thoughts were unreadable, but she detected emotion in the depths of his eyes. Was it anger?

"They made me an offer I couldn't refuse," Dr. Benton said with a waggish grin, paraphrasing a line from a popular novel.

"NASA hired you as a consultant, let's see—" she checked her notes "—five years ago. You went to work for them full-time three years ago and have worked here at the Space Center since then. Is that right?"

The scientist glanced first at her, then at Lij, who had spoken hardly at all. "That is correct."

Dr. Benton had an oddly formal way of speaking, as if he needed each utterance to be precise. He patted his mouth with a napkin and motioned toward Lij. "Now I am trying to get him to join me."

"Lij?"

Lij shifted impatiently in his seat. She needn't act so surprised. Some people thought he was handy to have around.

"He is a physicist, an astrophysicist, one of my best students," Dr. Benton explained. "The astronaut program is moving away from pilots and into specialties such as science and engineering. He's a natural candidate since he has a background in all of them."

Jennifer was momentarily excited by a thought. Lij would be a perfect specimen to follow if he did become an astronaut. She could write about his experiences. Little boys—perhaps big ones, too—would identify with him. They'd live and breathe his trials in the training program. With him, they'd survive the arduous tests, both physical and mental. It would be exciting....

Was she insane? He was just the type of person she wanted to avoid. Writing about him would throw them together for hours on end. No, no, no.

"In fact," the scientist said, reading her mind, "he'd make a good subject to follow through the training program."

Lij grinned sardonically at the look on Jennifer's face. She was about as thrilled at Benton's idea as Miss Muffit had been when the spider joined her for lunch. He perversely wished he could arrange it just to drive her mad. Only, he was the one most likely to go off the deep end.

"That's an interesting idea," she said, deliberately vague.

She steered the conversation back to the scientist's life and experiences while Lij gave her a knowing look. She and Dr. Benton talked for almost three hours, then Lij drove them back to the center. After dropping Dr. Benton at his building, Lij took Jennifer to the parking lot where her rental car was located.

On the way, Jennifer had rehearsed what she wanted to say. Now, taking a deep breath, she began her apology. She even managed a husky laugh at herself. "Forgive me for overreacting earlier. I didn't mean to lecture you. It's just..."

"What?" he asked. He pulled up beside her car and stopped.

"I didn't much like the military life."

"You were in the service?"

His presence filled the short space between them like an intriguing possibility she refused to acknowledge. "My father and grandfather were career navy men. The life of a military dependent isn't a life I'd choose willingly."

"What did you hate the most?"

She knew the answer to that question. Unable to sleep after Lij had left her at her room, she'd thought about the past. Her father had died in April 1963, just a few months before her fiancé. He'd gone down on the atomic submarine, the *Thresher,* ironically named after a shark, trapped eighty-four hundred feet beneath the sea during a test dive. It was still there. Sometimes she thought of those men, trapped beneath the sea....

She remembered her mother's loneliness each time the sub had left port, sometimes for months. She remembered the Cuban Missile Crisis, when her father had sent them a message to get off Key West and go to her grandfather's house in Washington until they heard from him. Then had followed days of not knowing where he was or what was happening.

"The loneliness," she said. "The uncertainty. The protocol. The unwritten rules that apply to wives." She paused, considering, and went on. "But mostly the loneliness and facing things alone. I was talking to one of the astronauts' wives the other day. Last year she saw him a total of two months, adding all the bits and pieces together. Two months. During his absence, their son got a tooth knocked out and their teenage daughter had a car wreck. Does that answer your question?"

"I believe it does," he replied. He reached across her and opened the door. "Did you get all the information you wanted about Dr. Benton?"

She nodded and climbed out. "Thanks for driving and for lunch." She smiled, closed the door and left.

Lij stayed where he was until she drove off in the compact car. He followed her out of the parking lot. At the exit, he turned toward the right, intending to visit Amy. Jennifer turned left, toward the hotel.

He recognized the scenario she scornfully spoke of. It was very much like the early days of his marriage, when he'd thought everything was fine.

He hadn't understood Rona's unhappiness, her inability to find a niche for herself among the other wives. Having Amy to take care of on his own after the accident had opened his eyes to a few things. Like the loneliness Jennifer had mentioned. Like responsibility. Like uncertainty.

Jennifer had learned some hard lessons about life. Well, everybody grew older and wiser, else they just kept repeating the same old mistakes. He'd learned his the hard way, too. And he wasn't about to repeat a damn one of them!

JENNIFER WORKED FOR two hours on her notes. She typed them up on the tiny portable typewriter she had brought with her, then reread them, adding impressions and follow-up notations in the margins.

Finished, she stretched, rubbed her tired neck and decided to go for a workout in the pool. She needed to get rid of some of the tension in her shoulders. And other places, she thought mockingly, reminded of her reaction to Lij's strong presence.

Lij's softly spoken taunt that he hadn't asked her to marry him had touched a nerve. No, he hadn't, but he was attracted. So was she, and that was a bad sign. She intended to take warning and not let anything develop.

If she was lucky, she wouldn't see him for the rest of her research period, which had about two weeks to go before she went back to Berkeley and started writing.

Of course, her luck was as lousy as ever.

Lij was in the whirlpool, set in a corner of the large indoor pool. Only two other people were about, which contributed an intimate ambience. Her first impulse was to turn tail and run, but her pride wouldn't let her reveal how he intimidated her. She smiled at him, fetched one of the big fluffy towels from the stack near the door and dropped it and her robe on a chair.

She dived into the clear water and came up swimming. For fifteen minutes, she did laps, forcing herself to go a little faster than her normal pace. Finally, she climbed out. While toweling her hair, she glanced with longing at the spa. Lij intercepted the look.

"Come on in. The water's fine," he invited.

His grin held an edge of mockery that grated on her nerves. She walked over, aware of his eyes on her figure, appreciation replacing the sardonic amusement of a moment ago. She gasped as she stepped into the hot, churning water, but not from the heat.

"What happened to you?" she asked, staring at the bruises she could see on his chest above the waterline and at those below when the bubbles momentarily eddied away from his body.

"A little difficulty with a . . . lady."

"Well, it couldn't have been the blonde from last night. She didn't weigh that much, and I don't think she could squeeze that hard, could she?"

"Hardly." He laughed, a rich, rolling sound that echoed in the cavernous room.

Jennifer grinned and sunk to her chin in the soothing water. "The warm water will be good for the bruises. It'll help take the discoloration away," she told him, remembering her Red Cross training. "What really happened to you?"

"I had to bail out of a plane. It was a little rough."

"An experimental plane?" she immediately asked. From her reading, she had a good idea of what they did at Edwards.

"Yeah." His tone didn't invite comment.

She laid her head on the tiles. Her legs floated to the top but she quickly pulled them under. "I thought you were going to take the afternoon off and go to the beach today."

"It didn't work out. My date couldn't go."

For a second, Jennifer saw something on his strong, angular face—loneliness, anger, regret? It was too brief to describe, but it left an impression on her memory. She ignored his statement about her refusal to go with him. Glancing at the wall clock, she reminded him, "I've been in here fifteen minutes. Twenty is the recommended max."

When she stepped out, he did, too. She was appalled by the bruises that climbed up his rib cage from hip to shoulder. "Some lady," she murmured.

Lij stalked over to a chair without a word. He pulled on a blue terry robe, slipped into deck shoes and started out without even a backward glance.

For some reason, he stirred her emotions. Why this man? she wondered. Was she just feeling sorry for him because of the bruises? No, it was more than that.

Perhaps it was the quiet way he moved and spoke and acted, as if he kept his thoughts locked inside. One thing, he hadn't tried to appeal to her sympathy because of his injuries. She liked that.

Men had been killed trying to eject from aircraft gone berserk. The bruises explained why he had so much free time when he was supposed to be doing his reserve duty. She was willing to bet his ribs were more than just bruised. There had to be a few cracks, too.

An irresistible wave of sympathy overcame her common sense. "How about dinner tonight?" she called after him. "I'm free if you are." He'd probably tell her to drop dead twice.

He stopped and faced her. For a second she thought he was going to refuse. Then he smiled, and Jennifer saw the same cynicism she had witnessed in Elaine. "Sure. I'll stop by for you at seven-thirty. The dining room here?"

"That's fine." All the way to her room, she tried to figure out why she'd done that.

JENNIFER THOUGHT ABOUT LIJ while she showered and dressed. Something had hurt him, but it was more than physical. He was bruised to the soul. Really? Since when had she become a mind reader, or a bleeding heart, for that matter. His woes were none of her concern.

Tossing the brush into her carryall, she quickly added makeup, then stepped into a black pantsuit, which was the latest in women's evening wear. A white silk blouse and Native American turquoise jewelry completed her outfit. She looked more establishment than Elaine. She plaited two tiny braids at each temple and added a black satin headband around her forehead. There, that was better.

When Lij knocked on her door, she slipped into black sandals and picked up an Indian-bead purse.

"Good evening," he said when she opened the door, his eyes appraising her outfit and coming back to her face. "You look beautiful."

"Thank you. You're not bad yourself... for a Montana cowpoke."

The teasing remark was deliberate. She meant to keep the evening on an even keel. He was too handsome in a dark blue suit and silver-gray turtleneck for her comfort.

"Yeah?" he drawled. "Waalll, ma'am, we do look in the Sears catalog to see what you city folks are wearing so we can keep up."

"Good thinking."

She stepped outside her door and let it close behind her. Lij took her elbow and guided her down the elevator to the fancy red-tiled restaurant. The maître d' seated them without a word about Lij's lack of a tie. The astronauts tended to casual wear, and since they set the trends around town, it became the style.

Their table was in a corner with very subdued lighting, she noted. "Did you pay extra for this?" she asked.

"Nope, pure luck." He gave her a wolfish grin and took the seat next to her rather than across the table. His knee brushed hers as he sat down.

He was different, she decided. Whatever had been bothering him earlier had been disposed of or relegated to the back of his mind. Now he was bent on being charming.

"The steak Diane is delicious," he said. "I had it last night. The lobster is fresh. I think I'll try it."

"Tell me about growing up in Montana," she requested after they ordered. "Were you really a cowboy?"

He nodded. "My folks own a spread near Libby."

He told her about snow and feeding animals before dawn, about how a person's hands could freeze onto an outside faucet if one weren't careful filling a bucket of water. He drew word pictures of his family life that made her long for the land and wide open spaces. To belong to one place and live there for years and years struck a bright green flash of envy in her.

"What about your misspent youth?" he asked after relating a humorous incident involving a mean horse and an overconfident teenager, which she took to be him.

She deflected him with a skill honed to butter smoothness. "Life as a navy brat wasn't very interesting. Mostly we moved from one place to another. That is, my mom and I did. My father was always sent ahead while we packed up. It must have been nice to live in one place and know everyone. Did you have a main street with all the stores on it in your town?"

Lij didn't deflect easily. "Yeah. Where're your parents stationed now?"

"My mother lives back East. My father went down in an experimental submarine back in sixty-three."

Lij caught several implications right off. She hadn't liked moving around as a kid. Some people needed a home base; maybe she was one of them. She'd resented her father's career in the navy. That he'd gone down in an experimental sub was significant. It explained a lot of things, like her attitude toward him.

"Is that why you avoid the astronauts?"

His softly spoken question startled her and her hand jerked as she picked up her water glass. "I beg your pardon?"

"I noticed at the party. You have a way of staying just out of reach. I wanted to talk to you that night."

"What about?"

He shrugged. He'd been attracted; he'd wanted to see if she felt the same. This didn't seem the time to admit it, though. "Growing up on a ranch in Montana. Living on military bases around the world. Do you speak any languages?"

"Some Greek, some Italian, a little French."

He asked more questions, which she reluctantly answered. But after a few minutes, she was finally talking freely. She laughed aloud as she told him about a misunderstanding between her and an Italian woman that involved a cake and a cat.

Lij saw more than humor, though. Slowly he constructed a picture of her life. With no brothers or sisters, she'd been a lonely child, moving from place to place for no reason as far as she could see, except that her father's job as a naval commander demanded it.

Lij understood her feelings and looked at her in a new light. He'd been intrigued by Jennifer Wright, the free-spirit who was so different from the other women at the party. He'd admired her take-charge ability in dealing with the blonde. He'd been impressed by the intelligence he'd observed during the interview with Dr. Benton. Now he found himself sympathizing with the child who'd longed for stability in her life.

It changed the nature of things. What had he had in mind when he first saw her? A hello and a quick trip to bed? Not with this woman. He sighed, disgruntled with life and all its complications, especially of the man-woman kind.

Her philosophy probably matched that of the hippie crowd. People who went around spouting Hindu proverbs and flashing the peace sign turned him off. They were a bunch of misfits and losers, in his opinion.

He studied Jennifer. No, she was too smart for that junk. And too lovely for his peace of mind.

When the hour grew late, she indicated she needed to leave. He insisted on paying the check, which obviously irritated her. She felt strongly about the woman's movement, that much was clear. He fought back a grin at thwarting her.

At her door, she held out her hand in that straightforward fashion of hers and looked him in the eye. "Thanks for a lovely evening."

He took her key, but instead of inserting it in the lock, he closed his hand around it and slipped his arm behind her. She was a challenge he couldn't ignore.

Jennifer saw what was coming and decided not to resist. There was speculation in his eyes. She wasn't going to give him any encouragement by playing hard to get.

The kiss was brief, sensuous but not sexual. It left her wanting more. His hand at her waist, the other just touching her face, tempted her to lean into him, to feel the solid warmth of his body with hers. She fought the urge.

"Good night," she said.

"There's a get-together Friday night at Dr. Benton's house. All the talk will be space technology. It'll bore you to death. Do you want to go?"

At his wry grin, she had to laugh. He expected a refusal. Was that why she was going to accept? "Yes, I'd like to go." Then, so he'd know it wasn't his charm that had decided her, she stuck on "I might get some good information."

"Fine. See you tomorrow."

He kissed her again, just a light brushing of his lips against hers. He was a man who knew when to push and when to hold back.

And she was a woman who'd better learn when to resist and when to run for the high country.

LIJ PROPPED HIS HIP on Elaine's desk. He picked up the lighter, flicked it and touched it to the cigarette she held. "Tell me about your friend," he invited.

"Who?" She knew very well who he meant, but she needed some time to think. Jennifer was a very private person.

"Jennifer Wright."

"What do you want to know?"

"What makes her tick?"

Elaine leaned back in her chair and blew a long stream of smoke toward the ceiling. "Ask her."

"I have. How long have you known her?"

"What's twelve from twenty-eight? Sixteen?"

"Sixteen years," he repeated. "You knew her when she lived at home and her father was still alive. She said she hated military life...the loneliness, the packing and moving around."

Elaine was surprised. "She told you all that?"

He nodded. "And that her father died in a sub."

"He did—" she tapped the cigarette against the ashtray "—a couple of months before her fiancé was killed at the Bonneville Salt Flats. He was trying a new type of engine, a rocket motor or something like that, when his car crashed and burned. He never got out."

"God!"

Elaine frowned up at him. "Don't bother her, Lij. She's had a man like you. Jeffrey was the same dare-devil sort, always after a challenge. She needs...security in her life, a man she can count on to be there."

"If I've ever seen a woman who can take care of herself—"

"Yes, she's built a life for herself...because she had to. She's earned her independence. Don't try and take it from her just because she didn't tumble for your charm at first sight." Elaine gave him a knowing glance. "I saw you watching her at my house."

"Is it a crime to look?"

"Maybe not, but it's a crime to hurt a person just because you can." Elaine stubbed out the cigarette and stared at him coldly.

Lij thought of Amy, of the loneliness that drove him at times. "You think I can?"

She sighed. "Yes. Because she's loved only two men, her father and her fiancé, both men like you. I don't know if she realizes that yet. So, yes, you could hurt her."

Lij wasn't sure he believed that. Jennifer, with her cool reserve and straightforward approach, wouldn't let herself be hurt. She'd been interested, but she'd held her emotions in check. She could take care of herself.

"What do you want from her that you can't get with ten other women?" Elaine said, relentlessly pursuing his conscience.

He shrugged. "What attracts any person to another? She's interesting, intelligent, lovely. We've both had difficulties in our lives. Maybe we'd be good for each other."

"I've seen the girls who hang around the bases. What difficulties have you had?"

Not allowing himself to recall the bitter memories, he simply stood and walked toward the door. "My wife died in a car crash two years ago," he ground out in a voice devoid of emotion. "And my daughter...was injured." With that, he walked out.

Elaine lit another cigarette. His wife dead, his daughter, injured. Did Jennifer know?

AT THEIR MIDMORNING coffee break, Elaine asked. She stubbed out her cigarette, lit another one and said, "Did Lij tell you about his wife and daughter being in an auto accident a couple of years ago?"

Jennifer's expression answered for her.

Elaine explained what little she knew.

"How did you find out? Did he tell you?"

"Uh-huh. About an hour ago, he dropped by my office and asked a lot of questions about you."

"About me?"

Elaine nodded. "I told him to leave you alone."

"Why?" Jennifer studied her oldest friend with a curious expression in her eyes.

"I don't want you to get hurt."

"Like you're hurting?"

Elaine tensed for a moment, then her shoulders dropped in defeat. "Things don't look good at Black Rock," she said with an attempt at levity.

"You think Mac is running around?" Jennifer asked. She remembered Sunday night. Mac wasn't usually a drinker; certainly he wasn't a womanizer.

"More than that." Elaine ran her fingers into her hair and rubbed her temples. "I overheard a snatch of conversation when he was on the phone last night. I think he may be involved in a..." She paused as if seeking courage to say the words aloud. "A paternity suit."

"Oh, Elaine, surely not."

"It happens. I heard a rumor last year about, well, someone else. It was all very hush-hush, of course. America's heroes can't have clay feet."

"Sometimes people say things like that just for publicity," Jennifer reminded her. "Singers and actors are involved in paternity suits all the time. Tell Mac what you heard. Silence only makes fears grow bigger."

Elaine looked around at the laughing, talking people at the nearby tables. Everyone was engrossed in his or her own group. "Isn't it ironic that Tissy, the one who swore she'd never marry, has been with the same man for almost eight years, six of those actually living together, and she's the only happy one of us."

"I'm happy," Jennifer protested.

"You live in a vacuum," Elaine snapped. She pressed a hand to her forehead. "I'm sorry, Jen. I'm terrible company today. I have an awful headache."

"Talk to Mac. Tell him how you feel."

"What do I say? 'Have you fathered a child with another woman? Is she suing you for support?'" She looked at Jennifer, her eyes misting over. "I refused to get pregnant last year when he wanted me to. He hasn't said anything about it this year. Maybe he wants to leave me and go to this other woman."

Jennifer listened. There were no words of comfort when a person was hurting. She knew that.

"Sometimes I wish they'd never invented the Pill. It takes away the element of risk. If I became pregnant accidentally..."

"That's a cop-out."

"Yes. Well, I'd better get back to the office. With your new badge, you're official and don't have to have an escort to take you around. Just let me know what areas you want to research next so I can clear the way with the department heads."

"I will." Jennifer glanced at the new ID badge clipped to her lapel. It had her picture and name as well as some numbers that apparently told the guards where she could go on her own around the complex.

"I'll keep you posted on things," Elaine promised. "Maybe we'll have the showdown tonight. If you hear any shots, duck." She stood and started to walk off. "By the way, Dr. Benton suggested that Lij be assigned to you for the rest of the week."

"What!" Jennifer bolted upright.

"The chief approved."

Chapter Four

Lij bristled with unspent energy. His stride was long, quick and forceful. Ergo, he's angry, Jennifer deduced. She followed after him like a pull-along toy on a string, stretching her pace to keep up with his.

"This is a clean area. We have to wear overalls," he tossed over his shoulder.

Behind his back, she saluted. He glanced back at that moment. Naturally. She gave him a level stare in return for his icy one. He wasn't enthusiastic about taking her around the astronaut-training complex, so it obviously hadn't been his idea.

"This wasn't my idea, either, you know," she said to his broad shoulders. "I didn't ask for you to show me around."

Lij paused with his hand on the doorknob of the clean room and faced Jennifer. Her perfume and warmth stroked his senses and made him acutely aware of how sweet and warm she could be—under the right circumstances.

She didn't know it, but she was just one of the pressures besetting him at the present. Another was his concern for his daughter. Just yesterday he'd gotten a letter from a lawyer hired by his former in-laws, informing him they wanted their doctor to perform psychiatric and skill tests on Amy.

To hell with that!

They hadn't been to visit the kid once in almost two years, and they lived just outside Austin. But now they'd decided he wasn't taking proper care of her by having her "institutionalized"—their fancy-lawyer term for the convalescent center—and wanted her checked by their own doctors. There had been a veiled threat of a custody fight in the letter.

Let them do whatever they wanted to him, but they'd better leave Amy alone. Outsiders, any kind of change, upset her, caused her to retreat inside herself. At the center, they'd worked hard for two years to make her more outgoing. He wasn't going to lose those gains on the whim of grandparents who had been too horrified to visit her after they realized the extent of her injuries. His in-laws had turned tail and run once they realized Amy would never be a replica of their daughter.

Not that he would have allowed that. He wouldn't have let Amy, with her sweet, loving ways, be ruined by them and turned into a spoiled woman-child....

"What is it?" Jennifer asked softly, touching his arm.

His eyes, dark and turbulent, looked at her hand. She removed it, feeling she had trespassed.

"Sorry," he muttered. "Something else...nothing to do with you."

"We could make this another time. I have other things to do."

He rubbed a hand over his eyes. "No, that's okay. I just didn't sleep well last night." Opening the door, he stepped back and allowed her to precede him.

They were in an anteroom. A pass-through was cut into one wall, disclosing another small room. In it were stacks of clothing stored on shelves. No one was in sight.

"Hey, Sam, we need dressing out," Lij called out.

A man shuffled in from the back. He grinned at Lij, looked both of them over and started pulling items off the shelf.

"Jennifer, this is Sam, the guardian of the clean room. He has to see that you're properly clothed before you go in."

"Hi," Jennifer said.

Sam had gray hair and dimples high on his cheeks when he smiled. He reminded Jennifer of an aging cherub. "Here you go," he said, handing her a stack of clothing.

Following Lij's lead, she pulled a pale green robe over her clothes, put a shower cap on her head, making sure all her hair was inside it, and tied booties on her feet over her shoes. Clean to NASA apparently meant spotless.

"Do we get mask and gloves, too?" she asked. They looked like surgeons ready for the operating room.

"Okay, you can go in," Sam said. He pressed a button to unlock a door at the back of the anteroom. She and Lij went in.

The room was white—everywhere, everything. Mounted like a fly in a web of scaffolding was the training module, an exact replica of the capsules the astronauts had flown in the Apollo missions. Two men, also dressed like surgeons, waited for them.

"Come on." Lij guided her up the steps. He told her to enter and be seated.

When she did, she found she was lying on her back, her knees curved over a sort of reclining lounger. "Odd kind of easy chair," she said, feeling just a tad nervous.

Lij smiled for the first time since she'd met him in Dr. Benton's office that morning. "I was a bit wary my first time in one of these, especially when they closed the hatch." He climbed in and took the middle of the three seats, leaving the left one empty.

His smile widened when she visibly jumped as the hatch slammed shut and they were locked in. "How do we tell them we want out?'' she asked, looking at the various switches and lights that lined the spacecraft over her head.

"There's a mike.'' He pointed it out. ''They're going to take us through a simulated lift-off, then we'll be in outer space. I thought you might like to get an idea of what the men actually go through.'' He showed her how to strap in.

"Oh, firsthand experience,'' she quipped. ''That should impress the students when they read my pamphlets.''

"These lights are connected to various systems,'' he began, forcing his thoughts to the task at hand. The ability to concentrate totally on the immediate task was one of the necessary traits of a test pilot. He put it to use.

He inhaled the subtle odor of Jennifer's perfume as the simulation tape began to play through the speaker. He glanced at her. A thin sheen of perspiration gleamed on her brow. Was she nervous about being confined in tight spaces?

The last thirty minutes of countdown became the last ten seconds. The count began: ''Ten...nine...''

Jennifer held herself very still as eddies of panic whirled around the edges of her mind. Not exactly panic—it was nothing that strong—but a sort of anxiety, as if she expected something to go wrong, to beset her. Then life narrowed to the last few seconds...

"Three...two...one...ignition. Lift-off,'' the voice over the speaker said.

The capsule filled with the roar of the rocket engine. It trembled...or was that just her? She closed her eyes and saw flames imprinted on the backs of her eyelids. She opened them and saw red, amber and green lights flickering over her head. The need to escape was sudden and urgent. Behind her, she could sense the hot breath of Death as it reached out a bony hand...

Stop it, she told herself sternly. Forcing her breath slowly from her body, she pretended to exhale the tension. It didn't do any good. She was locked in this tiny capsule, at the mercy of whoever was at the controls for however long they wanted to keep her here. She wanted out!

Lij flicked switches as if he knew what he was doing. He spoke in a normal voice, "All systems go. First stage burnout. Tanks are off. Second stage ignition."

She realized he was having a great time and that brought a certain amount of comfort. This was just a game, she reminded herself. She breathed a little easier. In a few seconds, she was relaxed once more, as much as she was going to be.

"Five minutes," Lij said.

She glanced at him. His gaze was filled with curiosity. Was there also sympathy? She hated feeling vulnerable. Her smile was cool and self-contained.

They went through second stage burnout, third stage ignition. Then the noise stopped. She and Lij were suspended in silence—deep, profound, total.

"We're in orbit now," he said. "That's it."

His announcement didn't register for a second, then the hatch opened, startling her. The real world intruded.

"How was it?" one of the technicians asked. He stood aside as Lij climbed out but offered his hand to Jennifer.

She exited the confined space. "Very exciting."

"You should go through it under pressure. That makes it seem real."

"It was real enough for me," she assured him, laughing now that it was over.

She followed Lij back to the anteroom and removed the clean-room garb. She thanked Sam for his help, told him she had really enjoyed the ride, then left, tagging at Lij's heels.

"Dr. Benton will join us for lunch. He's got some men he wants you to meet," Lij told her.

"Astronauts?"

Lij nodded. "The latest batch."

"We've had the First Seven, then the Next Nine. What are the new groups called?"

"It was the press that stuck the tags on. NASA calls them pilots or scientists, according to their specialty."

They went to the cafeteria and selected their food. Lij chose a large table. "Benton will be late. We'll start without him."

Jennifer took a seat. "You seem to know him well." There was a question in her voice.

"He was my graduate advisor." He laughed briefly, mockingly. "Once an advisor, always an advisor. He thinks I should be in the space program."

"I had wondered about that. I mean, about why you are here and why the air force assigned you to NASA."

Lij thought for a minute. When he spoke, his voice was soft so that it carried no further than the two of them. "This is off the record?"

She nodded.

"Politics," he said. "When the air force realized Congress was going to give their plum away to a civilian agency—it was called NACA in the old days—the top brass decided that if they couldn't have the whole ball of wax, they wanted to wield some influence. What better way than to have your best pilots become astronauts?"

"More astronauts have graduated from the naval academy than the air force academy," Jennifer murmured, recalling her notes.

"You're sharp," he complimented. "The navy must have decided the same thing."

His smile would turn the world upside-down, she thought, looking away with difficulty. She remembered how vulnerable she had felt inside the simulation capsule, lying next to him in the narrow space. Briefly, she had thought of her father and fiancé.

She pushed the memories aside. Being in the space module with Lij had been a different experience from those earlier ones. For once she hadn't been left behind to wait and worry. Not that she intended to wait for or worry about him.

She studied him while they ate. His smile turned into a slight frown as he became introspective. Something was troubling him today. Elaine had said his daughter had been injured. How badly? she wondered. And who was staying with the child?

"Is your daughter in California?" Jennifer asked with the innate curiosity necessary to her profession.

He erected invisible No Trespassing signs. "What do you know about her?"

"Only that Elaine said she had been injured in an auto accident and that your wife had died."

He placed his fork on his plate. Jennifer wouldn't have been surprised to see him stalk out. He spoke after a minute, "My in-laws are causing some problems."

"I'm sorry." She didn't pursue the topic although she burned to ask a thousand questions.

"Not your fault," he said gruffly. He ran a hand over his face, a gesture she'd observed in him when he was weary or resigned to some fate he couldn't control. "They're only one of the complications in my life right now." He looked directly at her. "You're another."

"I don't know what you mean."

"Yes, you do." His gaze held hers, refusing to let her pretend ignorance of the force between them.

Jennifer heard the heavy pounding of her heart, felt the contracting of nerves in vital places in her body. She longed for touching, caressing, stroking. . . . She looked away.

"Dr. Benton is a third," Lij continued. "He wants me to work for him, so he lures me with the promise of space flight. That's why he got me assigned to him while my ribs heal. Having me show you the ropes is just another lure. Space and sex. Why do people assume they go together?''

''Well, both are exciting possibilities,'' she suggested, a warning running through her at the intimate nature of the discussion. Just being around Lij was enough to start her mind reeling toward the more sensual side of humanness. The need to make contact with a living being increased. Not just any living being, she acknowledged. Lij Branigan was the one she wanted.

''Yes,'' he said.

His eyes roamed her face, focused on her mouth, then wandered down her throat to her breasts. By the time he returned to her eyes, she was frantically thinking of cold things—icebergs, frost, snowflakes, anything.

''But not between us.'' Her voice was a husky croak.

''You think not?''

Jennifer swallowed against the knot of longing that clogged her throat, making it difficult to speak. ''I won't let anything happen. I have work to do—''

''So what? What the hell has work or responsibility or anything else to do with this?'' His voice was very soft, almost caressing...hypnotizing.

''I won't be vulnerable again.'' She clamped her lips together, but there was no way she could recall the words.

''I know about your fiancé,'' he said abruptly.

''Elaine said you asked about me.''

He nodded. ''I was curious.''

''About what?''

''About a woman as beautiful as you running around free.''

She didn't thank him for the compliment. His manner was so matter-of-fact, as if he had stated the time or the weather, that a response seemed superfluous.

''So naturally I assumed there must be a reason.''

"There is," she snapped. "I don't need a man to take care of me. I've made a life for myself without depending on anyone else. I'm free because I want to be, and I intend to keep it that way."

" 'No man is an island,' " he quoted with a hard edge to his voice. "Everybody needs someone at some time."

"I have friends."

"But no lovers."

"I don't need one." She realized she'd given too much of herself away when he smiled. She was poised on the edge of her chair, tense and battle ready. She settled back and returned his steady perusal. "Was that what you wanted to know, Lij? If I had other lovers?"

The smile broadened. "Since I'm not one of them yet, I was wondering if you had *any*. Now I know the field is clear—"

"No, it isn't. I'd advise you to give up that line of thinking. It'll get you nowhere."

"A friend once pointed out to me that nowhere could also be pronounced now-here." He gave her a Gordo Cooper smile, that now-I've-got-you grin that had won America's heart when the first seven astronauts had appeared on national television. "And so I am. Here, with you."

Jennifer felt as insecure as an abandoned baby in spite of his presence. How had she lost control of the conversation?

His glance flicked over her. "Are you one of those rabid bra burners, Jennifer?" A smile played at the corners of his mouth. He was enjoying himself just as he had during their space flight. He loved a challenge.

"I'm a realist."

"Are you? I don't see you that way." His glance went right through her. "I think you're more of a dreamer than you're willing to admit."

"You must have X-ray vision," she mocked. "The Superman with lasers for eyes."

"The better to see you, my dear." He picked up his glass of water and saluted her before taking a drink. "Did you know the laser was used to measure the distance to the moon before Apollo 10 and 11 were launched?"

"No."

He brought the discussion back to the space program, telling her of technical breakthroughs that had made manned space flight possible. He stopped speaking when Dr. Benton came up.

The scientist took a chair beside Jennifer. "Did you enjoy the simulation this morning?" he asked.

He reminded Jennifer of Dr. Zorba, the elder doctor on *Ben Casey*. Like that other mentor, Dr. Benton was wise, shrewd and unsurprised at human nature.

"It was very realistic."

"Good. I have some other young men I want you to meet." He glanced from her to Lij and back. "We can't let this one have all your time, can we?"

"No," she murmured.

Two of the new astronauts joined them and Dr. Benton introduced them. "Tony and Steven will show you the altitude chamber this afternoon. You will find it interesting, I think."

"I'm sure I will."

"Now, are you coming to my party Friday night?" he asked. Having taken care of the business part of her life, he turned to the social.

"I'm bringing her," Lij spoke up.

"Good," the doctor said. "Good." He smiled with pleasure. "My wife makes good stuff to eat."

TWO DAYS PASSED before Jennifer saw Elaine again. They met in the cafeteria for a cup of coffee.

"You're killing yourself with those," Jennifer said gently as Elaine lit up a cigarette. "Haven't you heard the latest report from the surgeon-general's office? There's a definite link to cancer."

Elaine stubbed out the cigarette. "I know." Her smile was filled with despair. "I talked to Mac," she suddenly said.

"And?"

"We had a roaring fight."

Jennifer waited.

"I asked him about the telephone call. When he realized I thought he was involved in a paternity suit, he became furious."

"Did he explain the call or simply turn on you?" Jennifer asked. Sometimes people in their own guilt tried to turn the tables and make the other person feel at fault.

Elaine toyed with a cigarette without lighting it. "When he refused to answer, I asked him why. I had asked a simple question, was he involved in a paternity suit or not? Why couldn't he give me a simple answer?"

"Did he?"

"Yes." Elaine paused. Her smile was humorless. "He is."

"Oh, Elaine," Jennifer whispered.

"But not for himself. One of his friends from the academy. Mac is trying to get the girl to drop the suit without going to court and causing a big scandal. The Brotherhood sticks together," she concluded.

Jennifer sat up straighter. "Then it wasn't Mac!"

"Right."

Jennifer flinched at her friend's tone. Irony kept the despair at bay. Did people notice that astronauts' wives were always stoic in front of an audience? A brave front took less energy; she could pretend the fears didn't count. Jennifer knew all about it.

"So why aren't you beaming with joy and happiness?"

"You're always so quick on the uptake," Elaine complimented her friend. She lit the cigarette. "Mac was furious that I hadn't trusted him. He said if I had no more faith in him than that, we'd better forget the whole marriage bit. I agreed. Trust works both ways. He could have told me about the problem instead of leaving me to hear bits and pieces."

"So you've split up?"

"I suppose. Oh, he's still at the house—he moved into the guest room—but our marriage is definitely on the rocks."

"If he didn't leave and you didn't throw him out," Jennifer mused aloud, "I'd say you both want to stay close. Talk to him again. It's obvious you two love each other."

Elaine shook her head, her expression stubborn. "If he wants to talk, I'm willing. This time he has to make the first move.

"I've got to get back to work. Oh, I have something for you in my office."

Jennifer accompanied Elaine to the PR office.

"Here, something for you to browse through when you have a week to spare." Elaine handed over a manual.

Jennifer looked at the thick training guide for the astronaut program. Maybe what people needed was a training guide for marriage and other dangerous relationships, she thought.

Like the one developing between her and Lij Branigan?

Not on your life, she vowed.

"Hmm, these petit fours are delicious." Jennifer ate the last bite and licked her fingers. She felt pretty good. Her work had gone well that week. Only one more week to go, then she could get back to Berkeley and catch her breath. "Dr. Benton was right. His wife does make good stuff to eat."

The snacks at the party were all desserts and all scrumptious, drawing the guests back again and again to the table. Platters were kept full by a neighbor's daughter, who was hired to help out. She had confided to Jennifer that this was lots more fun than baby-sitting. "And it pays better, too."

She and Jennifer grinned at each other before the girl headed back to the kitchen to fill another tray with goodies.

"Friend of yours?" Lij asked, bringing Jennifer a glass of wine.

"A new one," she replied. "Her father is manager of Quality Assurance at MSC. Does everyone in Houston work at the Space Center?"

"Just about." He shrugged. "Who else would you expect to meet at a party given by one of the directors?"

Since that tension-filled luncheon, she had avoided Lij when possible; when not, she'd been cool and distant. He had found her attitude amusing, but tonight he seemed moody and not given to small talk.

For the next two hours he escorted her around the room and introduced her to his friends. Finally he took her out on the wooden deck that overlooked a small sloping backyard. Chinese lanterns set out on the lawn cast intimate shadows through the foliage. It looked romantic.

"I wonder where Elaine and Mac are," Jennifer murmured, an obvious distraction from the magnetic force of Lij, standing close beside her. "They were supposed to be here. I hope they haven't gotten into an argument again." She realized she was letting her worries about her friends show through.

"Do you always become involved with other people's problems?" Lij asked, correctly interpreting her sudden silence.

"Elaine is my best friend," Jennifer said defensively. "I care about what happens to her."

"That much caring can open a person to a lot of heart-ache," he suggested, his tone harsh.

"Not if you keep it confined to its proper place."

"Such as friendship?"

"Yes."

For a few seconds, they stood there in the flickering light of the garden with quiet all around them, each lost in thought, but she was acutely aware of him.

Jennifer glanced up at the moon. At its fullest point, it reminded her of an exotic fruit, ready to be eaten. "From here, it's hard to believe, isn't it—footprints on the moon?"

"Yes." He moved closer.

"Do you think it will bother couples on—" She stopped, but it was too late to recall the thought.

"A date?" he finished for her. "If I were parked at a quiet place with my date, I wouldn't be thinking about men on the moon. I'd be thinking of...more immediate matters."

He moved even closer. He didn't touch her, merely stood near her warming her with his body heat. She felt flushed and excited. Nervous. She fingered the beads that had been given to her by a Yakima Indian friend and tried to think of important things, like her job or the article she was writing. She couldn't. The moon was driving her mad.

"So you think the magic will stay the same?" she mumbled.

"Yes." His hands on her shoulders turned her to him. "The magic will stay, long after mankind has lost interest in the moon as a way station for astronauts." He rubbed his fingers along her collar bone, slid them over the beads and up into her hair. "The magic will stay, Jennifer, as long as there are people like you and me." His gaze was riveting...and so tender.

She backed off. "An astrophysicist and a reporter?" She laughed, a fine example of self-control.

He followed, catching her hands in his. "A man and a woman who want each other."

"I don't—"

"Don't lie."

Further argument died before reaching her lips. She was tired of the distance she'd maintained all week. She was tired of hiding and holding her emotions in check. She was tired of sparring.

Something about him appealed to her, something emotional as well as physical. He was a quiet man of deep reserve. He looked solid and dependable. Without thinking further, she rested her forehead against his chest.

His arms came around her, enfolding her within his soothing warmth. Tatters of old fears circled within her like scraps of confetti left from a parade. Lij was everything she should be wary of—a risk taker, an unsure element, a maker of turmoil in her life. She liked order around her and she liked being free.

But none of that mattered now.

She didn't know who moved first, whether she or Lij, or if it was a simultaneous coming together, like two magnets drawn to each other. One instant they were apart and separate, the next they weren't. Their mouths touched, and she was lost to reason.

It was so sweet, she wanted to weep. The kiss was a gentle merging, an act of discovery.

Her hands caressed him. She explored his back, his shoulders, the way his hair grew at the nape of his neck. With fingers that trembled with longing, she threaded her hands into the dark, shining waves and pulled him closer, locking them into the kiss.

"Let's get out of here," Lij murmured.

"Yes," she whispered.

They said good-night to their host and hostess and left. The drive to their hotel was ten minutes. It seemed to take forever; it took but a second. Jennifer didn't know which she preferred.

Lij took her to his room and she didn't object.

He turned on the radio to some slow music and pulled her into his arms. She smiled in surprise when he began dancing with her in the tiny space between the bed and the sofa.

"I've wanted to dance with you," he said. He kissed her forehead, her eyes, her ear where the peace symbol spoke of her values and views on life.

"Why?" she asked. She leaned against his arm. "Why me?"

Lij shook his head, a wry defeat in his expression. "I don't know. There're a thousand other women who'd be easier to live with than you—"

"Live with?" She looked shocked.

He gestured impatiently. "Do you prefer 'going steady'? Don't tell me you haven't thought of things developing between us? It's been happening all week, at least with me," he added softly.

"Lij—"

"Let it go tonight. Tomorrow we'll do the recriminations. Tonight, just come into my arms like you did there in the moonlight, soft and sweet and trusting."

"It isn't that simple." But she relaxed and let him guide her to the music.

"I know. Nothing ever is."

"Maybe it's because we're both away from our home bases and we're feeling lonely. That's why we're attracted."

"Jennifer."

"What?"

"Shut up."

She frowned at him.

He laughed at her.

The music washed over them. Lij recognized the song—the theme from Zeffirelli's *Romeo and Juliet*. Was there time in his life for this? For dancing with a beautiful woman and letting himself feel content just to hold her?

He needed it, he realized. It had been a long time since he'd felt like a man, a young man who liked a young woman, with no other complications or expectations for the moment. He'd forgotten what it felt like. He'd forgotten many things, simple things like dancing. Jennifer reminded him of them all.

"Jennifer," he said. He ran his fingers through her hair, all the way to the ends. She didn't raise a fuss about her hairdo. He gathered it into his fist and pulled her up to his lips. She let him. "God, you're so sweet."

Touching, Jennifer thought. She'd missed touching.

And strength. The hard, sinewy strength of a man's body.

And words. A woman liked words.

She let herself grow intoxicated with him. Oh, yes, she had missed so much. Elaine had been right: she had been living in a vacuum. The expressiveness of touching created a world of its own peopled only by him and her, she discovered.

They kissed.

He was so gentle; she felt as delicate as a rose.

She was so fragile; he felt as strong as an oak.

They turned to the music, around and around, dipping, swaying, moving in smooth steps, in tune with each other.

A tiny light flashed at the periphery of her vision. "You have a message," she said.

"It can wait." He kissed her nose.

But the blinking light intruded. The mood was destroyed.

"See what it is. It might be important," she said. She pulled out of his arms, releasing them from the spell.

He reached for the phone with one hand and grabbed her with the other. He brought her into solid contact with him and talked into the receiver with his cheek touching her temple.

"This is Branigan in room 421. You have a message for me?"

He nibbled on the beads braided into her hair, surprising her into laughter. She quickly muffled it so he could hear.

He listened. "Yes, I understand. No, you don't need to repeat it. Thank you." He hung up.

For a minute, he pulled her hard against him, as if he fought having to give her up. Then he raised his head.

"It's my daughter. I have to go."

"Is she ill?"

He hesitated. "A fever. She's very susceptible to colds and infections."

"Is she in Houston?" Jennifer had assumed the child was near Edwards, someplace in California.

"Yes, a children's convalescent center about a mile from here." Going into the dressing area, he quickly combed his hair smooth. All traces of her caresses disappeared.

"Do you want me to come with you?"

He shook his head. "Strangers frighten her." He rubbed a hand over his face, took a deep breath and let it out slowly.

Jennifer felt compassion twist her heart. The man she watched now was an entirely different person from the one she had held in her arms only moments ago. Then he had been the lover, gallant and exciting; now he was the father, anxious and concerned for his daughter.

"I'll walk you to your room," he said.

"That's okay—" she began, but he stopped her with an impatient gesture. At her door, he told her good-night and hurried off.

A lover and a father, she mused after turning out the light. Lij Branigan was a many-faceted man. His life was complicated. It didn't take a great deal of intuition to realize that. Too complicated for her.

But while they were dancing, it had all seemed simple.

A time for dreams. A time to share. A time... Really, there wasn't. There hadn't been any time for dreams in her life for six years. Oh, but it had been sweet while it lasted.

Her feelings for Lij were edging beyond her control. She'd best get back to Berkeley before she was sucked deeper into the tangled lives of these Space Center people with their strange life-styles that were quasi-military and part avant-garde. Her freedom was at stake.

Was she running?

Yeah.

Chapter Five

Amy was asleep, but Lij didn't put her in her bed. She lay in his arms, dressed in pink pajamas and smelling of baby shampoo and powder. Her hair lay close to her head in short blond curls. A thumb was in her mouth.

For the past two weeks, he had been with her every spare minute, comforting her when she cried with the aches of cold and fever, rocking her to sleep every night.

He rocked back and forth, feeling the fierce protective love that he sometimes experienced for her at odd tender moments. The trust with which Amy slept in his arms opened doors he'd rather stayed closed and sealed.

Like how it had felt to hold Jennifer.

Like how soft and trusting she'd been.

For two years he hadn't wanted to be that close to anyone, and he hadn't. Then he'd met Jennifer. A feminist. "Woman's libbers," the news commentators called them. A radical? No, but definitely a liberal and a strong-minded one.

She was also a woman who'd loved. A woman who knew what it was to hurt. Was that what he'd sensed in her when they met?

Kindred souls. He summoned a cynical smile. It didn't come.

Standing, he left the rocking chair and put his daughter into bed and tucked the covers around her. She opened her eyes slightly and smiled at him.

"'Night, Toots," he whispered, and drew a ragged breath filled with love so pure, it stung his eyes like sunlight.

She stuck her thumb back in her mouth and slept.

Out on the street, the sky was dark. It was near midnight. Lij drove to the hotel, his thoughts filled with images of a woman in his arms. The memory of Jennifer, all sweet, willing woman...

He cursed his body, his uncontrollable imagination, the lucid memories of their time together. After parking the rental car, he headed for his room. In bed, he cursed the restlessness that wouldn't let him sleep. It had been two weeks since he'd left her. At the end of this week, he planned to return to Edwards.

He tried to let the memories go, to crawl into sleep and forget her. He couldn't. Angry with himself, he made a decision. Tomorrow he'd ask Elaine for Jennifer's address. Saturday, he'd go see her on her own turf.

THE SCENE IN JENNIFER'S living room was not typical of a Saturday morning in her house. Everyone connected with the paper was gathered there to fold and stack the *Berkeley Free Press* into piles for distribution due to a breakdown of one of the machines—a not unusual happening with second- and thirdhand equipment, but the task was usually done on Thursday, so the paper would be on the streets Friday. They were way behind schedule.

Tissy, looking like an earthmother in a long tie-dyed shirt of many colors and Native American beads, her jeans so old, holes were almost as plentiful as material, gave out orders sporadically.

"Where are the labels?" Bradford demanded, his myopic eyes staring around the room from old-fashioned gold-framed glasses that looked as if they might have belonged to his grandfather. He wore a blue workshirt, jeans and sandals, and his long hair was held at the back of his neck with a rawhide string.

"Here." Handing him a stack was a government major in similar spectacles and a granny dress.

Sitting crossed-legged on the floor, they stuck on labels and stacked the papers for mailing or distribution to newsstands.

Jennifer, carrying a cup of coffee, yawned from the doorway and watched the activity.

"Come and help," Tissy said, handing her a bunch of labels. "We only have three thousand papers to prepare."

"Thank goodness the mailing list isn't any bigger," Jennifer said. She, too, sat on the floor and started sticking on labels.

That was where Lij found them three hours later.

He parked the car he'd rented at the Oakland airport in the narrow drive beside her house. In the detached garage he could see an old van. For a second he stared at the dilapidated vehicle. The psychedelic colors had faded from primary to pastel shades, but it was still wildly patterned. He remembered the stoned-out-of-his-mind driver of another van, also painted in swirling, disturbing shapes. The man had been laughing like a maniac in the emergency room where Lij's wife lay dead and his daughter bled internally, close to death.

Lij clenched his hands on the steering wheel and fought the terrible anger that welled in him. Slowly it passed. He got out of the car and went to the door of the old Victorian house. It was open.

Inside he could see a large hall and, in a room to the left, a gathering of people, talking in murmurs as they labored over some common task. Or was it some type of communal exercise?

He considered leaving without seeing Jennifer. This was not the place for him. Just then, she appeared at the back of the hall, carrying a coffeepot from the kitchen.

"Hi, come on in," she called. "We're in the living room."

When the student didn't respond, Jennifer glanced back at the tall male figure outlined against the sunlight. Her heart skidded.

"Lij?"

In the two weeks she'd been home, she'd convinced herself that whatever had blossomed between them in Houston had been a fluke, an instant out of time, never to be repeated. When she hadn't heard from him—not a phone call or card—she'd known she was right. She'd put him away with her other memories.

Now that he stood before her, she didn't know what she felt. Her reactions were all on the gut level—shaky hands, trembly legs, a giddy gladness she couldn't explain.

He stepped inside. She felt herself grinning like a perfect fool. He was dressed casually, just jeans and a sport shirt, tennis shoes on his feet making his tread cat soft, but he looked wonderful. She noted his quiet manner and quick appraisal. She wished she looked less like a wild Indian and more like a woman.

"We're getting out the paper," she said. "The labeling machine broke down. Again." She waved him toward a chair in the room. "Would you like a cup of coffee?"

He nodded.

"I'll get you a mug. Everyone, this is Lij," she called out to her friends. "That's Tissy. And Bradford. Janine. Ted." She rattled off the names of a dozen more students who were helping out, then headed back down the hall, coffeepot still in hand.

Bradford walked over and shook his hand. Tissy said she was glad to meet him, gave him a tense smile, a rapid survey and returned to her job.

The students' greetings were even more casual. "Hey, man," two of them chorused while the rest muttered, waved or just smiled.

Lij felt that he'd stepped into some weird pioneer scene straight out of *Star Trek*. Part of the group looked as if it had been dressed in leftovers from *Frontier Days,* while the rest were masquerading as Okies whose jeans and work shirts had seen their best, better and possibly worst wear.

Headbands rolled from firemen's handkerchiefs and rawhide thongs held the men's hair out of the way as they bent over piles of newsprint. One bearded student wore a leather vest, another a paisley printed one with a satin fringe.

They reminded him of the group his wife had run with. For a second, the anger resurfaced, but he fought it down. This was a mistake, he shouldn't have come.

Jennifer returned with a mug for him. She filled it, then poured coffee into others around the room.

"Here, you might like to read the latest edition," she said, picking up a copy of the paper and giving it to him. "We won't be much longer."

He read the questions in her eyes. She wanted to know what he was doing there. "Elaine showed me the article on the space program," he said. "That was good reporting. Honest. Fair."

"Thank you." She'd resisted the sex scandals Bradford had wanted and stuck to the facts: money for rockets versus money for the poor, for education, for social reform. In spite of her time at the Space Center and her awe of the Apollo triumph, she still felt the country's priorities were all wrong. She still wanted to change them, and she'd said so in the article.

She wiped her hands on the seat of her jeans, smiled self-consciously, then resumed her position on the floor and started working again.

Lij sat in an old velvet chair and watched. Jennifer was dressed in faded purple jeans and a loose plaid shirt. The size of the shirt didn't disguise the fact she wore no bra.

He liked the fact that she was disconcerted by his presence. He thought Elaine had probably called and warned her when he asked for the address. Evidently she hadn't. The element of surprise was in his favor, he surmised.

Jennifer's hair was pulled into a frazzly ponytail, leaving her neck bare. She looked vulnerable, sitting on the floor with her head bent to her task. She peeled labels and stuck them on the folded papers with hands that trembled slightly.

He studied her friends, Tissy and Bradford, and the students, forcing himself to be objective. Up close, they didn't seem so bad. They were quiet, serious and intent on their chore. No one appeared stoned, and there was no sickening sweet scent of grass in the air. He relaxed.

Finally, Jennifer rose. "I'm finished," she announced. She turned to Lij. "I need some air. Do you want to go for a walk?"

He agreed and followed her to the door.

Out on the street, she got right to the point. "What are you doing here?"

"Aren't you glad to see me?" he countered.

How did a man tell a woman about missing her? How did he tell her how scared he'd been when Amy's fever shot up and how much he'd wanted her there? How did he tell her he didn't want involvement and yet confess that each time he saw her, the sight lifted his heart like a balloon on a string? He couldn't give her that much ammunition. Women used a man's weaknesses against him.

She looked at him, her blue eyes dark and thoughtful now, not lighting up with gladness the way they'd done on his arrival. "I was surprised," she said.

"Your friends are a mixed bag," he remarked, looking at the students who ambled along the streets. He imagined them on a school day, hurrying to class with their books, ready to argue with their professors over life and its meaning.

"You didn't like them," Jennifer said.

That was it, she realized. That was what she'd felt when she introduced Lij to the group in her living room. His dislike. It had radiated like an aura from his lithe frame. Dislike and mistrust. Did Tissy, Bradford and the others remind him of the wife he'd lost? she wondered in quick sympathy.

Tension manifested itself in the thin line of his smile as he answered her. "I don't know them."

"But there's some reason you resent them," she continued. "Lots of people are afraid of others who wear long hair and beads." She smiled with sudden brilliance. "We're not trying to overthrow the government, only to make it more sensitive to the needs of *all* its citizens."

He didn't rise to her teasing.

She laid a hand on his arm. They stopped in the shade of a live oak. "What's wrong, Lij?" she asked quietly.

"You," he said. "And me. I shouldn't have come here."

She watched his eyes move over her. His expression was dark and moody, riffled with hidden tensions that brought a frown to his brow. She walked on up the street toward the university. "That's probably true, so why did you?"

"I was lonely. I thought of you."

His reply was so simple. And so complex.

"How is your daughter?"

"Fine."

Jennifer had only seen Lij briefly during the last week she had been at the Space Center. She had met him leaving the hotel when she was returning. She'd asked the question then. His answer had been identical, spoken in the same gruff tone, then he had walked out the door without another word. So much for solicitude.

His life was clearly off limits. Perhaps hers should be, too.

Before she could voice this, his hand caught hers. He slid his fingers between hers and pressed their palms together.

"I'm sorry. Amy had a flu bug. She has very little resistance to infection, and I've spent every spare minute with her for the past two weeks. I probably won't be very good company, but would you spend today and tomorrow with me? I have to go back to work on Monday."

Jennifer looked heavenward as if to ask why she was such a glutton for punishment. Being with him here would create memories she'd probably be better off without. It was becoming clear to her that their lives were in no way compatible. It was insane to continue seeing each other.

"Yes," she said, wishing she could just refuse and heave him out of her life. "I have a spare room. Do you want to use it?"

He glanced at her, amused. "Well, I'd rather sleep with you, but if you'd rather I didn't, the spare room will be fine."

"I think," she said with more than a hint of exasperation, "we should confine ourselves to being friends."

"You're probably right."

He was laughing at her now. He looked younger and more at ease. Meeting his eyes, she had to grin. Could they just be friends? Would that be enough?

Sure. For about two seconds.

TISSY STIRRED THE BROTH with a wooden spoon. "Taste this and see if it needs more salt."

Jennifer dipped the spoon into the pot-roast pan and sampled the juice. "That's enough for me. We might need more after the potatoes cook." She added the rest of the vegetables to the pot.

"I'll make cornbread," Tissy decided.

"With buttermilk?"

Tissy laughed. "Of course."

They had been living in this house for over five years and had formed an easy way of sharing tasks. Jennifer did most of the actual cooking while Tissy took care of setting the table and making the salad. Bradford cleaned up after the meal.

"How's Elaine and Mac?" Tissy asked. "You've hardly mentioned them since you got back."

Jennifer was reluctant to speak of them. "Not good."

Tissy raised her eyebrows.

"Elaine thought Mac was running around on her, then she overheard something about a paternity case. She assumed Mac was involved, but he was intervening for a friend."

"Oh-oh," Tissy said with a flash of comprehension in her eyes.

"They quarreled when Elaine asked him about it. He accused her of not trusting him."

"What did he expect?" Tissy snapped. "Did he think she was a mindreader or was maybe too stupid to notice that something was going on under her nose?"

"Apparently."

One thing about Tissy, Jennifer acknowledged, she went right to the heart of the matter, as she saw it, and spoke her mind. That had always irritated Elaine, but Jennifer found it refreshing.

"I never could figure out why she married that man. His family was enough to drive a person insane, what I remember of them when we went to the wedding. His mother kept asking the guests if they thought the couple was doing the right thing. I finally answered."

Jennifer grinned ruefully. "What did you tell her?"

"That I most certainly did not. I told her marriage was an antiquated custom dating from the days when women were chattel and that it served no purpose in society at present."

Tissy grinned with impish humor. "She didn't ask that question again."

Jennifer could imagine Mac's straitlaced family and their reaction to Tissy's outspokenness. "Do you really feel that way?"

Tissy considered. "No. Marriage is probably the only way to gain any stability at all in today's society."

"I'm surprised to hear you say that," Jennifer confessed.

"The world changes. The liberation movement has, too. At the beginning of the sixties, there was more idealism. What happened to Bob Dylan and the answers that were supposed to be blowing in the wind? Or not giving a damn about a greenback dollar?"

"They're still around," Jennifer insisted.

"The spirit isn't the same anymore. Young people join in because that seems the thing to do, but they're wilder than we were and more selfish. They don't really *care*. Or maybe we cared too much." She shrugged. "Who knows?"

"There're a lot of groupies these days," Jennifer commented.

"That was probably what worried Elaine. To sleep with an astronaut is the in thing, some of the students tell me. The pill may be the single biggest setback women have ever faced."

Jennifer put the clean dishes away. "Why do you say that?"

"It gives women no irrefutable excuse to say no and relieves men of all responsibility for the consequences."

"It gives us choices," Jennifer protested. "*We* can decide when we're ready for children. Speaking of which, Mac's family is pressing Elaine to have a baby."

"That's the last thing she needs." Tissy was emphatic.

"Why? Maybe it would cement their marriage."

"The only thing a baby cements is the woman in the trap." She waved her hands in an expanding gesture. "Did you know that when people divorce, a year later the man's living standard is forty-three percent higher, while the woman's is a third less? That means he has twice her income and only himself to think of, while she has herself and the kids to care for."

"That's terrible!"

"I want to run a series of articles about women and their lack of equal opportunity, but Bradford is reluctant. He's afraid of being labeled a feminist."

"Does he consider that worse than being called a Berkeley radical?" Jennifer asked with a laugh. After adding more garlic to the pot roast, she put the lid back on and turned the burner low. She finished stacking the plates on a shelf.

"Definitely, but I keep working on him. By the way, what's with this Lij Branigan? He's Establishment with a capital *E*. He'd want the same things Mac does, the wife to stay at home with the kids while he does his thing. Somehow I can't see you doing that." Tissy tilted her head and studied her friend. "Can you?"

Jennifer leaned against the counter and crossed her arms over her chest. "No. I accused him of chauvinism."

A dark, slender eyebrow shot up. "Wow, sounds like you two were into some pretty heavy cocktail talk. I thought you met him at Elaine's party."

"I did, but we saw each other every day after that. We talked of many things."

"Like shoes and ships and sealing wax and cabbages and kings?" Tissy suggested.

"Something like that."

"Far out," Tissy murmured. "We'll be hearing wedding bells for you next."

"No," Jennifer said sharply. "He was married once. His wife died. He has a little girl to take care of. The place where she stays . . . Elaine told me it was a home for retarded children."

"It is," a low, quiet voice said.

Jennifer and Tissy turned toward the voice. Lij stood in the doorway. His eyes lighted on Tissy, taking in everything from her beads to her bare feet, and the restless anger returned.

"She was nearly killed due to the carelessness of a guy in a van who thought he could go through a truck because his head was full of some psychedelic drug."

Jennifer understood his earlier tension. Seeing her friends, with their strange mix of clothing and life-styles, he was remembering the accident. He was equating them with the driver of the van.

"Tissy and Bradford aren't like that, Lij," she said quietly. "It isn't fair to compare them just because of the way they dress."

"Hey, man, lighten up." Bradford came up from the basement where he had been working on the printing equipment.

"Go to hell," Lij said. He heard the sneer in his voice and was ashamed of his actions. Jennifer was right. He didn't know these people. He was acting from past anger. "Sorry," he said to Bradford.

The weekend was going wrong and he didn't know how to right it. He'd planned no further than seeing Jennifer. Since he liked Elaine, he hadn't given another thought to Jennifer's Berkeley friends. He hadn't realized how much she identified with them.

Neither had he been prepared for a . . . a damned hippie commune complete with lots of single guys coming and going as they pleased.

"I'd like to speak to Lij alone," Jennifer said.

Tissy and Bradford exchanged glances, but they left. "I'll be in the basement if you need me," Bradford said.

"Thanks." Jennifer waited until her friends were gone and the door closed behind them. "Just what right have you to come in here and act like you own the place?" she demanded of Lij. "These are my friends, and I won't have them insulted."

His anger and frustration increased. He knew he should leave before he said things he'd regret. He knew he was going to say them anyway. "I doubt if that kind can be insulted. Pretty nice setup they have here—the run of the house, food service—" he pointed to the pot bubbling on the stove "—free labor, or did they pay you for your hours of work on the paper this morning? Or for the article you wrote?"

"Get out," she said.

"Just as I thought. They didn't." His dark eyes flicked over her. "They're using you for their own ends."

"They pay their rent just like the students," Jennifer informed him in the coldest voice possible. "They also pay half the bills. Before that, they helped me paint and fix up this place to make it habitable. Bradford is an orphan. He worked his way through Berkeley as a handyman."

"Good for him."

Jennifer ignored the sarcasm. She was certainly seeing a side of Lij that was eye-opening. "You're not welcome in my house. They are. We're not acid droppers here, Lij. I don't know the type of people your wife ran around with, but in this house, we warn kids about drug use. You'll find nothing stronger than wine here."

"Then you'd better check the third floor. It smells like incense burning up there. Or something stronger."

"I doubt it. You probably smelled patchouli oil. One of the students uses it for his weekly massage to drive out the bad vibes. The gang knows I have to pass inspection to run a rooming house. They wouldn't jeopardize my livelihood."

Lij ran a hand over his face. He'd blown any chances he might have had with Jennifer. Even a fool could deduce that. But he couldn't shake the feeling that he should grab her and get her away before something bad happened to her.

He didn't trust her so-called friends any farther than he could toss that stupid van in the garage. However, her friends were none of his business. She'd known them a long time, a hell of a lot longer than she'd known him. What right did he have to interfere in her life?

For the third time that day, he apologized. "You're right. How you choose to live it is up to you. I apologize for being obnoxious."

He walked over to her and touched her under her chin. lifting her face to his. "I've had some beautiful dreams about you the past couple of weeks. Thanks for those."

He stroked her cheek, then left. When he backed the car out of the drive, he glanced around for a second. No wonder the van had looked peculiar to him. It was an old hearse.

Chapter Six

Jennifer woke with a headache and a scratchy throat. She attributed the aches to a coming cold, not to the tears she wouldn't let fall. Throwing the covers back, she leapt out of bed and dashed for the shower before the cold of the early California morning penetrated her flesh. Would it be as cool at night on the desert as it was here in the Bay area?

She dressed, threw some last-minute items into her suitcase and snapped it closed. Tissy came out of her room across the hall, rubbing sleep from her eyes. "Ready?"

"Yes. Let's go."

"What about breakfast?"

"I'll have a doughnut at the airport."

Tissy frowned at this but said nothing. She quietly drove Jennifer to the airport.

Forty minutes later, Jennifer was in the air, flying south to Edwards Air Force Base. Home of test pilot Lij Branigan.

She wondered if Elaine had told him about the trip. He hadn't mentioned it during his brief stay at her house Saturday. Her mind had been on so many other things, she had forgotten it, too.

The landscape changed from coastal redwoods and mountains to Joshua trees, cactus and the buckled, arid landscape of the desert.

The sun was over the horizon when the DC-3 set down on the tarmac, but the day was still early. Jennifer's stomach growled. She'd get her rental car, check into the motel, eat breakfast... She looked at her watch and corrected her schedule. She'd drive out to the base, check in with the PR office there, then see about something to eat.

Within an hour, she had accomplished her tasks and was on her way, a plastic cup filled with the worst coffee she'd ever tasted clutched in her hand. She sipped it cautiously as she followed directions to the public-relations office at Edwards.

Her contact was a civilian, the base historian, Dr. Boone. He was waiting for her when she arrived.

"Is that Boone as in Daniel?" she asked with a cordial smile when they shook hands.

"Perhaps a cousin. I'm not sure," the man replied.

He was about sixty with salt-and-pepper hair, brown eyes and a sad face that drooped, from the corners of his eyes to the corners of his mouth, like a hound dog's. He was writing a history of the base and the planes that had been tested there.

"It's early yet," he continued. "The staff doesn't come in until eight-thirty. Let's go to the OC for coffee."

"Would it be all right if I had breakfast?" she asked. "I just had the worst cup of coffee in my life and need some food before it eats a hole in my stomach."

He grinned, the sags in his face barely lifting. "You must have gotten it from that place next to the rental-car agency. I think the owner boils out her husband's socks in it."

They were still laughing when they arrived at the Officers' Club. Lij was there, looking resplendent in an air-force dress uniform. Probably doing his reserve duty, she assumed.

She saw him as soon as she stepped over the threshold, sitting at a table with his friend she'd met at Elaine's house. Batman, she recalled, was his flying name; she didn't remember his real one. She realized she didn't know what Lij had been called in flight school.

Just as she remembered this inane fact, he looked up. As their eyes met, she looked away. Then back. He was still watching her, not moving, just watching. She nodded and turned toward Dr. Boone.

The historian gallantly insisted upon paying for her bacon and eggs, orange juice and coffee, which rather embarrassed her. They took a table next to a window, where she could look out on the desert and the hills in the distance. She was aware of Lij and his friend standing to leave, conscious of him walking over to her table. "Morning, Dave," he said to Dr. Boone. "How'd you get the prettiest gal on the base to yourself?"

Jennifer tried to objectively assess Lij. Like the first time they met, she sensed he was troubled. His smile didn't reach his eyes, and when he looked at her, he didn't smile at all. He merely stared at her in a manner so solemn that it made her uneasy.

Darn it, the element of surprise had been hers, she'd been prepared for a chance meeting. She wasn't going to get rattled, especially since he was calm as a cactus.

"I made an appointment," Dr. Boone said, his eyebrows rising in amusement at the inner edges, making him look even sadder than before. "Have you got one?"

Jennifer was pleased at this comeback. It put Lij in his place. Which was very low on the totem pole.

His eyes flicked over her briefly. She was willing to bet he could describe everything about her from the brightly printed scarf that held her hair back from her face to the tan pantsuit she wore. She picked up her orange-juice glass and sipped slowly, knowing she was hiding behind the action.

"Have I?" Lij turned the question on her.

"My schedule is full," she said.

"How about dinner tonight?" A sardonic smile curved his mouth into an attractive bow. She knew he was remembering that first dinner invitation, which she had refused.

She remembered a later date—the way he'd smiled and how his kiss had felt.... Like wow...like groovy...like outasight, as her student boarders would say.

"Should I perhaps introduce you first?" Dr. Boone inquired dryly.

"No need. The lady and I have met."

Dr. Boone looked startled. "I was going to ask Lij or Bill to help you with the technicalities," he said. "Since you know Lij, he can handle that end of things. I have all the names and dates pertaining to the space program and its development."

"Thank you, Dr. Boone," Jennifer interjected, "But I'm sure your office can supply me with everything I need to know. I wouldn't want to interfere with Major Branigan's schedule."

"No problem," Lij spoke before Dr. Boone could reply. "I have a meeting with some Pentagon brass this afternoon. After that, I can show you around as part of my official duties."

"I thought you were supposed to be flying," Jennifer said.

He frowned at her and his jaw hardened with determination. "It'll be a while before the next prototype is ready. I don't mind escorting a beautiful VIP on a tour of the base in the meantime."

His smile, sudden and beguiling, almost hesitant, disrupted any other arguments she tried to bring up. Dr. Boone demolished the rest of the effort. "That's a good idea. You can pick her up at my office in the morning." His eyes twinkled. "About tonight, you'll have to work that out between you. Now let us get on with our meal and discussion."

Lij accepted the dismissal with good grace. He touched his cap in a brief salute to Jennifer and left, his stride long and unhurried. Jennifer watched him go. With a sigh, she finished her eggs and stood to leave when her companion did.

The day proved tedious, the task of collecting facts arduous. She was assigned a desk in a room next to Dr. Boone's office, and there she read and made copies of fact sheets she thought teachers might want to use. She'd have to make the information interesting as well as informative or she'd lose her young audience.

Some of her work consisted of updating already published material. This she did first, making notes for later use as she went. At three, she cleared the desk and locked it, hoping she'd beat the commuter traffic.

The mid-afternoon heat was fierce. By the time Jennifer pulled into the motel parking lot, the back of her jacket and blouse were clinging to her body as if pasted on. She went inside and put on her bikini.

Was it too bare? she wondered. The bottoms seemed to get briefer each season. Picking up a towel, she opened the door to head to the pool.

Lij was leaning against the fender of a red sports car. He was dressed casually in white pants and a blue Hawaiian shirt.

"Quite a change, Major," she remarked, closing the door behind her after making sure she had the key.

"I'm off duty now."

"What are you doing here?"

"Waiting for you. I saw you leave the base and followed."

Her heart set up a terrible cacophony in her chest, which suddenly seemed empty of everything except the furiously beating organ. "Why?"

Lij almost smiled when Jennifer gave him her most direct look from those subtle blue eyes, a look that was calculated to wither a man's confidence. It demanded to know why the hell he was bothering her. He didn't have an answer, other than that it was important they reestablish the rapport he had first sensed with her.

"I wanted to talk to you. To start over," he added. "To say I'm sorry."

She pushed a strand of hair away from her face, and the towel slung casually over her shoulders parted. He saw the smooth expanse of skin along her throat and breasts. The bare curve of her waist beckoned his touch, her hips and thighs and calves demanded exploration.

The bright yellow material of the bikini contrasted with the honey tones of her flesh. Her toasty-brown hair with its blond strands lay over her shoulders in waves, a treasure waiting to be discovered. He had daydreamed of her...California dreaming.

He was filled with the longing to touch. He wanted to caress, stroke, taste, nibble...all the things lovers did to make each other feel alive and wanted. He felt weak with the awful need of it...of *her*. Jennifer, his California girl.

Quickly, before he made a complete fool of himself and she noticed, he spun away, putting inches and feet and yards between them so he couldn't reach out like a greedy kid and take what he so desperately wanted. Opening the door to the red Corvette, he climbed in and slammed it shut.

The loud metallic clink of the lock sounded final in his ears. He didn't know what was wrong with him in the first place. Seeing Jennifer again had upset his equilibrium. Whatever he had thought they might share was lost now. He realized that.

"I just wanted to tell you I won't intrude on your life again," he said with a smile of regret. "I'll have Bill or one of the other jocks assigned to you while you're here."

He noted the silky movement of her hair when she nodded without speaking. Swallowing against a tightness in his throat, he lifted a hand in farewell, then cranked up the engine and left.

Jennifer watched him drive away, feeling a terrible finality in the act. Should she have stopped him? Should she have told him she didn't want anyone else to show her around?

No, it was best to let it go now. Lij was everything she didn't want in a man. He was too complicated. There was a deep-seated antagonism against her friends in him. It was better not to get involved. So why did she feel like crying?

Crossing the parking area to the grassy verge, she went to the pool and joined a dozen others with the same idea for cooling off. The presence of so many kids prevented her from swimming her usual laps, and after a while, she gave up and lay in the sun, letting it dry her body as she wished that the restlessness would go away.

Happiness wasn't just a warm puppy, Charlie Brown, she reflected. Sometimes a person needed more.

Elaine and Mac were still separated although living in the same house. Tissy and Bradford were in disagreement over the inclusion of women's liberation articles in the paper. She and Lij were . . . what? Nothing, that's what.

She wrapped the towel around her shoulders and went to her room to shower. An early dinner at a local restaurant was peaceful. It was also lonely. She decided to call her grandmother when she got back to her room. She needed to touch base with someone who loved her without demands.

"Hi, Gram," Jennifer said, keeping her tone cheerful. "How are you doing?"

"Jennifer! Let me turn this television down so I can hear."

"Am I interrupting your favorite show? I can call back—"

"No, no. It's just a *Star Trek* rerun. Did you know it's not being renewed this fall? I was sorry to hear it."

Jennifer smiled at her grandmother's tone. The older woman was a bona fide Yankee, and her no-nonsense view of life seemed just what Jennifer needed. "No, I didn't know that. What have you been up to?"

Her grandmother talked of her garden and the battles she was having with the insects. Hearing the ordinary details of small-town life put Jennifer solidly on terra firma again.

"Now, child, you didn't call all this way just to listen to me rail about potato bugs. What's happening with you?"

Jennifer hesitated. "I've met a man," she said finally.

"Well, that sounds interesting. One of those young astronaut fellows I've been reading about?" Gram kept up with the world.

"Sort of. He's a test pilot now, but he's thinking of volunteering for the space program."

An awkward silence ensued while Jennifer tried to think of something to add.

"Ayuh," her grandmother encouraged, falling back into her New England twang as she occasionally did when deep in thought.

"There's nothing really to tell. We met in Houston. He came to Berkeley, and we quarreled. Then I came to Edwards. He works here. That's all."

Gram hadn't lived seventy-eight years for nothing. "What scares you about him?"

"He's totally different from me...you know what a rebel I've always been. I think he's a hidebound conservative. But he's had problems, he's gentle, and...and I like him."

Great, Jennifer, she chided herself. *That made a lot of sense.*

"Sometimes two people with differences can make an interesting combination," Gram told her.

"There are other things. He's involved in dangerous work. He didn't like Tissy and Bradford—"

"They take a bit o' getting used to," Gram murmured. She, too, had been rather shocked at the free-and-easy lifestyle of the residents of her grandaughter's rooming house before she'd grown to appreciate them and their impossible idealism and radical ways.

Jennifer, for all her twenty-eight years and the harsh tragedies that had befallen her, was still the quiet child who had loved fairy tales. *Tell me a story, Gram,* the older woman could hear her say. *Make it come out happy.*

Gram thought of her son's death, trapped beneath the sea. And young Jeffrey, going up in flames. Perhaps she should have taught her granddaughter that not all stories can have a happy ending. But she had never been able to make herself darken the shining trust in the young girl's eyes.

Right now it was the adult Jennifer who needed help. Gram could hear the doubt and confusion in the younger woman's voice. "Tell me how you met him."

Jennifer found herself telling Gram how Lij had helped her at Elaine's party—with a side excursion into Elaine's and Mac's problems—and of the days at the Space Center and the evenings at the hotel. "We're just too different to get involved. I mean, where would it lead?"

"Why don't you wait and see?" Gram suggested.

"You think I should see him?"

"Ayuh."

"I'll think about it," Jennifer decided. "When did you last see Mom? I got a letter last week."

They talked of family matters for a few minutes, then said goodbye. After hanging up, Jennifer pondered the conversation. Had she only called her grandmother because she knew Gram would advise her to follow her heart?

Gram was such a romantic, always making up elaborate stories to entertain Jennifer when she was a child, all of them with impossibly happy endings. *And they lived happily ever after and had four children and two dogs, a pet rabbit who could talk, and a magic horse that could fly.*

Jennifer sighed dispiritedly. "Beam me up, Scotty," she murmured. Any world in the universe had to be less troublesome than this one.

JENNIFER SAT ON THE hard chair in the briefing room and listened to an aircraft designer explain his design to Lij, Bill Davis and several other men, including an air force officer. Bill had taken her on a tour of the base yesterday, and today he had invited her to sit in on a discussion of a planned flight test.

"Just a routine test," he'd explained. "Nothing scary. Lij will be flying some loops and rolls to check it out."

"All right," she had replied.

When the briefing was finished, Lij came to them. He was dressed in a jumpsuit with another garment on over it. The outerwear hugged his torso and legs like some kind of kinky wrap.

"Did you get anything out of the talk?" he asked. His manner was easy and self-assured with no overtones of hostility that Jennifer could detect.

She shook her head. "Not much. Too technical."

He smiled. "What it amounts to is, I'm going to fly a prototype plane around for a while and see how maneuverable she is. If you want to watch, Bill can drive you out to the edge of the lake, unless you'd like to go up in a plane and fly chase."

"I'd rather stay on the ground."

His smile widened into a teasing grin. "I thought as much." He turned to his friend. "Bill?"

"Right. I'll drive her."

Jennifer felt a tingle of pleasure at Lij's thoughtfulness. She tried to ignore the one of apprehension for his safety. This was just a routine test. Nothing scary, Bill had said.

In a few minutes, she and Bill walked out onto the tarmac and watched Lij climb into a large plane. A smaller plane was attached underneath its belly.

"That's a bomber, isn't it?" she asked, puzzled. "What's the other one?"

The smaller plane looked odd. Its wings were angled sharply back from the body and looked way too small to support its weight. The apprehension she had felt escalated into a pang of fear.

"That's the one to be flight tested. At twenty thousand feet, Lij will climb into it and be dropped like a bomb. Then he'll crank up the X—uh, the plane and do the tests."

She noticed the near slip. "What do you call the test plane?" she asked.

Bill grinned. "Uh-uh, you don't catch me there. That's classified."

She watched the bomber taxi out on the runway and take off, carrying its load like a baby hugged to its breast. "Interesting wing design," she commented. Her mind had already sorted the experimental plane into a category.

"Come on." Bill grabbed her arm and raced her toward a side door. They went through it and out to a parking lot where he guided her to an army jeep. In a minute, they were off.

Bill raced along a desert road at a tremendous rate of speed. The road was unpaved but fortunately graded smooth. He drove until he came to a turnoff. He took it and gunned them up onto a small, steep hillock that gave them a wonderful view of the desert country beyond the base. He pulled two pairs of binoculars out of their cases and handed one to her. "Let's get out where we can see."

They stood beside the vehicle.

The bomber flew in a wide arc over the arid land, then headed toward them. When it seemed to be directly overhead, it released its load. The smaller aircraft fell away smoothly, shooting forward with the momentum of the mother ship. Jennifer saw the blast of smoke as its engines fired. The plane shot away and seemed to rise at an angle straight up from the desert floor. The other plane returned to the base.

A loud *boom* reverberated across the sandy spit where they watched. "He's sonic," Bill announced, his eyes lit with excitement as he followed the shining dot in the sky where it caught the afternoon sun. "He'll be lost to sight in a minute. I have a radio." He grinned at her. "Don't tell anyone."

He flipped on the switch and tuned in the special channel. Lij's voice came clearly over the airwaves. Jennifer could have imagined him safe back at the base had she not known he was forty or fifty thousand feet above them.

"Mach 2," he said. "She's looking good. Let's take her all the way." Then in a softer tone, "Come on, lady, show us what you got."

A vapor trail appeared in the sky, longer and thicker than the previous one. The dot shot up and out of sight. Jennifer couldn't see it by looking directly at where she thought it was, but by looking from the periphery of her vision, she thought she could detect the craft.

"Use the glasses," Bill advised.

She raised the binoculars to her eyes. Her hands wavered too much for her to keep the speck in view.

"Here. Lean on the fender. Wait until I put something on it, otherwise we'll burn our elbows."

He covered the hot metal with an old tarp, and they leaned their elbows on the vehicle for support. Jennifer scanned the sky for a long time before she spotted a tiny dot coming back into their field of vision.

"There he is." She fell silent, watching as the airplane nosed in a downward direction. It began a series of exercises that reminded her of a prankster having a good time. He waggled the stubby wings, rolled the plane, banked into turns, rolled out. It was impressive to watch.

When Lij stopped playing games and flew straight at them, Bill leapt into the jeep. "Come on. We'll meet him back at the base."

Jennifer was quiet for several miles, then she turned to Bill. "It's a rocket plane, isn't it? I thought the program was dropped in sixty-six."

Bill didn't say a word, but he gave her a startled glance before concentrating once more on his driving. Finally, just before they roared into the base, he said softly, "Lij said you'd done your research. Just keep this quiet, will you?"

"Mum's the word," she replied wryly.

She suddenly knew Lij had arranged for her to see him fly the experimental plane. It must have taken some pull to do it. She had confidential clearance; she had just witnessed a top-secret project. Mum was definitely the word.

When Lij came out of the flight building at five that afternoon, he was obviously surprised to see he had a visitor. Jennifer waited for him next to the red Corvette.

"You already have one of the requirements for an astronaut," she remarked. "They all seem to drive fancy sports cars."

A Florida auto dealer had made Corvettes available to the first astronauts, she knew. Lij, though, would have had to buy his own.

To her surprise, he looked embarrassed. "I did a commercial last year. This was one of the props, so they gave it to me."

"Nice work if you can get it," she said with a smile.

She watched as he looked her over, his perusal slow and careful, taking in every inch of her red skirt and tailored white blouse with a red bow adding a dash of color at the neck. Red-and-white spectator pumps matched her purse. She knew she looked vibrant in red and liked to wear it.

"Yeah," he said. He looked back at her face, his eyes meeting hers with a question in them.

Jennifer's smile faded. Neither of them seemed to know what to say or do next. Lij stared out across the desert, his eyes taking on the blue of his shirt and the sky.

Finally she asked, "Know a good place for dinner?"

His gaze came back to her. "Yeah. Are we starting over?"

"I don't know."

"I'd like the chance."

He sounded so humble, she wanted to hug him. Instead, she twisted the strap of her purse, giving her hands something innocuous to do.

"Give me an hour to get showered and changed," he suggested, very casual in manner, "and I'll take you to the best mesquite barbecue place in the West."

"All right."

His eyes seemed to change, going from cool blue-gray to a warmer shade. His smile promised anything she wanted. "Why'd you change your mind about us?" he asked, opening the door to her car and closing it after she was inside.

Because life is sometimes short and nights can be long, she started to say. *Because I saw you in that rocket plane and life at its fullest, with all the risks, suddenly seemed more important than life at its emptiest.* She said instead, "You called your plane a lady."

"I call her a lady when she's behaving. Otherwise, she's a bitch." His grin was sudden and charming. It made him seem younger and handsomer than ever before.

Jennifer realized he was happy. At this moment he was content with his world. It was the first time she had seen him this way. In Houston he'd had other worries on his mind, but now, with their truce, he was a young man, carefree and happy. It was very appealing.

"I'll see you later," she said with a catch in her breath.

"Roger that," he said. He leaned down and peered intently into her eyes. "One hour," he promised.

WHY WAS SHE DOING this? Jennifer wondered. It was too late to renege, but why had she suggested dinner in the first place? Answer: she wanted to see Lij. Caution be damned. She wanted the full-of-life feeling she got when she was with him. But why, some part insisted on knowing. Why? She didn't know.

Nevertheless, she pulled on a very short, brightly printed skirt over a form-fitting bodysuit, making the slenderness of her figure and the fullness of her bust clearly visible. Several gold chains dangling with charms went around her neck. Her earrings were a matched pair only if one considered a quarter moon hanging from one ear and a star from the other as a set. She pulled on white go-go boots, then added several rings to her fingers.

"Not exactly Twiggy and Carnaby Street," she murmured to her image in the mirror, "but certainly different from Elaine and her friends in Houston."

She realized she wanted Lij to accept her as she was—funky clothes, radical friends and all. Just as today she'd accepted his need to live on the cutting edge of science and technology. It was part of him.

LIJ BLINKED THEN SMILED at Jennifer's outfit when she opened the door. Gone was the businesswoman image of the day. Gone were the hippie jeans and shirt she'd worn in Berkeley. Now she wore the latest in pop fashion—miniskirt, boots and lots of jewelry.

He snapped his fingers. "I know—Nancy Sinatra doing 'These Boots Were Made for Walking.'"

"Nope, just Jennifer. Who you see is who you get," she quipped.

Lij ran a finger along her jaw line. "You'll do."

Jennifer looked troubled as she let him escort her to the Corvette. When they were both inside and he drove off, he asked, "Having second thoughts about coming with me tonight?"

"Yes," she admitted.

"Why?"

"You're a threat to my peace of mind." She laughed at this ridiculous answer.

"Well," he drawled, "that seems fair. You've destroyed my sleep for several nights."

"Can't we just be friends who enjoy each other's company with no...no other ties?"

She was afraid of getting involved, he thought. Afraid of getting hurt like she was after her fiancé died. Elaine had been right. He could hurt her.

"Sure. We haven't signed a pact in blood or anything. We'll play this strictly for laughs. How's that?"

She studied his profile as he wheeled onto a bumpy road leading to a restaurant on a hillock much like the one she had been on while watching him fly. His forehead was wide, his eyes deep-set with spiky lashes narrowed against the sinking sun. He was a man whose word a person would instinctively trust. She sighed in relief. "Super."

"Right," he said, his laughter a deep chuckle from his chest. "Super." When he parked and helped her out, his eyes were amused, as if secretly he laughed at their agreement.

They went into the restaurant and were seated next to the window, giving them a wide-open view of the sunset over the desert. "It's beautiful," she said.

"Yeah," he agreed, but he was looking at her.

"Jennifer?" Her name was spoken by a naval officer who stopped by their table, breaking the mood. "How are you?"

"Walt," Jennifer said. "What a surprise seeing you here." She introduced the men. "This is Lij Branigan. Captain Jacobs. The captain and I knew each other in Washington, D.C.," she explained.

"I served under her grandfather, Admiral Wright, until he retired," the officer added. "I understand he's advisor to the president?" He turned to Jennifer, excluding Lij.

Lij wanted to do something to make it clear that she belonged to him, he discovered. Except she didn't. He doubted she could belong to anyone—she was one of the most independent women he'd ever met.

"Yes. You know how you sailors are," she chided, teasing her friend. "They never retire, they just take a different job."

"Well, I'd better join my own party. Will you be in the area long?" The captain glanced furtively at Lij. "I'd like to see you."

"Just this week," she replied with regret in her smile. "I'll be busy with my research. Another time."

"Right." The man gave a half salute and left them.

"An old flame?" Lij asked. He knew it was none of his business, but he asked anyway.

"We dated a few times," she admitted. "It was nothing."

Because she hadn't wanted it to be, he thought. It didn't hurt a navy officer's career to have a wife who was granddaughter of an admiral and daughter of a dead hero, but

Jennifer obviously hadn't been interested. He remembered how she'd felt in his arms, moving against him, responding to him. She'd been interested then. A slow smile curled the corners of his mouth.

Jennifer tried to figure out what was so amusing to Lij. He seemed happy and content to be with her. And in perfect agreement that they stay on a friendly level, no more. That was fine with her.

Now if she could just stop thinking about how warm and strong his arms had been when he had held her that night in Texas. This was California ... another time, another place and a long way removed from that night and all the past nights of her life.

This was Lij Branigan and Jennifer Wright. Friends.

Right?

Right.

Chapter Seven

It was almost midnight when Lij brought Jennifer back to her motel. They had talked of inconsequential things during the evening and had laughed about silly incidents that had happened to them during their youths, and they had stayed away from controversial subjects.

At her room, she unlocked the door and turned to tell him good-night. He stood very close, close enough to shield her from the keen desert wind that cut through her clothing and sent chills along her arms.

"I have an idea," he said, his voice low, deep, caressing.

"What?" By contrast, her tone was wary and cautious.

His smile flashed white in the darkness. He rested his hand at her waist. "Would you like to go up with me tomorrow? I can arrange it."

"In what?" She thought of long planes with stubby wings. Rocket engines. Explosions.

"In a T-38. It's a trainer. Most of the astronauts fly them. It's a lot different from commercial aviation. I thought you might like to get a feel for *real* flying."

"A glimpse into your world?" she asked, feeling challenged.

"I suppose." He shrugged. "If you'd rather not...it was just an idea." His smile flashed again.

His manner was cool, as if it didn't matter to him whether she came or not. But the hand at her side bespoke tension in the tightening of his fingers.

"The experience might be good for my writing," she decided. "But I'm a terrible coward."

"This won't be frightening," he assured her. "A piece of cake."

"The last time I had cake, I think, was at my tenth birthday. I ate too much and got sick," she told him.

"I'll be careful with you."

The air between them trembled with possibilities and promises half spoken. Jennifer felt his hand move around her to caress her back and bring her closer. She lifted her face, expecting and wanting his kiss. Stupid. Foolish. Dangerous.

His mouth touched hers. His lips were tender, edged with passion kept in control, but there, like the implied danger of a carnival ride. She knew nothing was really going to happen, but there was always the possibility that it could. She had only to take one step back—a small step for a woman—and Lij would be inside the door, the invitation given and accepted. Her heart supplied the giant leap.

She put her hands against his chest, holding him in place while she stepped away.

He chucked her under the chin. "Good night, my friend," he said. "Bring some flat shoes."

She stepped aside, and Lij closed the door. The last thing she saw was the whiteness of his smile against the desert night.

The next morning, she labored faithfully at her texts, going over facts and figures, becoming fascinated with the evolving development of each plane and finding satisfaction upon fruition of a design into an operational aircraft.

But where, she wondered, did the rocket plane belong? What was the logical place for it? Something in space. That was the only logical conclusion.

Late that afternoon, after the regular work hours were over, Lij came for her. He was dressed in a flight suit and had brought one for her. "You'll need this."

She slipped it on over her slacks and shirt. She only had to roll the pant legs up once to clear the walking shoes she'd brought at his suggestion. At the hangar, he showed her how to wear a G suit over the other.

The plane he led her to seemed small and waspish. It had a sharp nose and swept-back wings. It was clearly made for speed and reminded her of a race car, its slender lines suggesting eagerness to be off.

Lij held a parachute pack for her and she slipped her arms into the straps, fastening them over her breasts and between her legs. Lij made the final adjustments, checking for proper tightness. His touch seemed impersonal until his eyes met hers. Then he grinned.

He secured her helmet and face mask and hooked her into the rear seat before climbing in and adjusting his harness. Jennifer felt awkward and bulky in the flight outfit. She also felt more than a little apprehensive. What if she made a complete and utter fool of herself? She'd probably throw up or faint.

Lij's voice came to her over the headset, directly in her ear as if he were lying next to her. It was an unsettling thought to add to all the others she had.

"Having second thoughts?" he asked.

The laughter in his voice told her he knew what she was going through. She gritted her teeth and vowed to take anything he threw at her. "No."

"Good. We're off."

The firing of the engine had her heart thumping like a bird's, about two hundred times a minute. By the time they eased onto the runway and got in a lineup behind two other planes, she was calm again. Deep bre??ing helped a lot.

She had to do her exercises a few n..nutes later when they took off—straight up. Or so it seemed to her.

"This beauty is a real lady," Lij murmured intimately in her ear after they had cleared the area.

Jennifer peered over the edge of the canopy. The sky was a great parabolic mirror. It reflected the tones of the sunset that was just beginning to paint the western rim of the sky in pink and gold. To the east, the mountains brooded in shades of lavender and plum. A nearby peak was ruddy in the glow.

"It's beautiful," she said.

Lij flew north and dropped the left wing so Jennifer could see the base painted a glowing peach in the dazzling ligh⁺. Then he dropped the right wing so she could look out that side.

"Can you take an Immelmann turn?" he asked.

"I'll try." She hadn't the foggiest idea what it was.

She clenched the edge of the seat and prayed not to be sick. The sky tilted to ninety degrees, then disappeared. Suddenly the earth was above her. When she peered out the window, she saw nothing but blue below them. Like a huge ocean with some whitecaps, she thought. For some reason, she didn't have the sensation of falling on her head. The plane completed the turn.

"Okay?" Lij asked.

"Yes," she said. She realized it was true. "Yes!"

"That's my girl."

His low chuckle in her ear sent frissons along her spine. Jennifer suddenly felt that she could do anything. She could fly. She could soar. She wasn't sure she even needed a plane.

"It's wonderful," she said, looking eagerly at the world far below. "I feel like a bird."

"How about a loop?"

"Uhhh," she hedged.

He laughed again. "Hang on."

The plane launched itself in a graceful backward somersault. Lij rolled out near the apex, saving Jennifer from the sudden downward drop. He tried a short dive. "How do you feel?"

"Queasy," she admitted. Elevator rides were not her favorite entertainment. "But not bad."

"You're doing fine." He spoke to the base, then to her, "I'll kick in the afterburner and take her up. You'll get some interesting G force before we go weightless at the top for a few seconds. That'll give you an idea of how the astronauts feel in space."

Before she had time to think, much less get scared, the plane leapt forward with a roar. She was pressed back into the seat, her skin pulled tight against her facial bones. She compressed her lips to stop the stretching sensation of her mouth.

Lij took the plane up and let her fall over into a gentle parabola. The weightlessness lasted only a few seconds. Jennifer released the breath she'd held and drew deeply on the air supply. They were pretty high now, much higher than commercial jets flew, she thought. She peered out.

The earth was far away, a hazy brown ball. She and Lij were high enough that she could see the tip of the sun again. Then as the plane descended, the sun seemed to sink again. Two sunsets in one day.

"Want a close-up of the desert?" Lij asked over the headphone.

"How close?"

"Five hundred feet."

"Upside down?"

"We can try it that way," he said.

She felt the aircraft respond to his touch. She thought of his lovemaking. He'd be like this, she thought. Confident.

Concerned. Gentle. He'd ask after her comfort and see to her pleasure. She wished she could see his face. How would he look when he made love? Did he close his eyes at the last minute? Or did he like to watch, gaining pleasure from hers?

"Okay back there?" he asked.

"Yes," she whispered.

"Jen?"

"It's wonderful, Lij," she said sincerely.

"All right. Get ready. Here we gooooo . . ."

His voice trailed off in her ears as they lost altitude. Near the ground—it seemed they must surely be touching—he rolled them in a quick flip. Viewing the world upside down was certainly novel. It was also upsetting her balance.

"You'd better get me right side up fast," she requested.

He turned them over. Jennifer laughed.

"Better?"

"Super."

He took them up to a few thousand feet. Another plane joined them. She heard Bill's voice on the headset.

"Move over, Cowboy, Batman is comin' through. Gonna wax your tail before y'all go home."

Cowboy. Of course.

"I've got a lady aboard," Lij advised.

"So I heard. Gonna wax her tail, too."

The plane screamed by, close enough for Jennifer to see Bill's huge grin. He rolled around their plane, climbed straight up and then went into a loop. She heard Lij mutter a distinctive curse, then roll out toward the left.

"That's what you think, ol' buddy," he told his friend. "Hang on, Jen."

"Right," she said. She was already clutching the seat edge again. She was afraid to touch anything else.

For the next half hour she was treated to a dog fight in the air. Lij explained the tactics to her as they swooped, rolled and looped. To wax a pilot's tail meant you closed in on him from behind, got him in your gunsights and didn't let him out. He was dead meat if the battle was real.

His explanation lead to another thought. "Lij, did you serve in Vietnam?"

"Yeah. Me and Bill and some others." His voice was flat.

Some others who didn't make it back? She didn't ask.

When they returned to the base and landed, Jennifer was still in the air. Her blood ran high from the mock combat. Neither man had bested the other, but she had experienced some exciting air acrobatics. Now if she could only capture that exhilaration on paper for the students.

Lij had to help her climb out of the cockpit and down to the ground. In her gear, still shaky with excitement, she could hardly stand, much less unfasten the harness.

"Okay?" he asked, his dark eyes looking her over anxiously.

She gave him a big smile. "A-OK." Then she threw her arms around him and hugged him as hard as she could.

"Hey," he murmured, arms going around her. "Hey."

"I can't tell you," she babbled against his chest. "It was so beautiful, the earth, the sky, the colors of the desert. And then the other. I wanted us to wax his tail," she declared, leaning back against Lij's arms.

Lij threw back his head and laughed. "Hey, Batman, the lady has issued you another challenge. She wants to win."

Bill Davis ambled over from the T-38 he'd flown. "What name we gonna give her? Gal with that much grit—"

"Lady," Lij interrupted. "That's her name. Lady."

"I was thinking more like Killer," Bill said, winking at Jennifer.

"Uh-uh." Lij shook his head. He put his arm around Jennifer's shoulders and led her toward the building. "She's a lady all the way."

"Right." Bill fell into step beside them. He looked at his watch. "Beer call."

"Care to join us?" Lij asked.

Jennifer hesitated, then nodded. She needed to see how they lived their lives. She *wanted* to see, she realized.

It was after dinner before she arrived back at her motel. Lij followed in his red sports car. He walked her to the door, holding her hand.

"You've seen my world now. What did you think?"

His manner was that of a challenge.

She chose her words with care. "Interesting. Demanding. Exciting."

"But?"

"Not for me."

He raised his eyebrows. "You enjoyed today."

"But today isn't the way it would really be. You'd fly like that every day, on the edge, in the thick of things. You'd get to do all the fun stuff. I'd get the leftovers." She grinned to show she wasn't angry, only practical. "I'll stick to my own thing, thank you all the same."

"Show me your world," he requested.

"You wouldn't last a week. We're too different. Not only our life-styles, but our beliefs. You're establishment."

"And you're a flaming liberal?"

He leaned over her, nuzzling her cheek and earlobe. His touch could make her forget a lifetime of principles.

"You're a flower, Jen," he continued, pulling her close, "but not a flower child. You have too great a sense of responsibility. Sure you're not hiding behind your radical friends? It's easier to love a cause than a person, isn't it?"

He had hit a nerve. "Are we talking about love?" she asked.

He hesitated just one second too long before answering.

She laughed ruefully. "No, we're not, but if we were, who'd be the one left at the castle while you went off to battle the dragons? I won't live within those confines. It isn't fair."

She realized that was what she had resented about her father's work. From a child's viewpoint, he always seemed to be off having great adventures, while she and her mother were left behind to attend to the details.

"When has life promised to be fair?" Lij demanded. "I didn't make the rules. I'm not challenging your freedom. Neither of us has commitments to others. We're free to come or go as we please. So show me your world and I'll show you mine. What can be the harm in that?" He paused and added, "I sincerely want to understand what you want from life with your crusades and causes."

With that earnest entreaty, how could she refuse without sounding like a shrew? Or a hippie who called everyone a pig without considering the individual? She had an inspiration.

"All right. There's a rock festival coming up in New York this weekend. I'm leaving Friday morning to attend. Do you want to join me?"

"I'll check my schedule." His grin disarmed her. "I have a beach house over at Santa Barbara. I had thought along the lines of a quiet weekend there, just the two of us."

"I've already agreed to cover this for the paper. It's paying my expenses."

He looked as if he wasn't sure what he was letting himself in for, but he was game. "You're on."

She stuck out her hand and they shook on it. Then he took her into his arms and kissed her.

"Why don't you invite me in?" he whispered against her hair sometime later.

Jennifer thought of the pleasure she'd find with him. She wanted him. Why couldn't she just say yes? What more had to exist between them than the moment? Lots of people she knew believed in the "love the one you're with" philosophy. However, she didn't. She needed to know her own heart before she committed herself to anything else between them.

"I don't go in for casual sex," she explained, wanting him to know where she was coming from. She wasn't playing the tease.

"Neither do I." He kissed her cheek, her jawline, her lips. "Whatever this is, it isn't casual."

He pulled back and looked into her eyes in the soft light outside her room. She felt like a kid with the light left on by her folks so she wouldn't linger in the shadows on the porch.

"What?" Lij asked, catching her change in mood.

She told him.

He smiled, but his eyes were somber. "We're not kids, Jen. This isn't a game."

"What is it?"

"I don't know," he admitted with a rough edge on the words. He sighed and rubbed his face. "The rock concert it is," he said. "I know of a plane I can use, a small jet. If we go by the regular airlines, we're apt to end up in Cuba, judging by the rash of hijackings lately. I'll see if I can clear a flight plan."

She was puzzled. "Will the air force let you borrow the trainer?"

"No way. My company makes one of its executive jets available for me, one weekend a month. I haven't used it lately. I'll call tomorrow and let you know if it pans out."

Jennifer thought this over after he left. She knew there was only one explanation for his company's acquiescence. The more dangerous the work, the more perks that went with it. Lij's test flying must be very, very dangerous.

She was awake most of the night. Instead of her fiancé emerging from a sheet of flame, she kept seeing Lij's dark, handsome countenance through the faceplate of the helmet. He kept dancing around her, leaving a trail of sizzling earth behind every burning footprint, until she was surrounded. Then there was only the two of them in a solid ring of fire. He held out his hand, waiting for her to take it ... waiting ... waiting ...

LIJ LOOKED OVER THE papers on his desk. Everything in order. The small plane he'd wanted wasn't available, but the large company jet was scheduled for a flight to New York. He and Jennifer would be passengers on it. After dropping off two of the vice presidents in the city, the pilot would fly them to their destination. Going east, they'd lose three hours; therefore, they'd have to leave before daylight to make it to the East Coast in time to settle in and get to the concert.

Four days with Jennifer. Tomorrow, Saturday, Sunday, then Monday for the trip back. What about room reservations?

His thoughts were interrupted by the ringing of his phone. "Branigan."

"Mr. Branigan? One moment for Dr. Chadwick."

Amy's doctor came on the line and Lij forgot flight schedules and all else. He listened intently while the doctor explained the results of the recent tests and asked several questions.

The doctor wanted to try growth hormone and thyroid extract to spur Amy's body. He explained the possibilities and the consequences. In the end, Lij agreed to the prescribed treatment, thanked the doctor for calling and hung up, feeling both elated and apprehensive. Amy had a chance. Perhaps she'd never be normal, but she had a chance at a better life. He'd take it.

For a few minutes he sat deep in thought, but he already knew what he was going to do. In order to be near his daughter, he'd volunteer for the space program. Dr. Benton had assured him there was a slot for him. Yeah, he'd be an astronaut.

Briefly, he wondered what Jennifer would say, then he went to tell his boss that he wouldn't be renewing his contract.

Chapter Eight

Friday, August 15, 1969

Lij and Jennifer left well before dawn for the Woodstock Music and Art Fair. "They're calling this festival the first Aquarian Exposition," Jennifer said, reading through the brochures. "I suppose that means there'll be another one next year."

"If this one comes off."

"You sound doubtful."

"I read in the paper that others hadn't made any money for their promoters."

"Umm-hmm," she acknowledged.

The businessmen were dropped off, then the plane took off again. Lij considered telling Jennifer of his decision to try out for the space program. He could appeal to her sympathy about being closer to Amy...no, he wouldn't do that. Besides, he wanted this weekend to be theirs, with no quarrel between them.

A short time later the voice of their pilot came on the speakers. "Lij, look below. You won't believe your eyes, man."

Lij and Jennifer peered out the tiny windows and gasped. People. People everywhere. The traffic was backed up along all the roads leading to White Lake, including the New York Quickway that ran nearby. It was a highway engineer's worst nightmare!

"How many would you say there are?" the pilot asked. "Quarter of a million is my guess."

"At least," Lij muttered. He looked at Jennifer, wondering what the hell she'd gotten them into.

She was still staring out the window. "How are we going to get in? They've abandoned their cars and are walking."

With all the turmoil, it was difficult to see what was happening. The pilot circled the area twice before heading for the airport at Monticello. "Good luck," he said after they'd landed. "I'll see you in New York on Monday."

Lij and Jennifer got off the plane, wondering how they'd ever make it back to the city in time to catch the flight. They weren't even sure they would make it out of Monticello.

"Where are we staying?" Lij asked.

Jennifer grimaced. "We have reservations at a resort in White Lake—if they'll hold them until we get there."

"We'll get there," he said with a tight smile. "How do you feel about riding a motorcycle?"

She stared at him. This whole trip was turning out to be entirely different from what she'd expected.

"Well?" he demanded.

"Why not?" She laughed. "This looks like it's going to be a weekend to remember."

He gave her a wry glance. "You'd better believe it."

THEY MADE IT. The trip took only an hour of weaving in and out of abandoned vehicles and teenagers carrying sleeping bags, blankets, radios and assorted baggage. Jennifer had a room at the resort, but only one. The rest were full of musicians, Woodstock staff and reporters.

"We can share," Jennifer decided. Lij quirked one eyebrow at her but said nothing.

He wondered, not for the first time, what he was doing here. The sight of long braids on one man prompted the memory of the accident that had changed Amy's and his lives so drastically. A remnant of anger settled on his neck.

He looked at Jennifer, dressed in jeans, a tank top and a man's long-sleeved shirt that hung off her shoulders. She wore her peace earrings and looked younger than twenty-eight.

This was her weekend, he reminded himself. He'd keep an open mind. That was only fair.

They left their bags in the room, strapped their jackets on the back of the big Harley motorcycle Lij had rented and headed for the Yasgur dairy farm at a top speed of ten miles per hour.

Jennifer, sitting behind him, hugged his lean waist and peered over his shoulder.

"How're you doing?" he asked.

"Fine," she answered. Her voice sounded husky.

Her body was cupped to his, her inner thighs touching his outer ones as she clung to him. He liked the feeling.

"Hey, man, save a place for me when ya get there," a young man sporting a fork-tailed beard called after them.

"Sure thing," Lij called back.

The teenagers around them laughed and moved aside to let them through. They seemed in the best of spirits and not at all angry at the delay or the mob. For the moment. What if the riot police showed up? Lij knew he'd hate to be in the middle of a confrontation between two opposing forces. Jennifer would probably love it.

"This must be the biggest bash ever assembled," a teen-age girl remarked excitedly. She wore shorts and a sleeveless T-shirt with gaping armholes, and she obviously felt a bra was unnecessary. Over her arm, she carried a bright Mexican shawl. Her hair was in two pigtails down her back. She looked young and fresh and pretty.

Her boyfriend slouched along beside her in jeans, T-shirt and sandals. His hair hung down his back in waves. He lugged a blasting radio tuned to a rock station.

"No eardrums," Jennifer said to Lij.

He looked over his shoulder at her.

Their mouths were close. He read the impulse in her eyes. She stretched forward and kissed him.

"Watch it. You'll make us have a wreck," he warned, but he couldn't stop the warm feeling that spread inside him.

She hugged him, obviously having no misgivings about the rock concert. The mood around them celebrated the joy of being alive and taking part in the event. He hoped it lasted.

He turned onto a road leading away from the dairy farm, found the dirt lane he'd spotted from the airplane that would take them back and turned left on it. He sped along it with no trouble.

They arrived at the six-hundred acre farm to find total chaos. Kids were milling around, standing around, sitting around. Off to one side was a hay field and a couple of ponds. Next to that was a copse of trees with a small stage nearby. A cornfield was directly to the south. Sandwiched between it and the West Shore Road were portable toilets, a hospital tent, medical trailer and three security trailers parked in a U-shape.

Lij stowed the motorcycle in the press-and-service vehicle parking area. Jennifer already had her notebook out and was scribbling away, making sketches of the Food for Love concession stands. There were sixteen of them. Enough to feed a small-sized army, but what about half million teenagers?

The stands were like a fantasy. Colorful braided ropes were attached to a center pole and wound around the support poles like captured rainbows. Tapestries interwoven with mirror cloth lent an exotic Arabian-nights appearance to the structures. Waving banners proclaimed the booths sold hot dogs, hamburgers, corn-on-the-cob, tacos, drinks, french fries, ice cream, even watermelon!

"Can you believe this?" Jennifer murmured, her eyes and pencil so busy, they hardly had time to note one item before jumping to the next.

Lij looked around. People...people...people. Everywhere.

"There's no way they're going to collect money from this mob," he announced, surveying the site with a pragmatic frown. "The logistics of it are impossible."

Jennifer recognized the hint of uneasiness in him. She'd asked quite a lot of him, she realized, challenging him to attend this...this sci-fi fantasy with her. Remembering that meeting her friends in Berkeley had recalled the tragedy in his past, she wondered if seeing this crazy mix of humanity would do the same.

The scene was surreal. Kids were coming in from every direction as if compelled by a force greater than their power to resist. Over to one side, she noticed a spindly fence had long since fallen and guards were hauling it away. What would happen if anger and frustration touched off a riot?

For the moment, the bonhomie was wonderful. All around her and Lij there were glad cries of friends greeting friends or making new ones.

"Peace, man. Where y'all from?"

"Montreal. How about yourself?"

"Kentucky, man. Glad to meet'cha."

Jennifer wrote as fast as she could. She wanted to capture it all: the air of excitement—everyone knew this was a real happening—the relaxed friendliness, the camaraderie, the feeling of being with a whole lot of people you just loved being with.

It felt good, she thought. She wished it could be wonderful for Lij, too. Now that they were there and it was too late, she worried about him.

They made their way to the front meadow. A huge natural bowl opened in front of the stage, which was set on the side of a hill. Lij, Jennifer and several couples who had swarmed in with them, arranged themselves at a comfortable spot off to one side about halfway back. The field was already thronged with people.

"Everyone is having a wonderful time," Jennifer said. "I feel sorry for the festival sponsors. They probably planned for fifty, maybe a hundred thousand."

Lij shook his head. "They'd better keep this crowd happy. I'd hate to think what would happen if they didn't."

Jennifer studied him while he assessed the situation. She sensed the tension in him, but it had been there from the start of their trip. In his jeans and open-throated knit shirt, he looked relaxed and at home in the bizarre scene, but there was something troubling him. She wondered if the problem concerned his daughter and his former in-laws, but decided not to ask. He would tell her in his own good time.

She sighed as she glanced around. Beyond the barbed-wire fence on the eastern side of the field, a herd of Holstein cows grazed. They kept a cautious eye on the strange creatures in the next pasture. Beyond them was another tiny stand of trees.

Asking the gang around them to save their places, she urged Lij to his feet. "We're going exploring," she explained.

They found the woods inside the fence had been laid out in romantic paths with strings of Christmas lights and shredded bark to guide the way to the camper and trailer parking. A helipad provided access to the outside world, a good thing because all the roads were clogged to a standstill for five miles around according to a radio report. There was even a park with swing sets and slides for the little kids.

Tom Law from the Hog Farm, a hippie commune, who had been flown in to help keep order and treat bad trips, climbed on the stage and led the hundred thousand or so attendees gathered in the first meadow in yoga exercises. Another eighty-five thousand kids milled around beyond the trees being entertained by strolling troubadours.

Several hundred thousand more settled in yards, the cemetery, on top of cars, or anywhere else they could find a patch of open space, and prepared to enjoy themselves just being in the vicinity since there was no way they could reach the dairy farm. Not being able to hear the festival, they simply tuned their radios to the same stations and danced to the music.

Lij ambled alongside the third pond on the Yasgur farm, still amazed and troubled at the size of the crowd and the fact that he was there. He agreed with someone in the vicinity who remarked that this was an "event, for sure." Yeah, he'd buy that.

He glanced at Jennifer. She was taking in everything and writing it in her notebook. "What do you put down?" he asked, curious about her job. This was the first time he'd noticed her acting the part of a super reporter.

"Everything I see," she replied. "And my impressions." She held the notebook out.

He read. "Early morning fog burned off—day fair, hot, about ninety. Young mother, long blue gathered skirt, floral peasant blouse, dk brn hair in Indian braids, two kids, boy 4, girl 3, sloping grn meadow next to pond. Happy, caring, gentle. A time for sharing."

Lij spotted the three. The mother was showing the children how to fold paper into boats. When each child had one, they set the toy boats adrift on the pond. The wind whisked the boats across the water at a brisk pace, and the three on shore laughed. Around them, people smiled indulgently.

The boy waded in after his paper boat when it bobbed into shore. The water rose to his knees, wetting his jeans. He looked quickly at his mother. She smiled. "Come. We'll take them off." She removed his pants and T-shirt. "There, now you can play in the water all you want."

"Me, too," the daughter squealed, and waded in to get her pants wet so she could take them off. The young mother rolled her eyes, but good-naturedly removed the girl's clothing and let her play in the water. Other parents did the same.

Lij thought of Amy. She'd enjoy the water, too. Hope crowded painfully into his chest. If she responded to the new treatment . . . He tried not to let himself hope for too much, but it was hard not to. He'd be grateful for small miracles.

He heard Jennifer laugh as she sketched the scene. He perused the crowd around them, and other worries cropped up. If anything happened to set them off, how could one man protect a woman from a mob this size? At the moment, it was all sunshine and sweetness, but what if things turned nasty? A lot of people would get hurt. Forcing his doubts aside, he returned his attention to the scene by the pond.

A young man, backing up to catch a hard-thrown ball, sank into ankle-deep ooze and fell backward into the water in a standard comedy of windmilling arms and startled expression. Again Lij heard Jennifer laugh, a real laugh filled with humor and the joy of living. The sound touched something deep within him, something young and foolish and hopeful, something he thought had been dead for two years.

"They're happy," she said.

The expression in her eyes, which seemed the same color as the sky today, caused emotion to clutch at his throat, making it difficult for him to speak. "Are you?" he asked.

"Yes."

She seemed hesitant, and her voice had a breathless quality, but she continued with her notes in a businesslike manner. She appeared cool and unruffled, not at all the way he felt.

He thought of that one bed in the room at the resort. Did she want him as much as he wanted her? The thought of caressing her excited him, but what would come after? He didn't know. Too many warring desires did battle in him. He turned them off. He had promised this weekend to Jennifer. He'd give her her time.

The young man pulled himself out of the mire and tried to slick mud off his arms and clothing. His actions only made the mess worse. "Well, heck," he said, "if they can go naked, I can, too." With that, he stripped and dived into the pond, coming up several feet from the churned-up mud. He rinsed the clay off.

"Say, that looks great!"

The stripper's friend threw his clothes over a bush and dashed toward the pond in the altogether. Soon the display of skin took on mob proportions as others welcomed relief from the heat and humidity. When a young man coaxed his girl into joining him, the scene became a Roman bath. Lij shook his head.

Jennifer, he noted, was taking it all in stride. She wrote steadily in her notebook. In a flash of insight, he realized she was as serious about her job as he was about his. It gave him a different perspective of her.

She'd never make a traditional wife. She had too much energy and curiosity about the world to be content to stay home. It was something he should perhaps consider before they became further involved. But perhaps he was getting ahead of himself. This was a weekend, nothing more.

"Shall we join them?" he asked, prodding her to remember his presence, surprised to find himself jealous of her concentration on her task. He watched her rather than the nude bathers, who were now painting swirls and floral patterns on each other with mud. She was much more interesting than the revealing flashes of skin.

Jennifer glanced up at Lij. A flutter ran through her veins as she thought of him, naked and magnificently male. She considered the young men diving into the pond children by comparison.

"Can't," she replied to his question with a droll grimace. "My notebook would get soggy."

She held up paper and pencil to indicate she would keep taking her infernal notes regardless of the circumstances. Lij studied the bathing scene and couldn't restrain a comment. "This is the generation that's going to change the world?"

"Maybe it already has."

"Maybe," he said, but he was skeptical. "We'd better eat while there's still food," he advised, changing the subject. He didn't want a philosophical argument.

They loaded up on hamburgers, french fries and Coke, then stuffed their pockets with candy bars in case the food was gone later in the evening. It was almost five o'clock and there was still no sign of the show starting, although a few announcements had been made about delays. The last one declared it a free festival.

Jennifer spoke to Lij over the clapping and shouting as they walked back to the meadow and their seats on the ground. "You were right. They're not going to try and collect the money."

Just as they reached their space, the crowd began to chant, "Jump. Jump. Jump."

Lij spotted a young man climbing the eighty-foot scaffolding that supported the sound system. At the top he waved his hand in the peace sign over the crowd, bowed to their applause, then flung himself off backward. He got up and walked off without a scratch.

Jennifer sank down weakly beside Lij. ''I'm not sure my heart can take this.''

''Bear up. It's bound to get . . . worse.''

She gave him ⅃ mock-ferocious frown, but he knew she wasn't really angry with him. He wished they were alone so he could kiss her.

His attention was claimed by movement on the stage. The performers were arriving and the lights came on. At 5:07 the Woodstock festival started with Richie Havens opening the show instead of Sweetwater. It was rumored the group was still stuck in traffic someplace sixty miles from there.

''Oh, no,'' one girl said. ''Helicopters were sent to pick them up. They'll be here in no time.''

''God, the cost,'' Lij mumbled.

He watched in amazement as Havens held thousands of young people enthralled with a series of songs. A string on his guitar snapped, but he played on. At the end of a Vietnam protest song, he segued into a chant. ''Sometimes I feel like I'm almost gone/Yeah, a long, long, long way from my home.''

For five minutes, Havens improvised music and words while the crowd chanted and clapped. Finally, still playing, he danced off the stage, came back to tremendous applause, waved and left.

''A capo,'' a man yelled. He was dashing around the edges of the crowd scrutinizing anyone with a guitar. ''Dammit, quick, we need a capo for Joe to go on next. Anybody got one?''

''Here you go.''

Lij recognized the friendly kid from Kentucky who'd introduced himself to everybody in his immediate range. He stood and tossed an elastic band to the man.

"Bless you a thousand times," the man said, and ran off toward the back of the stage.

"What was that?" Lij asked.

"A capo is a piece of elastic a guitarist wraps around the neck of his guitar to transpose a song to his vocal key. Joe McDonald doesn't have much of a range." She grinned as she gave out this piece of information, pleased that at last here was something *she* could explain to *him*.

"Show-off." Lij yanked on a curl hanging over her shoulder.

As Country Joe McDonald was introduced as the next act, he strolled onstage and saluted the audience after getting the capo fixed on his guitar.

"That's mine," the kid from Kentucky said in awed tones. "That's my capo."

Joe got right down to the nitty-gritty. He demanded the audience repeat four letters of the alphabet with him. The crowd responded to each request.

"What's that spell?" Country Joe screamed.

A half million voices shouted the correct answer—a popular four-letter word.

Jennifer looked at Lij defensively. "Well, I never promised you high art," she said.

Lij couldn't help himself. He whooped with laughter.

Up on the stage, Country Joe yelled, "One, two, three, four, does anyone know what we're fighting for?" then launched into his big Vietnam protest hit.

Jennifer wrote down each act and the songs performed: John Sebastian, then the laser light show that fizzled, the Incredible String Band that played for an hour and twenty minutes during an incredible molten orange sunset. Tim Hardin was next.

"He's a descendant of John Wesley Hardin, the out-law," Jennifer told Lij. Around them, this tidbit of infor-mation spread like ripples as the word was passed from one group to another.

Hardin had a silky voice that was shaky when he started, but improved with each phrase. Lij liked his gentle ballads best. "If I Were a Carpenter," "Reason to Believe," "Misty Roses." Soft songs that provided the perfect transition from light to dark.

The crowd mellowed after that, and Jennifer could feel the warmth of the many human bodies around her. Peace seemed a tangible quality of the air, penetrating through her pores. Lij reached over and squeezed her hand and she looked into his eyes.

In them, she saw all the promises of life, all the hopes she'd ever had. Shimmers of deep emotion played over her nerves like lightning over a network of cobwebs. She felt light, almost ephemeral, and yet solid, like part of the earth and people.

Desire flashed through her, making her want this one man more than she'd ever wanted anything in her life. She longed for privacy, for darkness and intimacy.

He kissed her with only their lips and hands touching. "Later," his kiss promised. "Yes," hers answered. Around them, others must have felt the same magic. Couples touched, kissed, then sat back to listen some more.

The storm came up at 10:30, out of nowhere, right in the middle of Ravi Shankar's sitar instrumental. It drenched and chilled the crowd, raged for fifteen minutes, then slowed to a drizzle and stopped. Bonfires sprang up in the meadow. The scene looked like a gypsy encampment. "Unreal," Jennifer wrote in her notebook, hovering under her jacket.

Lij agreed. He paid a kid twenty bucks for an umbrella and held it over Jennifer so she could keep her notes dry. *A real hero,* he thought, mocking his efforts. But still, he couldn't deny a basic need to protect her and to provide what comforts he could. He could feel himself drawn deeper into the emotional turmoil of a relationship that probably had no place to go.

Jennifer was apparently at home in this world. He wasn't. He'd shared some of the lighter moments, he appreciated the engineering skill that had turned a dairy farm into a rock concert, but he knew he didn't belong. He had too many responsibilities to take life as lightly as the group around him.

He almost resented their absorption in their "own thing." They ate, danced, kissed or smoked pot with complete abandon. As if there were no tomorrow. As if the outside world and its risks weren't real. He knew it was. Each time he went to visit Amy, he felt that reality. It made him want to hit out at a world that was unjust, that robbed the innocent of their future. Amy might never attend a rock concert or have a lover, a husband, children.

Jennifer touched his hand. Her glance was sympathetic, as if she understood what he felt. When he returned her anxious gaze, he managed a smile.

The show went on.

Melanie dropped by and agreed to perform. Bob Dylan, it was rumored, wouldn't be there. He was home with a sick kid. Lij felt a paternal kinship with the ballad singer and hoped Dylan's kid wasn't seriously ill.

Arlo Guthrie went on after Melanie. He sang his hit about the train that was named "The City of New Orleans." Then people began to sing with him when he played one of his father's songs. "This land is my land . . ."

Woody Guthrie had died a couple of years back, Lij recalled, and now his son had the same genetic disease hanging over his head. Lij realized lots of people had troubles not of their own making.

He heard Jennifer's voice beside him, singing along, true and sweet. She had a sort of husky way of singing as she swayed back and forth with the beat. When they sang the chorus again, he joined in.

Out on the small stage in the back—which was designated the free stage, although both stage acts cost nothing now—Joan Baez showed up and played for forty minutes. Then she came to the big stage and repeated her act. She talked about David, her husband, who was in prison for refusing to serve in Vietnam. She sang about peace and hope and beauty. She closed the show.

The first night of the festival ended a little after two o'clock. Unlike other festivals where all hell broke loose after the show, the Woodstock Nation simply rolled into their wet coats, blankets and sleeping bags and went to sleep. It was a phenomenon unanticipated and utterly right.

"I guess that's it for now," Jennifer said, glancing at Lij, unsure of his reaction to the long, tiring day.

A bonfire was lit next to them, and several young people held blankets up to dry. A young girl came dancing by. She wore a smile and several scarves tied around her body. Her long blond hair reached to her waist. She spun and dipped around the flames while everyone watched her. She seemed as insubstantial as a fragment of imagination.

When she danced their way, she smiled dreamily at Jennifer and Lij. Taking a daisy from her hair, she tucked it behind Lij's ear, blessed him by making the peace sign over his head, and danced off.

Lij left the flower where it was. It came to him that these young people were innocent of guile. They wanted love to prevail. They even believed it would, somehow. He realized he wanted it for them—peace and brotherhood and love. Something in him that had been tight and hurting suddenly let go.

Jennifer touched the daisy, then let her fingers trail along his cheek to the corners of his mouth. He smiled at her, but she saw the shadows in his eyes. Then his smile softened, became real.

She realized what a good sport he was. Not one word of disgust, irritation or regret had issued from his mouth during the whole day. Other than a wry grin and a comment or two, he'd been infinitely patient with the teenagers around them, had helped them find food and water or the medical tent for a bad case of cut feet, and had listened to them chatter of peace and brotherhood as if they were commodities that could be bottled and sold like soda pop.

She felt a stirring of emotion within herself. Feelings she'd suppressed pushed against the restraints she'd placed around her heart years ago. For a long minute, she sat very still and fought the tumult in her chest. Removing her hand from his face, she pressed it into her other palm.

"What is it?"

"Nothing." She stared at the empty stage.

The purpose of this weekend was to show them how ill-suited they were for each other. She thought it was showing her just the opposite. He was good, kind, patient and a thousand other desirable traits. Her feelings for him doubled in strength. She held her emotions in check, refusing to recognize the signs.

"Are you ready to go?" he asked.

"Yes."

"Save our places," he requested of the kids around them. "I'll take orders for breakfast now. You can have anything you want. As long as it's doughnuts."

"Orange juice?" said one girl.

"You got it," Lij answered.

"And coffee," her boyfriend chimed in. "Peace."

"Peace," Lij said. He pulled Jennifer to her feet and led the way to the motorcycle. Soon they were wending their way through the black shadows of the lane.

"A shower," Jennifer said, once they arrived at the hotel. But she felt suddenly nervous now that they were alone in the room. She'd thought she would face this moment with poise.

Lij studied her from beneath lowered lashes. He reached for her and murmured, "Relax. Nothing will happen that you're not ready for."

How could she tell him she thought it already had? Turning, she went into the bathroom and quickly undressed. In a few minutes, warm from the shower and in control once more, she let him have the bathroom while she slipped into her gown. The room had only one bed, a large one.

She chose the right side and propped two pillows behind her back while she reread her notes and added other thoughts and impressions of the day. When the shower stopped, her heart stood still, then thumped furiously.

Lij came out a few minutes later. When she glanced his way, she saw he was wearing only pajama bottoms.

Her breath ripped through her throat with a thin sound like tearing silk as she gazed at his chest. Thick, dark hair formed a loose diamond pattern on his body, spreading from a point below his throat outward to his nipples, then diving downward to disappear underneath the waistband of dark blue cotton.

"It's all right," he said.

His voice was the softest murmur across her ears. The tightness in her chest eased, then faded completely. She met his gaze levelly. "I'm not afraid."

"Good." He smiled as he advanced toward the bed. "You have nothing to fear from me, Jen, not ever."

He climbed into his side of the bed. In a second, he was stretched out on his back, one arm over his eyes.

She couldn't look away from the outline of his long, lean form. "Is my light bothering you?"

"No."

Silence batted between them for five minutes. Jennifer couldn't stand it another second. She put a period after the sentence she was writing and closed the notebook, then she turned out the bedside lamp and tried to settle down.

"How long before you're settled?" he finally asked when she turned from her right to her left side for the third time.

"I don't know."

She felt angry with fate, with him, with herself. She didn't want soft feelings. She didn't want yearning. Even more, she didn't want touching and all the things that would follow.

Except that she did.

She was desperate with longing. She wanted Lij's caresses in the most intimate way. She wanted his lovemaking.

Huffing out an irritated breath, she flopped over onto her back.

"That's it," he said. He turned on his light and reached for his jeans. "I'm leaving. You can relax."

"No, don't. I mean, you don't have to leave—"

"It's obvious you aren't going to sleep with me in the same room, much less the same bed," he snapped. "And I sure as hell can't sleep if you don't."

He began to shuck his pajama bottoms. "You'd better close your eyes," he suggested dryly.

She shook her head. He shrugged and let the pj's drop.

He was beautiful, from the long curve of his spine as he bent to slip into his pants to the muscular flexing of his thighs and calves as he balanced on one foot.

"You'll never find another room," she managed to say past a dry throat.

He didn't answer.

The earlier feelings, when the girl had given him the daisy, rose in her breast. "Where's your daisy?" she asked.

"In the trash can in the bathroom." He glanced around at her before stepping into the other leg of his pants. He stopped. "Jennifer?" he said quietly.

She met his gaze. "Stay."

"Heaven knows I want to, but...are you sure? I've given you all the slack I can. If I stay now..."

"Stay," she said, and knew it was what she wanted. Never would she be able to plead that she was bewitched or seduced or taken off guard. He was giving her every chance to escape.

Slowly he released his jeans and kicked them across the floor. He turned to face her. His body was powerful, his arousal plain to see. Jennifer drew a hard breath.

Instead of coming to her, he went to his weekend case. He returned to the bed and laid his means of protection on the night table. "I've been hoping," he said, a smile in his voice.

"I started on the pill a couple of weeks ago."

His smile moved to his lips. Hers did, too. She forgot about things like independence and order in her life, about things like not wanting anything too much, about avoiding men like him. Complications seemed desirable all of a sudden.

He sat on the bed and pulled the cover off her. With one finger, he slid the strap of her nightgown from her right shoulder. He did the same with the left. Her gown clung only to the plump dark nipples, visible through the lace edging.

"You're beautiful." He leaned over and kissed a point on each side of her throat. With his tongue, he flicked the material away from her breasts.

With a skillful move he lay beside her, his weight on one elbow while he guided the gown lower, past her waist to her hips. "Raise up," he ordered. When she complied, he swept the gown down her thighs. She lifted her legs, and it was off, tossed to the floor with his pajama bottoms and forgotten.

"I like your shoulders," she said.

She touched him, letting her hands roam the combination of bone and muscle. With just her fingertips, she trailed through the hair on his chest, down to his waist, over his abdomen, until she just brushed the most intimate part of him. He drew a quick breath and let it out slowly.

"What about the rest of me?" he asked.

"I like that, too."

She trembled on the brink of explosion. One tiny touch...

"Tell me what you want."

He was considerate as a lover, just as she had known he would be. "I'm not sure." It had been a long time, and she was too shy to make demands.

"Then we'll just experiment," he whispered close to her ear.

He nibbled on her earlobe while his body slowly climbed over hers, carefully, gently. First one leg, then the other slid between her thighs. He stroked her breasts, sides and back. He found she had tickle spots on each side, just above her hip bones. He avoided those.

He kissed her. Sometimes his mouth was soft, sometimes hard. Sometimes the kiss was long and slow; at others, it was a series of skimming touches. She had no preference. Everything he did felt wonderful.

His hands moved along her waist and hips. He followed the slanting line of her abdomen. When he at last touched her, she held her breath, not wanting any sensation but that of his touch.

"Open your eyes," he demanded.

She did, feeling as helpless as a hand puppet, able to do only his bidding. For a second, she thought of fleeing.

He must have sensed her uncertainty. "Stay with me," he whispered.

She moved her legs and felt the eagerness of her body for his. With a last coherent thought, she helped him find the empty space within her. Until then, she'd never realized how terrible the loneliness was.

He rose once and thrust deep, then was still. She knew neither of them could move or the moment would end too soon. She wanted the emptiness to stay filled, at least for a while.

"Don't move," she said.

"I won't," he promised.

With gentleness, he stroked her almost to the peak and each time, let her come back down. Then he moved again, slowly, then faster. His fingers played magic upon her and she burst into pleasure's mindless depths, crying his name once in fear and ecstasy.

With the greatest effort, Lij held himself back, although his body wanted to follow her to bliss. Not yet. He wanted more from her. He wanted her sated with as much passion as he could give her. When she was quiescent beneath him with only her heart pounding against his, he started again, building her to the peak, urging her to take it. This time, he couldn't hold back.

"You know how to please," he said, letting his weight hold her captive without crushing her. She was like satin inside, heated with the fire of their lovemaking, smooth and moist and welcoming. Like coming home.

She looked at him. There was nothing cool and distant in her gaze this time, he noted, but the emotion was still unreadable. A subtle woman, this Jennifer Wright.

Jennifer wondered how a heart could be so full and not split itself into pieces. The emotions she'd wanted to hide refused to be suppressed, yet she had no name for them. Did everything have to be tidy and labeled like a stack of compositions to be graded?

She smiled.

"What?" he demanded, lazily kissing her.

"An A-plus."

"You were grading me?" He seemed to find that amusing.

"Us."

"Yeah. We were good together, lady."

"That's what you call your airplanes. Lady. Or bitch."

"You pleased me," he said. He laughed and she felt his stomach move against hers.

"I might not always."

"Don't." He hushed her with his lips on hers. When he raised his head, he murmured, "Let's let it be a happening between us, this one thing, this one time. If we want more later, then fine, but for now, let's not question or evaluate."

"All right," she agreed. She felt him growing inside her. In a moment, he began to move and he filled her again, mighty in the way of a man but gentle in the way of a lover. She forgot to guard her independence and gave herself to the moment.

"WE SHOULD THINK ABOUT going back," Lij said late the next morning. They'd awakened, showered together and made love again. "I hope we can get back through the road."

"We could go across country on the motorcycle." Jennifer yawned and stretched, not tired but pleasantly lethargic.

He frowned. "Too dangerous."

"Are you protecting me?" she asked.

"It's a natural thing to do."

She decided she liked that. "I'm hungry."

"I promised breakfast to the gang." He slid from the bed. "Come on, lady. We have doughnuts to deliver."

They bought three dozen doughnuts, a dozen cups of coffee, milk and orange juice, then headed out to the farm.

"Drive carefully. I'm not sure I can hold all this," Jennifer requested. The sacks were balanced on each of her thighs.

They arrived at the farm without mishap and distributed the goods to a thankful group. Fortunately, the night hadn't been really cold and the damp clothing had soon dried from body heat and the bonfires. This morning everyone seemed cheerful enough, in spite of being a bit stiff.

"Hi," one of them said. "Did you guys sleep all right?"

Jennifer didn't look at Lij. "Yes. Did you?"

"I'll survive."

Lij glanced over the crowd. All around them, bodies lay in snug groups to share warmth. Some were starting to stir.

"A gigantic sleep-in," he said. "You'd better go to the latrine before the rest wake with the same idea."

The gang struggled to their feet, stretched their muscles and picked their way over to the portable potties. After washing up in Crystal Pond behind the free stage—more sleeping people as far as the eye could see—they returned for the breakfast Lij had brought for them.

The rest of the crowd woke slowly until some joker climbed on stage and bellowed, "Good Morning" into the mike. It came out as a roar through the powerful amplifiers. All over the field, bodies jumped to life as young people sat up.

The music started again a little after noon. The bass vibrations could be felt through the ground, coming right through the bones as well as the ears. The highlight of the afternoon was a new group, The Santana Blues Band, lead by Carlos Santana.

Jennifer and her friends loved the Latin rock. They stood and began to dance. Soon they were in a line, all making the same hand motions, which looked something like hitchhiking to Lij. He looked around and saw gyrating bodies in every direction. He imagined what the meadow must look like from the stage.

Jennifer broke away and danced over to him. With a lift of her hand, she invited him to join her. Her smile indicated her delight when he did. He danced with her and realized he was having a good time in spite of his earlier feelings. They moved to the beat for a long time before resting again.

At nine o'clock Saturday night, a group of hellraisers from New York pulled down several of the food booths and made a huge bonfire. The kids didn't join in. Their thing was peace and brotherhood, not torch and loot. Their attitude frustrated the city gang, and its members gave up when no one joined them. The destruction left only four concessions stands to feed the crowd, plus the Hog Farm's open soup kitchen.

Jennifer was worried.

"Everything's cool," Lij told her. "These kids are okay."

She glanced at the crowd. Some were singing to the music, others were swaying or dancing to the beat. Joints were being passed around in a friendly fashion.

Just as she decided to relax, a young man rushed toward them. He looked around, turning in a circle, his eyes wild with fear. With shaking hands, he showed them a Swiss army knife he had concealed under his shirt.

"They're after me," he whispered. "I won't let them get me."

All activity in the immediate area stopped as they stared at the newcomer. Two of the young men shifted in front of the women.

"Oh, hell," Jennifer heard someone mutter.

Lij stepped forward, putting himself in the first line of danger. "Who's after you?" he asked quietly.

"They are," the young man said. He whipped around as he caught a movement at the corner of his eye. The girl who had flicked the hair from her face froze.

"We're all friends here," Lij said in soothing tones. "I'm Lij Branigan. What's your name?"

"Chris."

"Well, Chris, why don't you come with me? I know where a doctor is. He'll take care of you. Come on over to the medical tent. No one is allowed to hurt anyone in there."

"Yeah?" Chris turned on one of the girls. "Is that right?"

She nodded, her eyes wide.

"Let's go," Lij urged. He draped an arm around Chris's shoulders.

"Someone might sneak in." Chris surveyed everyone around them as if looking for his enemy. He focused on Lij. Slowly the knife came into view. Jennifer bit back a cry.

"Naw," Lij said. "They keep watch. Come on."

They moseyed off, Lij talking the whole way over to the medical tent, Jennifer following a few steps behind. At the clinic, a psychiatrist stepped forward when Lij explained the situation.

"Hey, Chris," he said, "I'm a doctor. I know all these people. They're okay. No one will hurt you here. We all watch out for each other. Take a nap and I'll stand guard."

"I gotta keep this knife ready."

"Sure thing. Stick it under the pillow just in case. I'll give a yell if you need to use it."

Chris looked around the crowded tent. He nodded once and went to the cot. Carefully, he placed the open knife under the pillow and lay down. In less than a minute, he was sound asleep.

Lij grabbed Jennifer's hand and led her back to their place. "You're shaking," he murmured.

"I usually do when I'm threatened by a freaked-out guy wielding a knife." She tried to smile but failed.

The moment Lij had stepped forward, his life in jeopardy to protect her and the others, was the moment she'd known what she felt for him. All the turmoil he caused within her had but one name. She knew what it was. Love.

She was silent as they settled back on their damp coats. Lij told the group around them that Chris was sleeping it off.

At 9:30, the announcer told the crowd that there was some bad acid floating around. "Don't take the flat blue tabs," he advised. "It's not poison, but it's not good."

That ended a mass poisoning scare that had momentarily riffled through the scene. They figured Chris must have gotten hold of the bad stuff.

Jennifer had a sudden realization. She laid a hand on Lij's arm. "You could be court-martialled for being here," she said. "You're an officer. You could be sentenced for being around drugs, even if you don't use them."

"Yeah," he agreed. He laid his arm around her shoulders. "It'll be okay."

"Lij, I'm sorry. I didn't think about that before I asked you to come with me."

"Don't worry," he said. "Not even my own mother would expect to see me here."

Jennifer nodded ruefully. "No person of the establishment would expect to see one of their own in this disheveled, mud-splattered crowd." She gave him a shaky grin, insecure in her newly discovered feelings about him.

"I think we should try and make it to the hotel soon," he suggested. "There's another storm brewing."

She glanced toward the west. The clouds weren't visible, but the stars were blotted out on the horizon. She nodded. They listened to Grace Slick and the Grateful Dead, The Who and Jefferson Airplane. Jennifer wrote her impressions, and Lij kept an eye on the sky. When the stars disappeared above them, he gave her a nudge.

"After this set," she requested, wanting to hear Janis Joplin's numbers. When Janis finished, Jennifer had tears in her eyes. There was something so sad about the singer, as if she'd never found happiness.

Quietly Jennifer and Lij got up and went to the back of the concession-stand area, skirting the burned pile of booths that had been so lovely and medieval when they had arrived. The cycle was okay. Lij started it easily and they climbed on. In a few minutes, they were on the dark back road, trying to work their way around vehicles of every description that now clogged it, too.

Jennifer wondered when she would have to stop and think about all that was happening between her and Lij. Not now, she decided, nestling against him, her cheek pressed to his spine. Not now. She wanted the magic to last.

Lij was lost in his own musings. He thought of Amy, of the life he'd like for her. She needed a home. So did he. Pain gripped his chest as he wrestled with the tough decisions before him. He needed someone to share that home. He needed . . . a wife.

It was too soon to mention the future to Jennifer. She was having enough trouble accepting him just for the weekend. He couldn't suddenly start making demands for more.

Life was getting more complicated, but he couldn't see any way to change things. It frustrated him. He liked clear choices, firm decisions. There was no way he could see into the future. He'd have to take it as it came. Like the young people at the concert, he would live for today and not think about tomorrow. Not yet. Tomorrow might never come.

He knew that was a lie.

Chapter Nine

Muskrat, a hippie from New York, read the Sunday morning *New York Times* to the crowd while women from the Hog Farm dipped up cold mush on paper plates and passed it to waiting hands.

The dairy farm resembled a surreal scene from a war movie with bodies lying everywhere. Jennifer found it difficult to tell the well from the injured. Most of the wounds were cut feet. Nearly everyone was going barefoot. Rocks and glass were invisible in the muddy ooze due to another hard thundershower the previous night.

At the medical tent, she interviewed the doctors and nurses who had been helicoptered in to treat the increasing load of patients. She asked about Chris.

"He's helping over at the Hog Farm tent," one of the nurses told her. "It's part of the code—we help you through a bad time, you help somebody else."

Lij stood by while she did her job.

"I swear every hippie with diabetes came off without enough insulin," a medic said. "We've had to airlift about a thousand out just for that alone."

"Where do these people keep coming from?" a nurse wailed, looking at the line outside the medical tent.

"Some are leaving," Jennifer told the distraught woman. "When we came in this morning, we saw several groups heading toward their cars, perhaps thirty or forty thousand."

"A drop in the bucket," the nurse said with a sigh. "Next."

A woman with a child came forward. Blood was running from the little boy's bare feet. The nurse shook her head.

"Ready?" Lij asked Jennifer.

She nodded. He took her arm and they left the medical tent.

After reliving the moments of danger from the previous night, Jennifer admitted she was in love with Lij Branigan, daredevil adventurer, who thought nothing of putting his life on the line, whether in an experimental plane or up against a kid with drug-induced paranoia.

Before she had time to think through the implications, a voice over the speakers announced the arrival of food, another source of crisis in the Woodstock Nation. The resorts in the Catskills had answered the call for anything they could send.

"We need a circle for the helicopter pilot to target for landing. Join hands and form a circle, please." An older man dashed into the meadow and started urging everyone up. A group waded out of the pond where they'd been swimming.

"Come on." With a laugh, Lij pulled Jennifer into the cleared space and joined hands with the others to form a circle. Directly across from them were six naked young men. "Don't look," Lij advised. His grin was wicked.

"Right." She kept her eyes on him.

In less than five minutes, the helicopter landed. The pilot gave them a thumbs-up sign and opened the door. "Thanks for the landing pad," he yelled. "I've got the spaghetti. The sauce is coming on the next helicopter. Let's get this stuff unloaded so the next shipment can land."

Jennifer put her notebook and pencil in her pocket. She and Lij pitched in. Food became less critical by midafternoon. They had milk, cheese, ham, bread, peanut butter and jelly. Anyone who was hungry was given a sandwich and a paper cup of milk.

At two o'clock, the show started once more. Joe Cocker's rendition of "Delta Lady" set the crowd to clapping and stomping in time while he twisted and jumped and played an imaginary guitar. He gave his all to the song.

"The day would have gone fine," Jennifer wrote in her journal that afternoon, "if the daily storms had let up, but they didn't."

Joe Cocker grabbed the bottle of beer at his feet at the fourth crack of thunder and raced off the stage with the Grease Band right behind him. Other performers, gathered on the back of the bandstand, surged down the stairs or into the elevator.

The electrical crew swarmed onto the platform, putting plastic covers over the equipment, their faces grim in the fading light. If the storm tossed a thunderbolt at them while they were still on the stage, they stood a good chance of being electrocuted.

"My God, why don't they hit the main power switch?" Lij muttered.

Jennifer wondered, too. She heard someone scream for the crew to forget the equipment and get off the stage. At the foot of the platform, John Morris, one of the organizers, stood with a live mike in his hand and shouted directions. After getting the crew off the dangerous stage, he turned to the kids hanging from the speaker towers.

"Would you please get away from the towers? Clear away before someone gets hurt," he ordered. "Let's keep it nice and cool. Just sit down and be cool." Thunder drowned out the rest of what he was saying.

Jennifer wrote in her notebook, getting down the gruesome scene as the sky darkened by the second. The rain came, metal pellets that stung as they hit. The sounds of thunder and falling rain were tremendous.

She and Lij dove into the medical tent behind the stage and watched the downpour through the flap. Jennifer saw the movement first. She clutched Lij's arm. "The stage moved. Lij, the stage moved."

Lij's eyes narrowed as he studied the structure. Another gust of wind confirmed Jennifer's observation. The earth around the foundations was nothing but mud. It couldn't hold the massive structure on the hillside. As he watched, it slipped another two inches down the hill toward the crowd cowering under bedrolls and newspapers to escape the lash of the rain. Above them, the towers holding the sound equipment swayed dangerously.

"We've got to do something," Jennifer cried.

"Stay here," he ordered, then he was gone into the pelting rain. He caught a sound crewman by the arm and told him to cut the main power switch.

"I don't know where it is, man," the crewman said.

"Hell." Lij said, and ran around the stage.

That was the last Jennifer saw of him for several minutes. She was too busy holding the flap of the tent closed against flying debris. The wind raged down over the dairy farm like Death descending from a black carriage of clouds. It tore at the medical facility. The chief nurse held the center pole as if by dent of willpower she could hold the wildly gyrating tent on the ground. Her staff of nurses and paramedics scrambled to protect bandages and sterile gauze. Two empty cots collapsed and skidded under the edge of the canvas to disappear into the mud. Garbage, clothing and panels of plywood flew through the air.

This must be what war is like, Jennifer thought. *Or hell.* She saw the tears on the head nurse's face even as the woman gave out orders and reassured her patients. The wind tugged the canvas from Jennifer's grasp. Through the opening, she caught a glimpse of the trembling towers. Lij was on one!

Jennifer knew she'd never forget that moment of sheer panic as she realized the danger he was in. While she watched, he climbed halfway up the leaning tower and ordered a young daredevil down from the structure. When Lij and the kid jumped the last few feet, she wiped her face, not surprised to find tears there.

An electrician who took shelter with her said that one of the main electrical cables had been uncovered by the previous rains and the insulation worn off by thousands of tramping feet. With the wet ground and the lightning adding to the risk, thousands of people could have been sizzled like hot dogs in an electric cooker.

When the rain stopped a frenzied twenty minutes later, the electrical crew again got to work and transferred power to another cable. On the stage, Country Joe McDonald came through for the festival as he had the first day. Without power, he and the Fish performed their set, which looked like a pantomime to the audience. They loved it. A male dancer joined the action on the stage, stripping and dancing to the beat.

Lij returned to the medical tent. "Are you all right?" he asked, ducking under the flap and shaking water from his hair.

"Me?" Jennifer laughed, hearing the note of hysteria echo through the sound. She was suddenly furious with him. "You were the one on the tower. It nearly fell."

"Naw, I knew it wouldn't." He grinned at her, reckless, bold, handsome, desirable. "The stage was the main problem. It slipped six inches. They've got it shored up now on the front side. If it doesn't rain anymore, it should be okay."

"Fine," she said, and turned her back on him.

"What's with you?" he demanded, tapping her on the shoulder.

She whirled on him. "You just have to play the hero, don't you? *You* knew the tower wouldn't fall. *You* knew the lightning wouldn't strike. When did you become God?"

His expression became remote. "Is this a philosophical discussion? For a hippie who—"

"Don't label me because of your prejudice. I'm a liberal, not a dropout."

"For a *liberal* who believes brotherhood is the most important aspect of mankind, I'm surprised at your attitude. I didn't notice any of your friends getting that kid off the tower."

"So why was it your responsibility?"

She knew the answer. Lij would never consider the personal danger when other lives were at stake. He had confirmed his courage yesterday when he faced the youth with the knife and today when he braved the elements out of concern for another. It was the way he was made. But knowing that hadn't made her any less afraid for him.

Lij ignored her question. From the open flap he watched the weather grow calm. The last of the storm passed over the farm. The walls of the tent puffed and fell like the lungs of a strange beast as the wind surged, then died. Lij and Jennifer waited it out without speaking.

One of the nurses told Lij about the electrical emergency. He whistled under his breath. "We'd have been fried before we knew what hit us. All of us."

From the confusing scene of musicians, people, mud and flies outside the tent he turned his eyes to Jennifer. She met his gaze and tried to forget her terror.

"It's over," she said. "The danger's past."

He looked at her with a funny half-smile. "Is it? I wonder."

His cryptic remark should have made no sense, but she understood its meaning. She didn't want to think about their situation, not right then. Her feelings were too scattered by the realization of her love and by the fierce danger of the storm for her to sort them out. This was definitely a bad trip for her, one she knew she shouldn't have made.

JENNIFER LOOKED AT THE LIST in her notebook: Alvin Lee and Ten Years After; the Band; Blood, Sweat and Tears—she wondered if their lighthearted song about dying was apropos after the danger of the storm; Sha Na Na; Crosby, Stills, Nash and Young—who had joined the other three for this show—were names that would mean nothing to anyone who wasn't into the current music scene. They were all groups who had performed for the Woodstock Nation.

Sometime after midnight, first small, then larger groups began to leave. They left behind tents, bedrolls, blankets, radios and tons of junk and started home.

"They're exhausted," Jennifer said. "They've had enough of a good thing."

"Was it a good thing?" Lij countered, noting the sea of pale, strained faces whose owners looked as if they were just pulling out of shellshock.

Jennifer, over her personal fears, considered. "Yes, I think so. I know it's something I'll always remember. We all will, those of us who were here. The world will forget, but we won't."

They were quiet after that, just listening to the music. Lij realized that he, too, would never forget. It didn't make sense, but he felt he'd shared something with those five hundred thousand people at Woodstock. For a short time, they'd been of a like mind and spirit. It had been... awesome. He smiled.

"Do you want to go back to the hotel?" he asked.

She shook her head. "I want to get it all down. It's almost over. I want to capture the very last moment."

Sha Na Na went on as the sun was coming up Monday morning, their fifties' sound adding to the nostalgic mood. Jimi Hendrix came onstage at 8:30 to a crowd of perhaps thirty thousand, all that was left of the Woodstock Nation.

Jennifer and thousands around her wept as he played the "Star-Spangled Banner," "Taps," "Purple Haze," then launched into a long instrumental that left them solemn as the music ended.

The Woodstock Music and Art Fair was over.

THEY HAD NO TROUBLE getting to the city. After heading for the resort for a quick shower, they'd packed, returned the motorcycle and changed to a car. The roads were open and they zipped into New York City and caught the plane back.

"Glad to see you made it," the pilot welcomed them. "We're leaving in fifteen minutes."

Lij and Jennifer belted themselves into seats behind the two VIPs. Exhausted, they seemed to have little to say to each other. One of the men engaged Lij in a long conversation about the problems with an experimental plane until a steward served lunch.

Jennifer ate the chicken crepe and broccoli automatically. After that, she leaned the chair back and went to sleep. Sometime later she roused as Lij covered her with a blanket. She thanked him and closed her eyes again, ignoring the talkative vice president who gazed at her speculatively.

After dropping the men in Los Angeles, the pilot flew them to the Oakland airport. Lij insisted on taking Jennifer in a cab to her house in Berkeley.

Tree limbs blocked the street light and left the porch in deep shadow. Lij set her bag on an aluminum chair and took her by the shoulders. "When will you be coming back to Edwards?"

"I don't know. I'll write up what I have, then see what more I need." Jennifer intercepted his sharp glance. She could barely make out the features of his face.

"Let me put it another way—when will I see you again?" His smile flashed, white and brief.

She didn't answer. To tell him she didn't want to see him was impossible. Now that it was too late, she knew she had been foolish to let things go this far between them. She knew she should tell him not to come back. Would he understand?

"Jennifer?" His voice was deep, quiet, a slight huskiness to the faint drawl.

"I don't know," she said honestly. "I have so much work to do...." She let her voice trail off.

"Will you be going to Houston?"

"Yes. The man in charge of the brochures is there. He'll have to send my stuff around to be approved by the department heads and advise me of changes." She used the explanation as a shield against further questions.

"I see." Lij dropped her arms and was silent for a minute. "I'll be there soon."

"In Houston?"

"Yes."

"To help Dr. Benton?"

He didn't know any way to tell her of his decision except to say it. "I've decided to join the space program."

Jennifer stiffened. "When did you decide this?"

"Thursday."

"The day before we left for Woodstock. Why didn't you tell me then?" She thought of liquid oxygen, hydrogen, rocket fuel, all elements of death. Coldness swept over her like a chilling mist of the bay. "Why wait until now?" When she had already fallen in love with him.

"The time wasn't right." He spoke as if weighing each word. "Does it make any difference to us?"

"Yes, of course, it does," she cried. As if he didn't know. "It makes all the difference in the world."

"Why?"

"Because...because...it just does." All the tumultuous emotions he produced in her froze. She felt like an ice mass inside, cold and lonely and betrayed.

"We need to talk when we're not so tired. I'll come up next weekend if I can. I have a few loose ends to tie up—"

"No, don't. I'll be too busy to see you."

"When, then?" He was impatient.

"I don't know." She hated playing the coward, but she needed time to think. "We've each seen how the other lives," she said, forcing a reasonable note. "Our lives don't cross, not really. What would be the point of prolonging a relationship that's going nowhere?"

"Damn it," he muttered, and reached for her. He pulled her against him, his lips seeking hers. The kiss was long and demanding. "Why are you doing this?" he asked, lifting his mouth from hers only a few inches. He stared through the dark into her eyes, his gaze probing for answers.

Jennifer couldn't ignore the response of her body nor her heart to Lij's caress. She wanted to take his hand and lead him inside. She wanted him to hold her and never let her go. *Grow up.* This was the real world, and he was going to be an astronaut.

She thought of Grissom, Chaffee and White, consumed by fire in a routine test procedure, of four other astronauts who had gone down in T-38s. She couldn't bear it, not again. To risk seeing the person she loved going up in flames was asking too much. "I can't go through that again," she whispered. She touched his face. "I can't."

"So you'd just rather give up than face life," he mocked, his voice hard with anger. "Stay in your sterile world, Jennifer. Maybe you'll find what you're looking for among your friends here. Marry some Berkeley professor. That should be safe enough for you.'' He turned away in disgust.

Jennifer watched him stalk back to the waiting cab. *Let him go,* she advised. *Let him go now.* She fled into the house.

She found no comfort in her room. What difference did it make if he was an astronaut or a test pilot? None, really. Except Jeffrey had died in a rocket car trying to set a new land-speed record. She had a vision of Lij, strapped in the spacecraft while the Saturn rocket exploded as it raced toward the moon. Each time she closed her eyes, she saw Lij fly out of the Apollo module, his spacesuit all aflame, like a strange new star shooting through the night sky.

LIJ WAS CONSUMED BY a reckless, impotent fury the entire flight back to Edwards. For Jennifer to refuse to see him again after the weekend they had shared seemed a betrayal of their days together. For the first time in a long time, he had looked forward to something. He had thought of them in Houston, working on the same project, sharing thoughts and ideas as well as off hours. He had wanted her to meet Amy.

Well, old man, so much for that. The lady says no.

It was better this way. After all, what did the future hold for them? A long affair? He wasn't sure he had the time or that an affair would be enough. He had responsibilities. He had his work. Most of all, he had Amy. He leaned forward, stretching against the harness that held him in the copilot's seat, eager to see his daughter, suddenly wanting to hear her call him Da in her sweet little voice. He needed to share, to be important in someone's life, he realized. It made him feel humble. And lonely.

LIJ LISTENED TO AMY'S doctor with disbelief, rage and hope intermingling. "Why didn't this come up before?" he demanded.

Dr. Chadwick looked sympathetic. He had taken over the case only a few months ago and knew only what had been written in Amy's record. "It was the lack of growth that tipped us off. Often when the body had been through a trauma, it slows down, but Amy wasn't bouncing back. When we ran the tests, frankly I wasn't expecting the results we got. Hypothyroidism is difficult to diagnose. It can seem like a lot of other things." He smiled. His round head and unlined face coupled with premature baldness gave him a gnomish appearance. He looked both wise and kind.

"So what is the prognosis?"

"We'll have to see how hormone therapy goes," the doctor replied. "There probably is some brain damage, but it doesn't appear as severe as originally diagnosed. I think you'll be surprised when you see her." The young man walked with him to the garden door before turning back.

Lij crossed the patio and stood at the steps leading to the sun-parched lawn. He looked around for Amy and Mrs. Murrin, not sure what to expect, trying not to want too much, too fast, for his daughter.

It had been several weeks since he'd been in Houston. Closing out his office and quarters at Edwards had taken more time than he'd anticipated. But that was behind him now. The move to Houston heralded a new life. Yesterday he'd signed a contract on a town house in a wooded, spacious complex. He'd be moving into it next week, renting until the close of the sale.

He spotted Amy's nurse sitting alone on a bench. Where was Amy? Taking a deep breath as if he could draw courage from the hot September air, he strolled across the grass. The woman was busy with knitting needles and yarn.

"Mrs. Murrin," he called when he was within speaking distance.

"Mr. Branigan," she exclaimed, lifting the yarn from her lap.

"No, don't get up." He walked over and looked around. No Amy. A group of four children, golden in the Saturday morning sun, were playing a game, a relay carrying a ring on a stick held in the mouth, led by a bossy blond teenager with a full set of braces on her teeth. "Where's Amy?"

Mrs. Murrin smiled grandly. She pointed one of the blunt-nosed needles toward the open space in front of them. Lij glanced around and frowned. He didn't see Amy anywhere. She wasn't sitting on the ground in her placid manner, vaguely watching the world go by. He peered around the laughing kids. She wasn't on the nearby swing, watching them play.

He sucked in a hard breath as he caught sight of her. "My God," he said. "It's Amy."

She was one of the children, gilded by the sun, her short blond curls bouncing around her face as she waited for her partner to tag her. When the boy rushed up and handed over the stick and ring, she took them and carefully rushed across the grass.

Lij watched her shuffling trot, her gait not quite coordinated, her elbows swinging with more energy and enthusiasm than balance, but she was moving. Not sitting, not locked in her own world, but playing, laughing, taking part. Hope, feeble as a newly emerged butterfly's wings, beat through him. Amy was playing!

"It's like a miracle, isn't it?" Mrs. Murrin said softly beside him. "Soon she won't need me."

"You think not?" When he spoke, his throat felt as if a cork had been wedged in sideways.

"Amy," she called when the relay was over. "Look who's here."

Amy pivoted. "Da," she yelled, her face alight with instant recognition.

"Hey, Toots."

He met her halfway. When he lifted her into his arms and tossed her into the air, he knew there were tears in his eyes. He didn't care. Amy had come home.

BRADFORD PULLED HIS WILDLY curly blond hair behind his neck and tied a rawhide thong around it, thus keeping it out of his way. His blue pencil skimmed over copy as he read the article. "This is pretty heavy stuff," he said when he finished.

The article expounded upon single-parent families, mostly females, and the struggles they had in raising their children. Many states wouldn't honor another's award of child-support payments, and there was no national policy.

"'So, while the man lives the bachelor life with full wages and no responsibilities, the woman and children suffer in poverty,'" Tissy concluded, reading over Bradford's shoulder. "Other western countries take the payments out of a man's wages, like taxes. If he ducks out, then the money he's paid to Social Security is used to aid his kids. That seems fair to me." She tossed her braid over her shoulder and looked defiant.

Jennifer had never heard her friend speak so vehemently on the subject. With sudden intuition, she wondered if part of the problem wasn't personal. Last week she and Bradford had cooked a big dinner and cake to celebrate Tissy's twenty-ninth birthday.

"One more year," Tissy had said with a catchy little laugh, "then it's all downhill."

Was that what was bothering her? Later she had mentioned her age and the fact that, if she wanted children, she'd better start thinking about the time element. "The biological clock'' was the way some women referred to it. Time running out...

Jennifer thought of her own birthday, coming up in January, right after the new year. Twenty-nine. She never felt older or wiser with each new year. There still seemed to be a young, restless spirit in her that yearned to be free. Free from what? To do what?

"I'm not sure feminist issues are that important to a college-oriented readership. Our circulation is already down."

"Feminist! Important!" Tissy fumed. "What about the protest of the Barnard women over being segregated into dorms with much stricter rules than the males? Women want equal rights!"

"Well, maybe if we have space—" Bradford began.

Tissy whirled and stalked out of the basement office in a ruffle of patterned skirt and outraged womanhood. In a second, they heard her bare feet on the stairs.

Bradford sighed. "I guess I blew that one. I don't know what's come over her. Used to be, I could reason with her."

Jennifer removed a page from the ancient typewriter in the editorial office. She checked it over and laid it with the rest of the article she was writing on child-care facilities at the college. "Why don't you talk to her?"

"About what?" he asked. He tossed the article on his desk.

"About being nearly thirty. About having children. About the future she can expect with you."

"What?" he said, suddenly attentive. "Do you think... Is she...has she said..." He collected himself. "Is she pregnant?"

Jennifer shrugged. "You should know that better than me."

"But she's never said..."

Jennifer watched startled thoughts chase across his face. "Then maybe it's time you asked," she suggested. "And she's right about women's issues. More and more women are demanding better pay, help with child care—"

"Okay, I get the message." He threw up his hands. "We'll run the article." He started out, stopped. "I think the paper has run its course. I've been thinking of looking for a job."

Jennifer knew it was a hard admission for him. He loved putting out his own news. "Maybe it won't be as stifling as you think. There are major papers that print in-depth stories."

"Yeah." He looked glum as he started for the stairs. "Perhaps it's time to move on to other things. Like raising a family and all that." A smile appeared on his face. "Like wow," he said softly, and ran up the steps.

Jennifer drifted up to the first floor and went into the living room. Settling in a chair, she watched a tennis match on TV. The announcer said if Rod Laver won, it would be his second grand slam.

One of the third-floor boarders came in with a friend. Both young men were carrying sandwiches and cans of beer. Jennifer looked them over thoughtfully. "Who's your friend, Ted? Haven't I seen him around here a lot lately?" She didn't permit any free boarders. Her budget wouldn't allow it.

Ted plopped on the floor, his eyes on the tennis match. "This is Buster. He was in lab class with me. This is our landlady, Witch Hazel." He grinned through his scraggly beard. "Also known as Jennifer Wright."

"'Lo," Buster mumbled around his bite of sandwich.

"Hi," Jennifer returned, her manner friendly. "How long are you visiting with us?"

Buster looked uncertain. He glanced at Ted.

"Until he decides what to do," Ted offered as an explanation. "The feds are after him. He lost his college exemption. Told you to keep your grades up."

As Ted directed this last statement to his friend, Jennifer caught on. "He's been drafted."

"Yeah. He doesn't want to go to Nam."

Jennifer could hardly blame Buster for that. "It's tough," she said sympathetically. "But Canada is a very nice place. They've been wonderful to—"

"I don't want to go to Canada," Buster put in.

"Where are you going? No other country has offered asylum."

"I thought he could stay here," Ted said.

She shook her head. "I don't want anyone here to get in trouble."

"Ah, come on, Jen, lighten up," Ted cajoled. "Nobody will know he's on the place."

His patronizing tone stung. "There are six other people in this house, Ted. I have to consider them."

Tissy and Bradford came down the stairs. They were holding hands. "What's all the shouting?" Bradford asked.

"Ted's friend here. He's evading the draft. I told him he had to leave."

"Why?"

Jennifer frowned at Bradford. "Do you want to be arrested for harboring a fugitive? You could, you know."

"I think we should take a stand and help him," Tissy declared.

Jennifer considered, then shook her head. "He's the one who needs to take a stand. Hiding out isn't going to solve his problem." She turned to the young man. "Did you register as a conscientious objector? You would get medical duty or something like that instead of combat."

He looked horrified. "I don't want to do anything."

Jennifer thought of Lij, who'd flown missions in Vietnam and lost friends there. She thought of him at Woodstock, putting his life on the line to help others. She perused the young man who apparently didn't care about school or war or anything but his own skin. Her sympathy faded. "Then you'd better move on north," she advised.

"I thought you were on our side," Ted exclaimed.

"I am," Jennifer said. "Don't I write articles and organize marches? Do I call the police every time a draft dodger crosses my path? Hardly. All I'm asking is for Buster to make a decision and act on it without harming others."

"I've invited him to live here—"

Jennifer whirled on Ted. "Since when did you start running things around here?" It was the first time she'd ever had to remind them it was her property, and she felt embarrassed, as if she were one of the capitalist pigs the hippies screamed about.

"Look," Buster said, "I don't need this. I got other places to go. No sweat, man," he said to Ted. "I can make it." He ambled out, leaving his used dishes and empty can on the floor.

Ted followed. "I'm leaving, too, as soon as I find a place," he tossed over his shoulder.

"Fine. I wish you both every happiness," Jennifer called. She remembered an old Chinese curse. "May you live in interesting times," she yelled, irritated by Ted's grand manner.

"They won't know what that means," Tissy said, smiling.

Two of the student boarders had been into Zen Buddhism. Their precept was to try for serenity through meditation. Interesting times, meaning times of turmoil and conflict, were anathema to them. Jennifer had picked up the curse from them.

Gathering the dishes, Jennifer started toward the kitchen. That was another thing she had rules about—leaving trash around the common living room. Oh, well.

"By the way," Tissy said, causing Jennifer to halt. "Bradford and I have decided to get married."

"What!"

They both grinned. "We want children. It's only fair to give them a secure home and legal protection." Tissy glanced at Bradford with a meaningful smile. "Such as it is."

"I give," he said. "I'm convinced."

"Congratulations to you both." Jennifer set the plates down and rushed across the room to embrace her friend. "So, am I going to be a godmother soon?"

"Not for at least nine months," Bradford said.

Tissy gave him an exasperated glance.

"I thought we were going to start as soon as possible," he said, his smile innocent, his gaze tender. Jennifer knew all at once why Tissy had fallen in love with him.

"Married," Jennifer mused. "I think we're all a bit more traditional than we'd originally thought." She smiled at Tissy. "You'll be my friends, the old married couple, instead of my friends, the radicals. Darn."

They delved into an eager discussion of the future, the earlier debate forgotten.

"Elaine will probably laugh when I call and tell her," Tissy complained. "She'll say I've bought the great American dream."

"Haven't we all?" Jennifer asked philosophically. "I mean, at one time or another, haven't we all believed in Santa Claus?"

When she finally made it to the kitchen and put the dishes in the sink, she realized Tissy and Bradford would probably be leaving soon. Suddenly she felt as if life were rushing past her without a second glance. It was an odd feeling.

Chapter Ten

"You've passed the first part of your physical," Dr. Benton informed Lij. "Heart, lungs, gall bladder, et cetera, check out okay." He gave his former pupil a dry smile. "I don't think you'll have trouble with the second part. How will you do on the psychological battery?"

Lij was surprised by the strange question. "All right, I suppose. Why? Do you think I won't?"

"You've had things on your mind lately. How's Amy?" the doctor asked abruptly.

"Fine. She's..." Lij shook his head, unable to summon words. "She's a living, breathing miracle. The rate she's learning...it's as if she's trying to make up for the past two years."

"And the other?"

"The other?" Lij echoed cautiously.

Dr. Benton made an impatient gesture. "The woman. Jennifer? Wasn't that her name?"

"I haven't seen her in a while," Lij admitted.

"Hmm," Dr. Benton said, making Lij's admission sound like a life-threatening situation.

"There's nothing between us." Because she'd wanted it that way. He hadn't seen her since leaving her at her door after the Woodstock weekend. He'd called twice, but she'd been preoccupied, too busy to talk long.

"I see," the physicist said wisely. He checked his watch. "It's time for my lecture to you new recruits. Are you coming?"

Lij followed his mentor along the hall, his thoughts running off on their own. Jennifer. He wondered what she was doing now. Not that it mattered. She'd made it pretty damned clear that he had no place in her life.

After Dr. Benton's lecture on travel among the stars, Lij separated from the class and went to the lounge. The coffee machine took his money but refused to give him a cup. He watched his coffee go down the drain.

"I have some in my office," a voice said behind him.

He turned to see Jennifer's friend Elaine standing in the doorway. "Thanks. That was the last of my change."

In her office, Elaine efficiently poured them both a cup of coffee and settled at her desk with a cigarette. "How's it going?"

"The training? No sweat."

She grimaced. "Of course you're not having any trouble. Men rarely do."

"Do I detect a note of bitterness in that last statement?" Lij studied Jennifer's friend curiously. Elaine was harder, more career driven than Jennifer, he thought. There was a softness in Jennifer. She was independent as hell. Her feelings about astronauts were clear, yet she was a fair person. He didn't think Elaine was.

Elaine puffed out smoke. "Ignore it." She sighed. "Mac and I are getting a divorce. Men aren't number one on my list of goodies these days."

"Sorry. Any particular reason for the breakup?"

"Why?"

"Jennifer seems to have a problem with astronauts, too."

Elaine shrugged. "You know about her past."

Lij took a long swallow of the coffee. It was as bitter as Elaine's attitude. "Yeah. Life's taught her not to get involved with a certain type of man. I think she's afraid of any type of commitment because she's afraid of getting hurt. I don't think it matters what the man does."

"Thank you for that insight, *Herr Doktor*," Elaine said with a caustic arch of one eyebrow. "I'm sure the women of the world will appreciate it. The trouble with most of you men is that you want cheerleaders for wives. Jennifer isn't one. I'll tell you that right now and save you a lot of trouble."

Lij finished the coffee, crumpled the paper cup and tossed it in the trash can. He walked to the door. "When you see her, tell her I said hello."

"I will," Elaine assured him, crossing her heart. She smiled when he raised his eyes heavenward. He saluted and left. As he walked down the hall, he admitted talking to a woman with a bruised heart wasn't the smartest thing to do. He felt sorry for Elaine. But when, he wondered, was Jennifer coming to Houston?

"Speak of the devil," Elaine said an hour later when Jennifer strolled into her office.

"Were you talking about me?" Jennifer dropped in the chair next to Elaine's desk and stretched her feet straight out in front of her.

"Lij was." Elaine noted the stillness that came over her friend, then the pretend busyness as Jennifer searched in her purse for a tissue. "He was trying to pump me about you."

Jennifer glanced up. "What did you tell him?"

"Nothing. I figured if you'd wanted him to know you were in town, you'd have contacted him yourself."

Jennifer breathed again. "I—we're not seeing each other."

"Why?"

"It's better this way."

"He wanted to know what you had against astronauts." Elaine paused, then added, "He says you're afraid of getting involved with *any* man. That you're afraid of getting hurt."

Jennifer blew her nose and threw the tissue in the trash. "How astute of him."

"Do you have a cold?" Elaine asked.

"Hay fever. Are you ready for lunch? I didn't get time for breakfast this morning. I was still unpacking."

"Do you like the efficiency apartment?"

Jennifer nodded. "It's cheaper than eating out all the time, too. I'd rather fix my own meals."

Elaine looked her friend over critically. "I think we've both lost some weight."

"Are you going through with the divorce?" Jennifer asked.

Elaine nodded. "Whatever we had, it's gone. I don't even know what happened. Let's not talk about it."

Jennifer thought of Elaine and Tissy and herself, fresh out of college and off to conquer their respective worlds. Then reality had set in for all of them. Life wasn't as easy as it looked from the hallowed halls of academia. "I have some news," she said. "Bradford and Tissy are going to get married. They want children. She's going to call you as soon as they arrange a date."

Tears leaped into Elaine's eyes. She shook her head slightly. "Well, good for them. Let's go eat, shall we?"

The cafeteria was noisy and crowded. Elaine and Jennifer finally found a table with two chairs in the far back corner. While they ate, they talked about Jennifer's contract and how the brochures were going. Elaine flung down her napkin as soon as she finished. "Drink your coffee and relax. Dillon won't be able to see you for another hour. He has a meeting. I've got to run. Come by at one thirty."

Jennifer felt somewhat abandoned by her friend's hasty exit. She ate the last bites of her lunch, then sipped her coffee while watching the space workers come and go. She saw Lij when he stood and came toward her. Her heart beat rapidly for a second before settling into a hard thumping rhythm.

"Hello," he said, taking Elaine's empty chair. "Long time, no see."

"Hello, Lij." She was surprised at how quiet she sounded.

His dark gray eyes skimmed over her, making her aware of her eyes, her face, her lips. She raised her cup and took a rapid drink. He smiled. She couldn't tell if it was a friendly smile or not. He looked ... wonderful ... exciting ... dangerous. Pick one.

"Five weeks," he continued as if she hadn't spoken, recounting the elapsed time since they'd parted. "Is this just a quick visit to the Space Center, or are you staying awhile?"

She considered lying, then quickly decided on the truth. "I've taken an apartment here for the next two months. One of the directors requested that I do the series on the astronaut training next. They have a new group just starting."

Lij frowned. "That wouldn't have been Dr. Benton, would it?"

"I don't know."

"He likes for everyone to be married. Thinks it makes the men more stable and less prone to recklessness."

At Lij's soft, cynical laughter, Jennifer glanced at him. Her gaze lingered. His hair was as unruly as ever, his eyes as dark. She still couldn't read his thoughts. Was he glad to see her?

Was she glad to see him?

The rumpus her heart had kicked up at his appearance suggested she was. Crazy heart. "How are things going with you?" she asked.

A startling smile brightened his face. "You wouldn't be-lieve what has happened. Amy is much better. She's grown an inch, and she chatters like a grackle."

"Grackle?"

"A blackbird with a long tail. You see them a lot in Texas." He grinned. "My daughter is relearning to talk."

"Has something different been tried with her?"

He nodded. "The doctor tried a growth hormone. Also, her thyroid was impaired. She's taking an extract that has helped her a lot."

"That's wonderful, Lij," Jennifer said with sincere warmth. "Will she be all right?"

"It's too early to tell, but I've got my hopes up."

She worried about his hopes. What if the effects were only temporary? What if the little girl had an adverse reaction?

"I'd like you to meet her," he suggested.

"I'd like that," she said without thinking, and was im-mediately sorry. To meet his child would mean further in-volvement.

After seeing him fling himself into danger twice at Woodstock, she knew exactly what she would be letting herself in for if she continued to see him. He'd be in the very thick of whatever life threw at them. It was his nature.

"Watch it," he warned her with a teasing grin. "I might think you mean that."

"I do, but I shouldn't."

They looked at each other.

"I still want you," he said softly. "I've missed you."

She looked away. "Don't."

"Don't what? Want you? Ask me to stop a train with one hand. It'd be easier. Miss you? Take away the nights so I don't have to go to bed and realize that for two nights I held you all night. To give that much then take it away was cruel."

His voice was so low, she had to concentrate on his lips to understand him. A shiver rushed along her spine at his accusation.

"Lij, I'm sorry. It was wonderful, but—" She bit her lip, unable to explain her need to get away from him. She had felt she was being sucked into quicksand, getting in over her head with no control over the future. She felt the same way now.

"Don't sweat it," he advised with a half smile. "I'll survive."

She wondered if she would. He changed the subject to Space Center happenings. She asked about his training.

Dr. Benton drifted over on his way out. "Well, I see you're already at work. Has Lij been complaining of the indignities he's suffered this past week?"

She shook her head.

"He's passed the first part of the physical—"

"They take you apart and shift every cell through some damned test or another," Lij interrupted. "Then they have the nerve to tell you you're fine. I need a week in the hospital to recover."

"Pay no attention. They all say that." Dr. Benton smiled at her and his former star pupil with paternal indulgence. "Tomorrow he will go in the comet. I think you'll find it interesting."

"No!" Lij broke in again. "She's not going to watch while I'm made a fool of."

"I'd be delighted," Jennifer asserted. She realized she had probably committed herself to seeing Lij through his training. She looked at Dr. Benton, who was smiling happily.

"Good," the doctor said as he left them.

"That's the first time I ever realized Cupid was also a mad scientist," she muttered.

Lij chuckled as realization of what she'd just admitted washed over her features. "Felt the twinge of an arrow or two?" he inquired gravely.

"No." She returned his gaze as steadily as she could with her heart racing like a runaway engine.

He became serious. "We climb aboard the monster machine at 0900 sharp. Shall I pick you up at your place?"

"I've leased a car."

"Then I'll see you around." He got up and ambled out.

Jennifer finished her cold coffee, smarting under the fact that he could be so cool while she was in turmoil, then went to see Dillon about the next series of brochures. She was the worst person to write about astronauts, she thought. She didn't even like the breed!

THE MONSTER MACHINE was similar to a carnival ride. It could spin around all three axes to imitate the yawl, roll and pitch of an actual spacecraft. It measured a person's ability to take that kind of punishment and still function.

Jennifer clicked her pen in and out as she waited in the observation booth for the test to begin. Four men would be put through the machine that morning.

"I hope you have a strong stomach," one of the engineers said with a rueful grin. He was near her age and good-looking. At her questioning glance, he explained, "They usually get sick. That's why some people call it the 'vomit comet.'"

She smiled. "As long as I'm not the one going around, I'll be okay. What's the machine really called?"

"The multi-axis training simulator."

"Okay," the test conductor called out, "Branigan's first."

Jennifer sat on the edge of her seat and watched as Lij was strapped into the machine. He wore coveralls resembling a light-weight spacesuit.

She could hear the men talking over the speakers in the control room. Lij's deep voice answered "Check" to each question and instruction. He knew what he was doing.

When he was finally installed in the machine and the medical people were satisfied his blood pressure and pulse were okay, the test started. He was spun in circles and flipped head over heels—all in the name of science. Inside the contraption, he performed some simple instructions during the commotion.

Jennifer took notes and asked questions when a procedure wasn't clear to her. The young engineer was very helpful. When the test was at last complete and everyone was preoccupied in removing Lij from the machine, Jennifer slumped into her chair. Against her will, memories pushed into her mind.

She remembered Jeffrey's car tumbling over and over until the sheets of flame enveloped it entirely. Sweat broke out across her forehead as if she felt the hot wind of death breathe on her. She pushed her bangs off her forehead. Through the window into the test chamber, she met Lij's gaze as he was helped out. He gave her a thumbs-up. She felt vastly relieved. Her smile stretched from ear to ear.

The technician held a bucket toward Lij. Lij laid a hand over his stomach, but shook his head. The men around her laughed.

"He did good," the young engineer told her. "Most of them don't make it halfway into the test."

"He's been through that before," she said, remembering the rolls and flips they'd done in the T-38. "He's a test pilot." Was that pride in her voice? She had no right to be proud of him. He was nothing to her.

By the end of the month, she'd given up trying to convince herself of that lie.

JENNIFER, LIJ AND THE other three astronaut candidates who were tested with him became a familiar sight around the Space Center. The five of them went to lunch together daily. One of the other candidates and the test engineer who'd explained the comet test were very interested in her. Aware of their feelings, she was careful not to be alone with either of them. Lij watched her maneuvers with sardonic amusement in his eyes, which she ignored.

"Well, if it isn't the nifty five," Elaine said one day at lunch, surprising Jennifer by joining them. "Got room for one more?" They slid chairs around until she was fitted in. "What have they been doing to you poor souls this week?"

Ken, the youngest candidate, spoke up. "Giving us quizzes for a psychological profile. At least, that's what one of them said. Personally, I think it's some kind of diabolical plot. You should see the questions they ask us."

Jennifer and Elaine glanced at each other and managed to keep solemn faces. They'd read the test questions over the weekend and had been astonished. The ones about sexual preferences and habits had been revealing and startling. Some of the queries had caused them to howl with laughter as they imagined the men's answers.

"Hey," Ken said, "you guys don't get to see the answers, do you?"

Elaine assured him that only the psychiatrist in charge had that privilege. Ken was clearly relieved. Jennifer wondered about his answers. She glanced up to find Lij's gaze on her. A slight smile played at the corners of his mouth. He knew she had seen the test and was wondering just how the men had responded to the more personal questions. The rat. He was laughing at her.

Elaine finished her meal, then she and two of the men left. Ken, Lij and Jennifer remained at the table.

Jennifer glanced at her watch. One more hour before the men had to report for another probe into their psyches. She decided to go to her office and write up her notes from the morning.

"Uh, Jennifer..." Ken began with a scowling glance in Lij's direction. He paused a second too long.

"How about a movie tonight, Jen?" Lij interjected lazily. "Also, I thought we might take my daughter on a picnic tomorrow. Or are you going to work on Saturday as usual?"

The gentle inquiry didn't fool Jennifer. With the one question, he had made it clear he was quite knowledgeable about how she spent her Saturdays. With the statement about Amy and a picnic, he had made it clear she was part of his personal life.

The younger man looked defeated. He picked up his tray. "Well, I have some studying to do. See you two later." Without looking at either of them, he hurried off.

"That was mean," she said.

"It was less bruising than getting a refusal. You were going to refuse him, weren't you?"

"Of course."

"Of course," Lij repeated. "The lovely Miss Wright is not at home when it comes to men."

"Pettiness doesn't become you."

He let his gaze travel over her. Her skin felt several degrees warmer all at once. "What do you want in life, Jennifer?" he asked. "Give me an answer in one paragraph."

"Was that one of your test questions?" she asked.

"No, they wanted to know why I wanted to join the space program in a hundred words or less." He grinned, disarming her with his humor. "Do you realize you often answer a question with a question?"

"Journalism 101," she intoned. "'Your job is to find out who, what, where, when and why. And spell their names correctly.'"

They laughed.

"That's the first time I've heard you laugh since Wood-stock," he said. He settled deeper into his chair. "Not going to answer?"

What did she want in life? Once it had been the tradi-tional home and family and security, but she'd grown out of that. Nothing was certain in this world. Besides, she was confident she could make it on her own without a man to be the breadwinner for her. That made the whole question of marriage a different proposition.

"I don't know," she said truthfully.

"Fair enough."

"Do you?" She couldn't resist asking.

"Yeah. I think I do. Now."

"What?" Her throat was so parched, she would have croaked on a cracker.

"To have Amy happy in whatever she's capable of doing."

"Oh."

"To have a friend."

"You have several of those."

"A special friend," he murmured.

She wouldn't touch that one with an eleven-foot pole.

"Are you going to ask what I want from this special friend?"

Jennifer shook her head.

"Too bad. I might have told you." He stood and picked up his tray. "But then again, I might not." He left.

She considered throwing a soggy napkin and hitting him in the back of his arrogant head. He had been deliberately leading her on, knowing she was on the edge of her chair waiting to hear what he was going to say next. He was ex-asperating.

Ever since she'd been at Houston, she'd waited for him to make some move, but he'd been remote, although friendly at all times. It was enough to drive her crazy.

So what did she want? That he should throw himself at her feet and beg for her attention? Well, that would be a start. With a wry smile, she put her tray on the rack and went to prepare for the meeting with Dillon.

"WE'D LIKE FOR YOU to cover it for us," Tissy said.

"That's only five days away," Jennifer protested. "Wednesday, the fifteenth, is right in the middle of the week, too. I'm observing underwater tests next week."

"This is going to be the biggest peace march of the century," Tissy warned, going for Jennifer's reporting instincts. "It'll show Nixon we mean business."

"And revenge Agnew's calling the war protesters a bunch of effete, intellectual snobs?" Jennifer suggested.

"Your understanding of human nature is exquisite," Tissy complimented, then spoiled it with a laugh. "You know you want to go, so just say yes and save my long-distance bill."

"Why don't you and Bradford go?"

"We're the publisher-editor staff. You're the reporting staff."

"I get the picture." Jennifer laughed. "Okay."

"Okay? Does that mean you're going?"

"Yes. Right. Affirmative. Okay," Jennifer repeated.

"Great. Your tickets will be waiting for you at the airport. Have you got a pencil? Here are your flight numbers...oh, you'll need a room. The return flight is the next morning."

Jennifer jotted down the information on her calendar pad, said goodbye—

"Wait a minute," Tissy broke in. "I just wanted to tell you you're going to be a godmother. Bye," She hung up.

Tissy pregnant.

It seemed ironic that Tissy and Bradford, the most liberal of her friends, were on the verge of becoming the most domesticated.

Trying to work after that was impossible. Besides, it was four o'clock on Friday afternoon. Most of the workers were leaving for home and a busy weekend with their families.

She straightened her desk and locked up. Slinging her purse over her shoulder, she joined the crowd. Once in her car, with the windows open to cool out the day's accumulated heat, she thought of marriage and babies and life.

Six years ago she had put all that behind her and set out to build a career that would let her live a life of independence. She'd succeeded, but was it enough? Lately, she wasn't sure.

Glancing in the rearview mirror, she saw a familiar red sports car. Lij. He gave her a half salute. She lifted a hand from the steering wheel and waved back. To her surprise, he turned when she did and proceeded to follow her home.

"So this is where you hide out," he remarked when they stopped in the parking area and got out of their respective vehicles.

"Yes." She looked at it through his eyes. It was a rather expensive apartment complex, built since the Space Center had opened. The grounds were attractive with green lawns, palm trees and oleander bushes, which were still in bloom.

"Would you like to go to dinner with me?" he asked.

She looked into his eyes. All the longings of the past weeks seemed to leap through the air, making her skin tingle. She could feel her body changing, becoming softer, warmer, waiting for him.

"Or we can fix steaks at my place," he suggested.

She shook her head. She might be crazy, but she wasn't *that* crazy. Alone with him at his place...

"I want to talk to you, that's all, just talk."

"What about?"

"My daughter."

She stared at him. "Your daughter?"

"Amy. I need your advice."

Jennifer laughed shakily. "I'm not the world's foremost expert in raising kids. You'd do better to read Dr. Spock."

Lij shook his head. "You're intelligent and able to think objectively. I'd like your opinion."

Curiosity got the better of her. "All right," she said, keeping her tone cool. "Let's go to the King's Inn. They do a good prime rib there."

He chuckled. "Don't trust yourself alone with me? Most women are bowled over by my charm."

Jennifer had to laugh as he assumed a modest tone, which was patently fake. "About seven?"

"Why not now?"

"It's too early for dinner. I want to do my workout first."

An interested light gleamed in his eyes. "Perhaps I could join you for a few pointers—"

"Not on your life. I'll see you later." She walked up the path toward her building.

"You won't always be able to resist," he muttered at her back. She wasn't sure if she had been intended to hear or not. She kept walking.

Lij OPENED THE DOOR and stood aside for Jennifer to enter. He'd asked her to come to his place because the restaurant had been noisy with the Friday night TGIF crowd. He wondered what she thought of his home.

It had none of the lived-in, comfortable ambiance he'd found at her house in Berkeley. Her living room had been colorful with wallpaper, pillows and bright knitted afghans. His was blah.

The carpet was beige, the walls off-white with matching drapes. The sofa and wing chair were brown velvet, the reclining rocker that he favored was brown leather. A basket of dried straw flowers and a couple of art prints were the only color.

"This is very nice," she said.

"Have a seat. I'll put on some coffee." When he returned from the kitchen, he found Jennifer had kicked off her shoes and was curled into the big rocker, a magazine open in her lap. At once the room seemed different.

Cozy.

Comfortable.

Homey.

"I'll build a fire," he said. A husky note had crept into his voice. He laid on some wood and lit the gas jets to start the flame. Had he brought her there to discuss Amy and his in-laws or to seduce her?

He sat on the hearth, which was a step above the floor, and looked at Jennifer. Her eyes were half closed; her expression was dreamy. She had on the black pantsuit that was so damned sexy. A silk blouse of vibrant blue made the most of her eyes. She was lovely, and he was filled with desire for her.

He sensed she might be vulnerable to him tonight. But she'd hate him for taking advantage of a weak moment when the morning came. He gritted his teeth and controlled the impulses that threatened to drown his common sense.

"Would you like a brandy?" he asked.

She nodded. "Only a little."

He fetched snifters and poured them each one, his body needing the movement to help quell the restlessness. "Are you coming in the pool with us next week?" he asked.

The astronauts would be performing tests in a swimming pool, dressed out in space suits to simulate the lesser gravity of the moon. She shook her head. "I'll observe from the side." She paused. "I won't be in Houston all week."

"Going back to Berkeley?"

"No. Washington, D.C." She laid the magazine on the table and sipped the brandy. "Taking part in a protest." She said it as a challenge to him.

Lij stared at her, his mind conjuring up TV pictures of fights breaking out between police and demonstrators. "What kind?"

"A peace march to protest Vietnam."

He thought of Nam, the heat, the flies, the smell of mud and dung hanging over the fields. He hadn't liked the war, either, but he'd been a soldier and he'd done his duty. A man should at least do that.

He frowned at Jennifer. She was so cool, he wanted to shake her. Instead, he tamped the feeling down. There were other problems besides their differing views on Vietnam. Didn't she realize the danger in these mass meetings? Things had a way of getting out of hand.

"I'm covering it for the paper." She surprised him with her next words. "Want to go?"

He remembered Woodstock. People. Music. Laughter. Rain. Making love in the night. Yeah, he especially remembered that.

His thoughts must have got through to her. Her hand trembled on the snifter when she raised it to her lips. So she wasn't so cool, after all. Neither was he.

"What did you want to ask me about?" she prodded.

The fire had caught and was driving the October chill from the air. He sat on the sofa. Watching the swirl of brandy in his glass, he thought of his latest problems.

"My in-laws are trying to get a court order to force me to let Amy undergo an extensive IQ evaluation from their doctor. The clinic just completed a whole series of tests. I've offered to make the results available."

"That seems fair."

"Does it? I've tried to remember they're her grandparents. I suppose they love her in their own way."

"What were the results?" Jennifer asked. "Is—is there no hope for her recovery?"

Lij shook his head. "You'd have to see it to believe it. Every time I go over, she's learned something new. She's still behind a five-year-old, but she tests in the normal range for a three-year-old, which was her age when she was hurt."

"Why, Lij, that's wonderful," Jennifer exclaimed.

He found himself explaining everything that had happened over the past two months, pausing only to bring in their coffee. Jennifer was an attentive and understanding audience. He poured out his heart, his hopes, his fears, his plans for the future. "She will probably be able to come home in about a year if she keeps on like this. She may even go to a regular school when she catches up."

"And if she doesn't?" Jennifer's voice was gentle but practical. He realized she didn't want to dash his dreams, but neither did she want him living in a fantasy. Such as he'd built around him and her during one weekend in New York?

"Then she'll continue at the center," he answered easily.

"Good. I think you have things under control."

"You don't think I'm being unfair to Rona's parents?"

She replaced her cup on the tray while she considered. "Send them the test results and invite them to see her for themselves."

Lij thought it over. "Maybe that would get them off my back. Or they might decide on a custody battle. They've implied as much before."

Jennifer was sympathetic while he talked of his problems. When he finished, she stood. "It's getting late. I should be home. I've got work to do in order to take off Wednesday."

"What flight are you taking to Washington?"

"The Tuesday-night red-eye."

He grinned at her disgruntled tone. "Coming back the next night, same flight?"

"No, the ten o'clock flight on Thursday morning. Everything else was booked solid."

"Hmm."

Jennifer glanced at him as she slipped her shoes on. She couldn't tell a thing from his expression. So what else was new? She picked up her purse, and they left after he closed the fire screen around the dying embers.

At the door to her efficiency, she thanked him for the meal and the evening. "It was pleasant."

"Even though I dumped on you?" he asked wryly.

"I was glad to share," she said simply.

He laid his hands on her shoulders, his fingers caressing her through her clothing. "I believe you were."

Jennifer saw the longing in his eyes as he bent toward her. Helpless, she raised her face and accepted his kiss. It was brief. Sighing, she put her key into the lock and stepped inside. When she flipped on the light, she saw him take a peek into her domain.

"It's not much," she said. "A place to hang my hat."

"I'd know it was yours," he told her. "Books and papers, your typewriter, peace earrings on the table. I recognize your touch."

"Are you saying I'm messy?" she asked with mock indignation.

"Naw, just . . . you make a place your own."

The words hung suspended in the cool darkness. She fought a desire to invite him into her world. But they'd done that, and look how it had worked out. She frowned. Actually, he'd fitted in. But Woodstock had been a temporary thing, a long weekend, not a lifetime.

"How would you like a partner on your jaunt to Washington?"

"What?" She stared at him stupidly.

"I've decided to join in the march."

"You'll be court-martialed."

"Not if I don't become involved in a brawl and get arrested."

"Lij—"

He laid a finger across her lips. "Maybe you're right," he said. "Maybe it's time this war was over and our boys brought home." He turned and disappeared into the night.

Chapter Eleven

Wednesday, October 15, 1969

"I can't believe this."

"What?" Jennifer glanced up from her notes.

"You. Me. This." Lij waved a hand at the gathering crowd. "I don't know why I'm surprised. I should know by now that when you invite me to attend anything, it's a happening."

The woman behind them, over thirty, nice slacks and a sedate wool jacket, spoke up. "The radio says police are estimating the crowd here in Washington at forty-five thousand. In New York, it's one hundred thousand. Bill Moyers is reading the names of the dead on the steps of Trinity Church. Chicago, Los Angeles, everywhere, people are taking part in the war moratorium. Two hundred fifty thousand people, marching together." She looked at them with tears in her eyes. "My brother was killed in Vietnam."

"I'm sorry," Jennifer murmured, touching the woman's arm in sympathy. "I don't have any brothers, but two of my friends from school are MIAs. It's been over eighteen months, and we don't know whether they're alive or not."

The woman nodded. "That's why I'm here today. I'm not a radical or anything. I'm just so sick of hearing about Vietnam on the news every night."

"So are a lot of people," Jennifer agreed. She glanced at Lij. He was focused on some inner vision. She wondered if he was remembering buddies who hadn't made it back. "Lij?"

The sound of his name jerked him back into the present. For a moment, he'd been in Nam, the shells whizzing all around him while below and behind his plane Agent Orange plumbed out like a giant ostrich feather and settled on the jungle.

"I'm hit! I've taken a hit!" his best friend had shouted into his radio. Lij had watched him go down, had seen the billow of smoke and fire as the plane exploded. He'd written the letter to Brenda, telling her she was a widow.

"You're remembering," Jennifer said. "You were there, too."

Around them, people chanted, "Peace *now!* Peace *now!*"

"Yeah."

"Do you wish you hadn't gone?"

"I wasn't given a choice."

She chewed on her lower lip. "You could have refused."

"Only women have the luxury of choice. A man either goes or he hides." His face hardened. "I was a soldier. I had a duty and I did it." He touched her arm. "Drop it, Jen."

"Don't you feel it was wrong—"

"No," he said. "Whatever you civvies were doing stateside, it didn't have an impact on us in the field. Our only shame was being soldiers who weren't fighting to win. We didn't understand that."

"My brother wrote me something like that," the other woman broke in. "He said he couldn't figure the people out. He was fighting for them, but they didn't want him. He didn't know who the enemy was. At times he thought it was himself. It was all very...strange."

For the first time, Jennifer saw the war through the eyes of those who fought it. They were young men, idealistic, but somehow the ideal had gotten twisted. "It wasn't your fault," she said. "It was Johnson and McNamara and a Congress of old men who didn't know what was what."

"And they still don't according to your way of thinking?" Lij asked.

"No." She met his gaze squarely, refusing to back down.

He drew a deep breath. "Maybe you're right, but it's the vet who's getting hurt by the controversy. He's caught in the middle, ridiculed by his peers if he goes, imprisoned by his government if he doesn't. It's hell either way."

"I hadn't thought of it like that," she admitted. "But the war itself is wrong. Only Congress can declare war. The president hasn't the authority, but we've been embroiled in Korea and now Vietnam. For what reason? National security? I doubt it."

The issue was a stalemate between them, Lij saw. His point about the soldiers' quandry made no difference. It was just another tough fact of life to the marchers. He glanced at the sister of the vet. She was sincere. She wanted to stop the war so other young men wouldn't have to die. So did Jennifer. He could buy into that.

He held his peace and followed her through the crowd while she interviewed individuals on their reasons for participating. One veteran, his legs gone, spoke from his wheelchair. "My kid brother is coming up on eighteen. I don't want him to go to Nam, and I don't want him to slink off to Canada like a dog, either."

The injured vet looked fierce and protective, like a tribal chieftain. He wore a red bandanna around his head and sported a great, shaggy, red-gold beard that belonged on a Viking conqueror. Jennifer asked him about his experiences in the war.

He gestured toward his body. "Men die or lose parts they'd rather keep. That's enough reason to stop the war," he growled, tears forming in his eyes.

Jennifer thanked him and walked on. Lij stayed close. He could see she was troubled. He watched as she stopped and looked up at the Washington Monument.

"We never learn, do we? Humans seem destined to go from one war to another, and we never learn a thing from all the others." She rubbed an impatient hand over her eyes, swiping at the moisture that collected. Turning, she gazed through the bare October trees toward the Lincoln Memorial.

He hesitated, then put an arm around her, drawing her to him. "Just strategy and tactics for the next war," he affirmed, feeling the tension in her slender frame.

She suddenly relaxed against him, letting her body lean into his side, her curves molding to his angular lines. Whatever barriers existed between them, lack of trust wasn't one of them, he surmised, feeling strong and protective of his woman.

His woman?

Yeah.

Wasn't that the main reason he'd tagged along? He'd been worried about her safety and he'd wanted to be with her. Could they recapture a little of that magic they'd shared at Woodstock?

A need grew in him. He couldn't define it, but he knew it was there, in him, waiting to be acknowledged. It centered on this elusive, independent-minded, free-spirited woman, who was so self-sufficient it scared him.

He pulled his coat closed against the fall chill in the air and tried to listen as Mrs. King spoke of her husband's dreams for a united, loving America. When night fell, he and Jennifer joined the other marchers in lighting candles and marching solemnly to the gates of the White House. They sang softly, "We shall overcome . . ."

When the march ended, the crowd dispersed with murmured goodbyes and silently faded into the dark. He and

Jennifer walked along Pennsylvania Avenue, close in spirit if not in attitude toward the Vietnam question.

"I couldn't get a room," she said. "All the hotels were booked. I thought I'd stay at the airport." There was an unspoken question at the end of her statement: What are you going to do?

"I called last Friday," he told her. "I have a room at the Hilton. I'll let you share if you pay half."

"I can't stand people who plan ahead. But I'll take you up on your offer," she added quickly. She stole a glance at him under the street light while they waited to cross the street. She wasn't sure where she stood with him.

Lij let out a piercing whistle. A cab whipped over to the curb. "The Hilton," he said, ushering her inside.

They were silent on the short ride. Lij paid the driver, tipped the doorman and led Jennifer to the elevator. He studied her face while they ascended the three floors to his room. She in turn studied the various components of the compartment as if she were researching an article on elevators. He took her arm and guided her to the room. When he had the door open, he stood aside.

Jennifer had felt the tension like an electric current in the air all the way to the hotel and in the elevator. It escalated when he opened the door to his room. With a straight back, she walked inside after Lij flipped the light switch. The room leapt into view—two chairs, table, TV. . .two beds.

Oh.

"Choose whichever you like. I'll take the other," he said.

Such manners.

She looked up at him. His smile was grave, his gaze tender. There seemed to be a certain wistfulness in it. Lij Branigan, wistful? *Come off it,* she scolded her imagination.

"You can use the bathroom first."

She washed up, brushed her teeth and came out in the robe provided by the hotel. Since she hadn't been able to get a room before she came, she had brought only her makeup and toothbrush in her purse. She laid her clothing on a chair, waited until he was in the bathroom, then discarded the robe and jumped into bed, pulling the covers up to her neck.

When Lij finished and came out, she was pretending to be asleep.

"Here," he said. Something landed on her bed. "You can use the top. I never do."

She opened her eyes. His pajama top lay on the cover. She snaked one arm out and grabbed it. Pulling it under the sheet, she struggled into the garment, buttoning it to the top. For some reason, she felt better. Decent. Proper. Covered.

"I know what females look like," he said with a caustic edge to his voice.

And exactly what I look like. "Good night," she said. "Thanks for the pj's." She snuggled under the covers like a mouse hiding from the house cat.

He turned out the light.

Darkness seemed to descend on the room with a thud. She lay there, hearing every noise in the building—a couple laughing as they walked along the hall, someone getting a Coke from the machine nearby, Lij turning over. The darkness magnified every sound.

She tried counting her heartbeats. She tried humming dreamy songs, silently, of course. Nothing helped.

Lij was awake, too. She could tell.

"Why are you so good-natured?" she finally demanded. "Why are you so reasonable? Why haven't you called me a bitch like you do the planes when they don't act right?"

"Aren't you acting right?" He sounded cautious.

His niceness only set off her temper. "Yes, of course, I am."

After all, she'd acted in both their best interests in refusing to see him again. In the two months since their Woodstock weekend, he'd not said one recriminatory word to her about it. It *had* been for the best. So why was she feeling guilty?

Why was she angry?

Because he hadn't grabbed her and tried to make passionate love to her, she admitted, ever honest with herself. He'd been harsh but considerate, even compassionate today when he'd held her and comforted her.

"Lij, I'm sorry if I've seemed difficult."

"You haven't been difficult. You've been truthful. That's a rare quality in a person, man or woman," he said.

His voice was soft, so near and so far in the dark. He understood there was no future for them, she thought. She let her body relax and soon her eyelids grew heavy and she slept.

Before dawn she woke.

Tears were in her eyes and she felt terribly sad. Her dreams had made no sense, just a lot of jumbled running with a sense of gloom and disaster to them. But over all was the sadness. She tiptoed to the bathroom, found a tissue and blew her nose, then tiptoed back to bed.

He spoke to her from the darkness. "Jennifer, are you all right?"

"Yes."

A long silence. "Are you crying?"

"Yes. My dreams were...sad, I think. I'm not sure."

"Go back to sleep," he advised. "It's only three."

She lay there for a few minutes, remembering another room with only one bed. Sharing it had been so sweet. In his arms lay peace and forgetfulness as well as the most intense excitement she'd ever experienced. If she asked, would he...

"Lij?"

"Yes." Patient, composed.

"May I sleep with you?" She'd made the first move. Would he be offended at her boldness?

"Yes. Shall I join you—"

She was out of her bed and into his before he finished the question. He pulled her into his arms.

"Nothing like an eager lover," he said, trying to cover the throat-tightening way he felt before kissing her with the pent-up hunger of weeks, their differences forgotten.

There was nothing to compare with a man's strength, Jennifer thought as she snuggled closer, or the warmth of his body. She felt secure even as she experienced the rising tide of passion through her veins.

His hands—oh, heavens, his wonderful hands—unbuttoned the pajama top, and then he touched her. He cupped one of her breasts, and she felt the nipple grow hard against his palm. Slowly he kissed along her neck, down her throat, following a line to her breasts. His mouth replaced his hand, and he stroked each tip with his tongue, causing shivery sensations to delve deep into her.

"God, I've missed you," he muttered fiercely. "Don't you ever do this to me again."

"No," she promised, hardly aware of the words. She knew only the needs he aroused in her. Only with him could she find release.

He arched over her and moved inside, claiming her and giving himself at the same time. She sensed it was the moment when neither of them could go back to the distant friendliness of the past weeks. They were beyond that point.

But where?

She buried the question under the desire that spread from their intimate point of contact to every part of her. There was only them and this and now.

"SO, ARE WE ON AGAIN or what?" he asked the next morning, his voice deep, quiet and full of contentment.

Jennifer yawned and rubbed sleep from her eyes. She nestled against him, her curves fitting his perfectly. "Were we ever on?"

"At Woodstock."

"That was a time out of context," she reminded him, aware of all the problems that existed between them. Someone had to keep a clear head. "A long weekend that can never be repeated."

"Oh, I don't know," he drawled, keeping it light. "Last night was pretty good."

She raised up on an elbow and studied him. "Don't look so smug," she ordered. "It didn't solve anything."

"Don't be such a worry wart." He wanted no postmortems this morning. "For a free-spirited liberal, you sure do think a lot."

"Somebody has to," she grumbled, punching him on the chest, then letting her hand linger to caress him. She trailed her fingers through the dark whorls of wiry hair, liking the feel of him. His skin was tan and firm, the muscle hard beneath. Without meaning to, she leaned down and kissed his nipples.

She felt his breath still for a slow count of ten, then he sucked in a deep draft. "Jen," he said huskily.

The tenderness caused her anguish. She didn't want tenderness. She wanted forgetfulness. She wanted to live for the moment and not think of tomorrow. She couldn't.

"What did you think of the march?" she asked.

He pulled her over on him for answer and kissed her neck. She felt his rising desire and experienced a surge of heat through her own body. He stroked her back from her neck to her legs, sliding over her hips with familiarity. "Come to me," he said.

And she did.

It was much later that he answered her question. "I think the marchers are like children, enjoying the excitement of the moment."

"You don't think the moratorium did any good?"

"Some. It'll make the president and Congress take notice. But the real way to change things is to infiltrate, work your way up the chain of command, then begin a campaign to redirect the thinking of the organization as an insider."

"A mole, like in the espionage books," she concluded. "I don't like the image. It seems underhanded."

"Sometimes life is that way. You have to be, too. Come on, we have a plane to catch."

While they showered and dressed, Jennifer tried to imagine herself as a mole. The image didn't fit. She hadn't the patience or nature for it. She considered Lij.

He could handle it. Even if he didn't believe wholeheartedly in the goal, he would do it if he thought it was his duty. Therein lay a major difference in them. Could they somehow meet on a middle ground? Was their attraction strong enough to overcome their basic beliefs? Neither seemed able to compromise on principle. So where did that leave them?

Nowhere, she concluded. Absolutely nowhere. But there was no reasoning with him. Men thought if all was fine in bed, all was fine everywhere, or at least solvable.

They took the shuttle to the airport and caught their flight. When they arrived in Houston, he invited her to his place.

"Why don't you come home with me?" he asked, holding her so close she could hardly breathe. They stood outside her apartment. "There's plenty of room. You could use the den as your office, keep all your papers there. You wouldn't have to return to Berkeley to write up the pamphlets."

"I've already taken this place for two months." She met each kiss he dropped on her lips with growing need.

"So?"

"I feel better having a base of my own."

He drew away and frowned at her. "A hiding place, Jennifer?"

"You might find you hate having me around by the end of a week," she warned him. "I tend to scatter things around—"

"Good. My place needs some scattering. I'll help you pack."

In the end, she compromised. She took a change of clothes to his town house, but left the bulk of her belongings at the flat. In case things didn't work out.

They ate pizza for dinner, put her toothbrush in the master bath next to his and installed her typewriter on the desk. He scattered her papers over the neat surface. "Does that look about right?" he asked, solicitous of her comfort. "Is that messy enough, or should I spread them out a bit more? Here, I'll toss a few magazines on the chairs and sofa."

She hit him with a yellow note pad.

With a low growl, he grabbed her, threw her over his shoulder and proceeded down the hall to the bedroom. He made fierce love to her until she was exhausted with pleasure. Maybe it would work, she thought before falling asleep.

Looking for a happy ending?

They happen only in fairy tales. Get real, Jennifer.

SATURDAY WAS A PERFECT DAY for a picnic. Lij carried the basket that he and Jennifer had prepared across the grounds of the convalescent center. Children and parents formed happy groups here and there. Jennifer felt like an interloper.

"There she is," Lij said. He set the basket down and cupped his hands around his mouth. "Amy," he shouted.

A little girl, small and delicate, stopped her chatter to a nurse and another child and ran toward them. "Da," she cried.

Lij held out his arms and scooped her into them, lifting her high into the air, then holding her tightly while they kissed. He turned back to Jennifer. "Amy, here's a friend I want you to meet," he said. "My special friend, Jennifer, the one I told you about the other day. Remember?"

The child nodded and twisted around in his arms, her blue eyes fixing on Jennifer as they came closer. She looped one arm around her father's neck, seeking security. The gesture wasn't lost on Jennifer. She remained seated on the ground and waited for Lij to make the introductions.

"Amy, this is Jennifer. Jennifer, this is my daughter, Amy. Can you say hello, Amy?" he encouraged. She stuck her thumb in her mouth and looked at Jennifer with big eyes.

Jennifer smiled with an effort. She noticed Amy's eyes were the color of the afternoon sky, a deep, pure blue without a hint of Lij's gray. Her mother's eyes?

"Hi, Amy. We have a picnic lunch here." Jennifer spoke as if she and Amy were old friends. "We made your favorite sandwich, peanut butter and strawberry jelly." She opened the basket and shook out the blanket, then began placing items on it. "Roast beef for your father, pineapple and cream cheese for me. Lemonade for everyone. Do you want a big cup or a medium one?" She held up two paper cups for comparison.

After a hesitation, Amy took her finger out of her mouth and ponted at the big cup. "That one."

"The big one it is." Jennifer poured the cup half full and set it down. "Sit over there," she ordered casually. When Lij and Amy were seated opposite her, she continued setting the food out.

Jennifer and Lij talked about the weather and the food while they ate. "This is really good," he said. "Didn't Jennifer make us a good picnic lunch? We'll have to give her a gold star."

Amy smiled suddenly. "Star," she said. "I have one."

Lij looked surprised. "No. A star? For what?"

She pointed to her teeth.

"For brushing your teeth?"

Amy nodded, obviously pleased about the reward. "All week," she said.

"You remembered to brush your teeth all week all by yourself?" he asked, amazed.

Amy was very proud. She nodded vigorously, her soft curls bouncing about her face.

"Like wow!" Lij said, laughing and hugging his daughter. Amy laughed, too, and patted his face.

Jennifer looked away. Lij was a good father. His gentleness was unlimited, his love for his daughter uncomplicated. He should have other children, she thought. That much natural parenting talent shouldn't be wasted. He was a family man in his heart. Even a fool could see that.

She chewed on a piece of pineapple, unable to get it down to a size that would get past the lump in her throat. She thought of balancing a job, husband, children, all the tasks involved in running a large household, the demands that love placed on a person. Life seemed terribly complicated again.

When they finished their meal, Lij wiped Amy's mouth and hands with a damp towelette.

His eyes met Jennifer's. They held hers for a long second, a message clearly in their depths. Jennifer saw his love for the child, so fierce, so gentle. She wondered how it would be, to be loved like that.

"Play," Amy said, breaking the mood. She stood up, her movements not quite fine-tuned yet, but more graceful than anytime during the past two years. She stopped, looked back and smiled. "Bye, Da. Bye…" She frowned as she thought.

"Jennifer," Lij reminded her.

"Jen-fer," Amy repeated. She started off, but stopped again. "Thank you," she said very clearly. Then she ran toward a group of children who were playing tag in a circle.

Jennifer couldn't read the thoughts in Lij's eyes as he watched Amy scamper across the lawn, but she saw him swallow a couple of times as if he fought emotion. She felt a rush of tenderness for him. His life hadn't been easy, but he had accepted it with courage and love. He hadn't withdrawn from Amy, which he could have easily done. Her love for him deepened.

"Today was good," he told her later, lying side by side in his big bed. "Amy liked you."

"I liked her, too. She's a fine little girl." She traced a pattern on his chest. "You're a good father, Lij."

"I'm getting better," he said quietly. "Not long ago, I resented the past and what had happened, but I'm learning to let go. It's the future I think of now."

A premonition feathered over her skin, leaving a faint chill. Was she included in his thoughts?

AT THE TRAINING CENTER, Jennifer agreed to take one of the milder simulator tests so she could get a real feel for what the astronauts went through. "Not that horrible multi-axis thing," she protested.

"Chicken?" Lij inquired with a definite twinkle in his eyes.

"Realistic," she retorted.

"Okay, if that's the way you want to be. How about the 5DF?"

"What's that?" She wasn't going into anything blind.

"Five-degrees-of-freedom trainer."

"That sounds interesting. Name the five degrees."

"Come on."

She soon found herself strapped into a chair that let her move backward and forward—degrees one and two—or she could roll forward into a somersault, sideways in a cartwheel or turn completely around like a ballerina in a pirouette—the other three degrees of freedom. The machine made it easy. She felt as graceful as a swan as she glided and turned.

Next, Lij and his fellow trainees insisted she try the spacewalk simulator, a chair on a hydraulic arm.

"Just push the button," Ken instructed her.

She pushed the button and went whizzing off in the opposite direction at a great speed. The men guffawed at her startled yelp. In a minute, she figured out the machine's operation and flew about the room like a great seated bird, up and down, forward, back, sideways. The microgravity training chair let her make tremendous leaps at one-sixth her normal weight.

"No wonder men love this," she argued with Lij at lunch. "It's fun and games."

"It can be dangerous," he reminded her.

"When it comes to the real test," she acknowledged. "But it's also exciting. Women should get an equal chance to try it. We'd be wonderful in space. We're smaller and more agile. More patient, too."

"Spare me a list of your virtues." He picked up her roll and stuck it in her mouth with a mock-fierce scowl.

LIFE SETTLED INTO a routine. They spent several evenings and most of Saturday and Sunday with Amy, who soon grew used to Jennifer. On Halloween, which fell on Friday night, Amy came home to spend the weekend with them.

Lij lit the fire in the grate although it wasn't dark yet and the night chill hadn't penetrated the room. He just wanted the glow. It matched the way he felt inside.

From the bedroom, he could hear Amy's piping voice and Jennifer's quieter one. The girls were putting Amy's clothes away and decorating the room. Jennifer had taken him shopping the night before; now she and Amy were arranging the bean bag chair, the desk and the chalkboard in suitable locations and putting posters on the wall.

The girls. His girls. He realized he had begun to think of them collectively and possessively. They were a pair and they belonged to him.

Don't rush it, he advised himself. He suspected Jennifer wasn't ready for any long term arrangement. Was he? What did he want? For life to go on just as it was now. He was happy. Amy was happy. Jennifer seemed content, although once in a while her eyes took on a distant hue. Did she think of her fiancé?

He felt no jealousy, only a bittersweet grief that life hadn't worked out for her. That was the way he felt about his marriage now. He would probably always view it with a haunting sadness for what might have been, but he no longer felt the sharp anger, nor quite so much guilt for not making wiser decisions about him and his young wife. They'd both made errors; they'd both paid.

The doorbell rang, followed by a spate of giggles. "Trick or treat," a chorus of goblins yelled.

"I think we have our first guest," he called. "Are you girls going to get it?"

"We certainly are," Jennifer replied.

She came into the room. Amy jumped out from behind Jennifer. "Boo," she yelled.

Both were dressed as witches with horrible masks complete with warts and hairs. "Good grief," he exclaimed.

Amy jumped up and down. "Did we scare you, Da?"

Lij clutched his chest. "I nearly fainted." The doorbell rang again. "Get the door," he ordered. "I think it's some of your friends."

He watched them go into the foyer. A mama witch and a daughter witch. Catching a glimpse of himself in the mirror over the mantel, he realized he was grinning like an idiot. Well, why the hell not? He was having a good time. He ambled to the doorway to watch Amy and the spooks.

When she opened the door, ten kids screamed "Trick or Treat" at her. Amy was overwhelmed. Reacting instinctively, she turned and ran for the bedroom, leaving them standing there.

Jennifer took charge. "I'll give out the goodies. You go explain things to Amy."

Lij quickly went down the hall. Amy was facedown on the frilly bedspread Jennifer had selected.

"Hey, Toots," he said, sitting beside his daughter. He laid his hand on her head, noting how large he seemed next to her smallness. "Hey, those were just kids, dressed up like ghosts and monsters, just like you're dressed as a witch. It's all pretend."

"They yelled at me," she sobbed.

"That's what you're supposed to say to people. 'Trick or treat.' It's just for fun." He felt infinitely patient as he stroked her soft curls. He'd lived with fear too many times to take another's terrors lightly.

He coaxed her with gentle words until she was ready to face the world once more. Finally they washed her face and returned to the living room just as the doorbell rang again. Jennifer cast them an uncertain glance, then opened the door.

"Trick or treat, smell my feet, give me something good to eat," sang out one brash youngster. His little sister cowered behind him. "Come on, say it," he told her impatiently. She wouldn't. He sighed in the manner of older brothers. "Her, too," he said.

Jennifer treated both of them.

"I'll do it," Amy said decisively after they left.

When the next bunch arrived, she was ready. She solemnly held out the candy bowl and let them select their own goody. One brave little witch, Lij thought, ignoring the burning in his eyes. One brave, beautiful little witch, warts and all.

And one beautiful big witch.

A powerful surge of yearning rocketed through him. He wanted more, he realized. He stepped forward instinctively and put his arm around Jennifer's shoulders. When the door opened, a flash of light momentarily blinded him. When his vision cleared, he saw a man, another father, he assumed, taking pictures of the little goblins coming up his front walk. With a smile, he went to find his own camera.

"Hold that pose," he said. "I want a picture of my two favorite witches."

Jen and Amy hammed it up for him.

LIJ READ THE LETTER from Rona's parents for the third time. They wanted custody of Amy. They were prepared to go to court with proof that he was an unfit parent. Enclosed was a picture of him with his arm around Jennifer in her witch's outfit while Amy held out a bowl of candy. It looked so innocent. Their innuendos made the evening sound like something lewd and ugly.

He'd have to tell Jennifer. First, he'd have to come to a decision about them.

He gave a silent snort of laughter and flung the letter on his desk. He could hear Jennifer in the kitchen, rattling pots and pans as she prepared dinner. It turned out she liked to cook. The quality of his meals had improved with her around so much. She still had her efficiency apartment and sometimes retreated to it to think out her work plan, she said. He wondered.

Did she just need space around her once in a while? Was he too close? Did he smother her?

Was there really a decision to be made? When it came to his daughter's future, he knew what had to be done. Setting his lips firmly together, he knew he would do it. But not yet. Maybe he was a coward, but he couldn't do it yet. The time had to be right.

He laughed without humor. Yeah, timing was everything. Especially when it came to goodbye.

Chapter Twelve

Friday, November 14, 1969

Jennifer sat in the visitors stand at the Kennedy Space Center, Florida. With binoculars pressed to her eyes, she viewed the Saturn V rocket, its nose pointed skyward, and waited with several thousand other people for the second attempt to put a man on the moon. Conrad, Gordan and Bean waited inside the Apollo 12 spacecraft for take-off.

Somewhere above them, out of sight, two chase planes flew in broad circles, also waiting for the lift-off, cameras ready to record the event. Lij was in one of them. It was customary for astronauts not assigned directly on a mission to fill in other slots on the work force. Flying chase was one of the fun jobs.

She rested the binoculars on her lap. Lij. Something was eating at him. Never a talkative person, he had become even quieter of late. She hoped he would share his thoughts soon. She didn't like being left out, she discovered.

Around her, she was aware of people—movie stars, congressmen, TV newscasters. Out on the launch pad, the huge rocket steamed as vapor formed and was whisked away by the ocean breeze. Around the launch vehicle, the structure of steel beams and work platforms looked like something out of a science-fiction novel.

Over the speakers, she could hear the voices of the flight engineers in the control room located in the nearby VAB going through the countdown procedures. When they reached the last ten minutes, the tension in the crowd went up by several degrees. Then it was ten seconds and counting...

"Ignition. Lift-off," came the voice over the speakers.

It was impossibly beautiful, incredibly awesome in real life. Jennifer realized seeing it on TV couldn't convey the excitement of being there. The ground shook under her feet. In a few seconds, the sound reached her ears like the low rumble of a mighty beast awakening. It escalated into a deafening roar.

Smoke. Flames shooting out to the side through the flame-deflector pit. A million gallons of water pouring over the structures to keep the service towers from melting.

A shout went up. Apollo 12 was off!

With her binoculars, Jennifer could detect a small dot in the sky, streaking after the rocket. Lij or the other pilot, doing their job.

"T plus one and counting," droned the voice over the speakers.

LIJ FELT THE G FORCES slam into him as he kicked in the afterburner and reached for a piece of the sky. He kept the rocket and spacecraft in view as long as he could, filming the first stage burnout for the scientists who would study the flight from every angle to see that all went well. When the Saturn sped by, leaving him in a cloud of vapor, he turned toward Patrick Air Force Base, just south of the launch complex.

Two weeks, he thought. Two weeks and he still hadn't talked to Jennifer about the future. He'd have to do it soon. He shrugged his shoulders against the harness, not liking the feeling of being pressured. He'd hired his own lawyer, who had reviewed his situation and assured him the Colburns had no case. That had given him a little more time. Still, he felt uneasy.

The first phase of his astronaut training was completed. He had made the cut. Phase two was due to start. It would whittle the number to a final count between twenty and thirty. He felt confident, without being arrogant, that he would make it.

He landed, refueled and checked the plane for the return flight to Houston. Then he waited.

Jennifer showed up within the hour. She waved as she climbed out of the VIP car. He smiled, knowing he liked seeing her too much. She had become too important in his life to let her go easily. It was a sobering thought.

"That was wonderful," she exclaimed, running up to him. "Are we ready to go?"

He nodded and helped her in. They buckled up and took off for Texas. She chatted to him about the excitement of watching the launch in person rather than on television. She thought firsthand experience was good for writing the brochures.

"Lij?" she said. "Are you there?"

"Yeah, I'm listening," he said. "So you really liked it?"

But her heart had gone out of the discussion—monologue, she corrected. She was the only one doing the talking. When she got a spare minute, they were going to talk . . . seriously.

SOMEHOW THE MOMENT was never found. Jennifer worked long hours at the Space Center. The second moon journey and walk had been completed. She had witnessed the astronauts' safe return to earth, and their pick-up at sea by a nearby cruiser after a perfect splashdown. She wrote up her notes and composed the brochures, passing them to Elaine and Dillon to begin the "approval" circuit. Finished, she prepared for Thanksgiving. She was going home.

JENNIFER STEPPED AROUND LIJ as she packed. All her clothes had ended up at his place before October was over. The efficiency apartment had been vacated well before the rent was due again.

"You'll be at your grandmother's house?" he asked.

"Yes. My mother will be there tomorrow and Thursday, then she's going to visit friends. I'll stay with Gram until Sunday."

"I could fly up on Friday and bring you back Sunday. I'll have a plane."

She looked at him with a question in her eyes.

"I have to get my flying time in with the air force since I'm not out of reserves yet. Dr. Benton will get you approved as a passenger for research purposes."

"It must be nice to be able to pull strings," she remarked.

"Yeah," he agreed.

He was becoming irritated with her. She could tell by the tightening of his mouth and the stiffness in his shoulders. He'd detected the coolness in her voice when she mentioned pulling strings. The fact that he had strings to pull brought home to her the reality that he was thoroughly entrenched in the established order of things, the very order she wanted to restructure.

"I suppose that offends your liberal soul," he commented when she said nothing.

She straightened a blouse and laid it in the suitcase. "Yes, it does. Not everyone has access to the good-ol'-boy system of favors and opportunities."

"Everyone does favors for friends, even you. You use your position here to write articles for your friends' radical paper."

She felt a surge of heat along her neck. "An article doesn't equate to a favor," she said. "However, you're right. I'm being sanctimonious when I have no right to throw rocks. I apologize."

He ran a hand through his hair. "How the hell did we get on this subject? All I'm trying to ask is if I can see you over the weekend. Is that possible?"

She drew in her hackles and went to him. "Yes, very possible. Gram is dying to meet you."

"Your grandmother knows about me?"

"Yes."

Lij closed his arms around her slender waist. "Since when?" He inhaled the subtle fragrance of her hair, wanting her with a sudden, possessive desire. Was now the time to talk? No, not when she had a plane to catch in a couple of hours. He sighed and contented himself with kissing along her hairline.

"Months ago," she confessed, leaning against him.

Desire sharpened his senses. He was aware of her body, the solidity of her bone structure, the strength in her hands as she caressed his neck. She was slender, but not delicate. When they made love, she came to him with as many demands as he.

"I need to finish packing," she reminded them both.

"I need you," he murmured, wanting her one more time . . . one last time?

When he guided her to a chair, she didn't resist. He saw her eyes go dark and knew she wanted him as much as he wanted her. In a few minutes, they were joined, their bodies gliding easily as he held her on his lap, her legs straddling his.

Later, after the fires had been banked, he drove her to the airport. They were both quiet. She kissed him goodbye as if it were forever instead of just three days. He'd join her on Friday after spending Thanksgiving day with Amy.

"Don't forget to give Amy the turkey," she admonished just before getting on the plane. She had bought a ceramic one, brightly painted, for Amy's room.

"I won't." He watched her leave, his brow puckered with thoughts as ominous as a Montana thunderhead crackling with heat lightning. Friday, he promised. Friday, they'd talk. He needed more than just the quick relief of lovemaking, he realized.

He also needed to know where he stood with her and where they were headed. It wasn't in his nature to let things drift along. He wanted a solid foundation with Jennifer.

Other problems loomed, adding to the urgency to formalize his relationship with her. The Colburns were threatening a custody battle again. As a family, he and Jennifer could provide a stable home for Amy. He knew she loved the kid, and Amy loved her.

He turned from the window after Jennifer's plane taxied down the runway and lifted into the sky. Whatever Jennifer's feelings about marriage, he had to have a commitment from her. It was an inescapable fact: he needed a wife. He wanted her in the role.

FROM BEHIND THE FARMHOUSE in Maine came the steady chop of an ax on wood. Her grandfather, retired admiral and consultant to the president, was splitting wood. He stayed in shape that way. Lij was helping him.

"Tell me about this Lij Branigan," Gram invited. She picked up her knitting needles and resumed work on a sweater in smoky-blue yarn, the same color as her granddaughter's eyes.

Jennifer gazed into the fire. Lij had arrived the previous day and fitted right in with her family. Her mother had looked him over with approval before she left to spend the weekend with an old friend from school days.

Her grandfather had been won over when Lij helped him haul in a fallen log for chopping and splitting into firewood. Gram was a little more discerning.

"You know most of the details," Jennifer said.

Lij had kept them laughing with his stories of growing up in Montana. Underneath the banter, he'd managed to convey the sense of a boy growing up in a warm, close-knit family. As a man, he came across as decent, respectable and dependable, with the ability to laugh at himself and life. As a father, he showed concern and love for his child. Patience, humor and humility were other traits glimpsed through his funny anecdotes.

"Then tell me about Jennifer Wright." Gram serenely worked a cable stitch into the sleeve.

"A disaster. You wouldn't want to hear," Jennifer said with a soft laugh.

"You're in love," Gram prompted.

Jennifer clenched her fists. "Yes, but I think he's wrong for me. We seem to be at cross-purposes more and more these days."

"Is it his being an astronaut?"

Jennifer met the wise, gentle glance defensively. "That's part of the problem."

"Life with the man you love is worth the risks," Gram told her. "Was your life wonderful before you met Lij?"

Jennifer thought of it. Elaine had been right. She'd lived in a vacuum for six years. But it had been easy living without emotional ups and downs. Peaceful. *Barren, empty,* her heart supplied.

"We seem to be on the brink of a quarrel a lot recently," Jennifer confessed. "I don't know what's wrong. Perhaps he's trying to think of a way to say goodbye." She smiled wryly.

"Where's your spunk, child?" Gram demanded, the anger in her tone startling Jennifer. "If I had a fine young man like your Lij seems to be, I'd grab hold with both hands."

Gram's eyes sparkled with righteous fire. Her cheeks were flushed. She almost looked young and girlish. Jennifer felt a rush of love for her grandmother. "It isn't just his career."

She told Gram about Elaine and Mac. "Three years ago, they were so in love, I thought nothing would ever part them. Now they're getting a divorce. If that could happen to them, what chance do Lij and I have? We're so different."

"Are you?" Gram pushed her glasses to the tip of her nose and peered at Jennifer over them.

"Yes. Of course we are."

"No 'of course' to it. You're both adventurous. He's more physical, in the way of most men. You're more verbal. Women are."

Jennifer had to smile. Gram's view of life and love seemed too simple. "So we just ignore the differences and stick to the similarities?"

"You're both more alike than you know. You just need to remember to give each other some space."

Jennifer laughed at Gram's use of current psychobabble. "Amen," she agreed.

The two men came in, their noses and cheeks red from the cold. A light, teasing snow was starting to fall.

"Warm up the cider, Alice," Jennifer's grandfather requested. "Lij and I are colder than a wet hound dog."

Jennifer suddenly wished she and Lij had been married fifty years with all the problems between them laid to rest ages ago. Did life work that way? Maybe her grandparents didn't reveal all there was to their marriage. Did they ever quarrel? Next time she talked to Gram alone, she'd ask.

But she and Lij left before she got the chance. Lij was navigator on the return flight—flying sideways was the way the crew referred to the position. The pilot had been at the military academy with Lij, and Jennifer was treated to some shavetail stories that kept her laughing on the trip home.

When they arrived at Lij's town house, they found an invitation to Tissy and Bradford's wedding. It was to be at the Berkeley campus, under the tree where they had met during a student sit-in. The reception was to follow at Jennifer's house.

"I'm to be Tissy's best person," Jennifer read. She looked at Lij. "You're invited. Do you want to go?"

"Yes."

He picked up their suitcases and went into the bedroom, but not before Jennifer had seen a ripple of emotion pass through his eyes. She tapped the letter from Tissy against her palm. When she went to Berkeley for the wedding, perhaps she should stay.

THE PACIFIC FOG BANK snuggled against the western hills, dipped down along the water's edge and obscured the pilings so that the Golden Gate Bridge seemed to float in the crisp December air.

Across San Francisco Bay, mist clung stubbornly to the hilltops, defying the noon sun. Beneath a live oak tree on the Berkeley campus, an event was in progress.

A group of minstrels, dressed in Elizabethan costumes, played quaint tunes on lyres and flutes while the wedding party assembled.

Lij glanced around wryly. He and the justice of the peace were the only men in suits. Around him, people gathered on the lawn, appearing from the thin mist like wood sprites. The men wore jeans or faded cords; the women were in long flowing dresses with flowers in their hair.

Unreal, was the term that came to mind.

The music paused, then began a new tune. Lij saw Bradford and his best man—or should he say best person?—walk through the small crowd, kissing both men and women on the cheeks. They stopped in front of the justice.

A new melody was begun, one that was haunting and beautiful, played on the flutes with only a soft strum of the lyre for backing. Tissy and Jennifer wended their way among the group.

The two women stopped by him. Tissy, wearing a tiara of white flowers and dressed in a shimmering gown of red silk with embroidered flowers along the sleeves and hem, lifted her face for his kiss. He bent and touched her lips. She tucked a small mum in his lapel and drifted on without saying a word.

Jennifer solemnly handed him a tiny net bag tied with a bit of lace. She raised her face. Lij knew he would never forget that moment...the sun shining through the mist, Jennifer dressed in a long blue dress with a golden rope around her hips, a circlet of flowers in her hair. The lilting music piped a magic spell.

A chorus of women began a chant. "'The Lord is my shepherd; I shall not want/He maketh me lie down in green pastures...'"

Lij cupped Jennifer's face in his hands. He felt the living warmth of her and was filled with the sharp pain of desire, not sexual, although that was there, but with feelings far more complex than any he'd known before.

He touched her lips. Her mouth trembled under his. Sweet, she was so sweet, a taste of honey and spice. He let her go.

"'...surely goodness and mercy shall follow me all the days of my life: and I will dwell in the house of the Lord for ever.' Amen."

When the psalm was finished, Tissy and Jennifer stood beside the groom. The music faded as the minstrels walked toward the back of the crowd, then stopped.

The justice of the peace intoned the purpose of the gathering and spoke of the bonds of marriage and its greater good beyond that of the couple's happiness. "Bradford and Theresa will now exchange their vows," he finished. The couple turned to each other.

"I, John Bradford, come to you with little more than you behold this minute, yet if you choose to cast your life with mine, I pledge you my love, my loyalty and my life. I want to be your companion, your lover and the father of your children. I will endeavor to assume the responsibilities of a husband and to do good by you and our children."

"I, Theresa Irene, do choose you for my husband. I will be a loyal wife to you, John Bradford Wilson, and will put you first in my heart. Together, our lives will count as more than the sum of our individual selves. Any good that we may accomplish will serve as our legacy to our fellow creatures and our children as our faith in the future. This I do pledge."

"I, John Bradford, give you this ring as the token of my pledge."

"I, Theresa Irene, give you this ring as the token of my pledge."

"I call you wife."

"I call you husband."

"Amen," the justice said.

The ceremony was over.

Lij released the tension in a long breath. Weddings, even do-it-yourself ones, were hard on the nerves. The couple turned toward their cheering friends and bowed, hands clasped together. The music started again, a joyous ode to tradition.

"Are you ready to go?" a voice inquired at his side.

He managed a tight smile, which faded at the solemn expression on Jennifer's face. "Sure."

She drove quickly to the house. "Fill the punch bowl, will you?" she asked as soon as they were inside. "I'll see if the cake arrived." She was gone in a swirl of silk, leaving the scent of perfume, powder, shampoo, soap and all the mingled surprises that were her wafting gently around him. "It's here," she called from the living room.

The time was near, he thought with a tightening of the stomach. He followed orders. When the rest of the wedding party arrived, the refreshments were ready.

The bride and groom cut the cake. Guests laughed and made teasing comments, some bawdy, drawing more laughter. It was a traditional wedding reception.

The musicians arrived. They played a lilting tune and a chorus of women sang, "'Summer is a-comin' in/Loudly sing cuckoo.'" "Scarborough Fair" was their second number. Lij moved close to Jennifer when Bradford and Tissy took the floor for the first dance. They performed a 'roundelay' to the delight of their audience. Tissy moved gracefully around Bradford, their clasped hands held high as he turned with her, his eyes never leaving her.

When the music ended, there was a hushed silence before the guests applauded. The musicians changed to modern instruments and started a rousing rendition of "Proud Mary." In a single measure, the mood changed from ballad to rock. People gyrated to the beat, filling the living room and hall with ecstatic bodies dancing as singles, couples or whole groups.

"Shall we?" Lij asked. He held out his hand.

Jennifer turned toward him and put her hand in his. Her fingers rested lightly on his palm. She smiled at him, friendly, cool, unreadable. It was like their first meeting, as if they hadn't been lovers at all.

He didn't expect the pain. It hit low, fast and hard, throwing him into a tailspin of mixed emotions. He needed a wife; Jennifer was the woman he wanted. Would she have him?

She must have sensed the turmoil, for she looked questioningly at him. He shook his head slightly. Not yet. He needed a little more time to hold her, to savor her.

They danced around the small space in the living room, closer now that other guests had joined in. He inhaled her fragrance, the essence of her, knowing it might be the last time. The music ended all too soon.

Lij and Bradford changed partners for the next song.

"I'm glad you could come," Tissy said. Her smile was sincere.

"Thank you for inviting me," Lij replied. "Would you mind if I told you how extraordinarily beautiful you look?"

"Not at all."

He perused her red dress, the dark tumble of hair under the wreath of white flowers. "You look like one of the elven ladies of Lothlorien. Are you familiar with the name?"

She laughed and shook back her hair as if pleased. "From Tolkien's *Lord of the Rings,* isn't it?"

"Yes." Briefly, he thought of the elven queen in the trilogy who had loved a mortal and married him, forsaking immortality and her people to stay with her love. A romantic fantasy. "I liked your wedding ceremony."

"Did you? Some people would probably think it was hokey, but I didn't want the usual 'til-death-do-us-part vows. This is a new age...for men as well as for women."

"Is it? How?"

"As women gain in the marketplace, men will no longer be expected just to be the breadwinner. You'll be able to tune in your deeper feelings, to touch your inner selves. There will be a more equal sharing of family responsibilities."

"How? Will parents take turns working and looking after the kids?" He shook his head. "It doesn't seem feasible."

Tissy smiled. "Why not take children to work? Once, they saw what their parents did. Now, work is done at some mysterious place far from home. I think that's wrong."

Lij was skeptical of her vision. "I can see Amy in a space suit," he said with a laugh. "She'd love it."

To the tune of "Green Sleeves," Tissy introduced Lij to her parents and those of the groom, all four of whom seemed to be relieved that the couple had finally legalized the relationship. He had to smile in sympathy. It was hard to tell about young people these days, whether they'd be responsible citizens or dropouts. Already the sixties were being called the Decade of Dissent.

At four, Tissy and Bradford left. The wedding guests tossed the packets of birdseed at them. "Birdseed," Lij murmured to Jennifer. "It figures."

"Yes, it does." She laughed.

When the other guests left, Jennifer began cleaning up and Lij helped her. "You don't have to do that," she said.

"I know but I want to." He hesitated. "I want to talk to you when we finish."

Jennifer glanced at him. Did he realize she had brought all her stuff with her when she left Houston? She planned to stay in Berkeley for a while. To think. Or was she running? *No!*

"Okay." She went to the kitchen for a trash bag. They emptied the cake crumbs into it and threw away the used napkins. There were several pieces of cake left, which Jennifer put away. It took a while to clean the dishes and carry all the wedding gifts upstairs to the couple's room, but finally it was all done.

"Would you like coffee and a sandwich?" Jennifer offered when they returned downstairs.

"Yes." He followed her into the kitchen.

She put the coffee on. "I'm going to change to something comfortable. How about you?"

"I brought some jeans."

She went into her bedroom and closed the door. Lij came in right after her. "My bag is in here," he said.

"Oh, yes. I'd forgotten."

She pulled a sweatshirt and pants out of a drawer and went into the bathroom. Feeling ridiculous in light of the fact that he had undressed her more than once, she left the door ajar. In her bedroom, she heard him unzip his luggage, then the rustle of clothing. She took the flowers off her head and pulled her hair back with combs on either side. When she had changed, she went out. Lij was in jeans and a flannel shirt.

His masculinity struck her anew. A tall, broad-shouldered cowboy who spoke with a faint drawl. A keenly intelligent scientist who understood physics and rockets. A daredevil of a man who liked a challenge. Her lover.

They returned to the kitchen where she made thick pastrami sandwiches with hot mustard and sour pickles. Sitting at the table, they ate almost in silence.

"A piece of cake?" she asked, pouring two cups of coffee.

He grimaced. "I think I've had enough."

"Me, too. The icing was so rich I could hardly eat it. Shall we go to my office?" She sounded formal, as if they were going to have a business conference.

Her office was next to her bedroom. It was more private than the living room, which was shared by everyone in the house. "Ted and his friends—they were the musicians—will probably be back soon. They went out for dinner."

"Are you over your quarrel with him?"

She'd told Lij of the debate concerning the draft dodger. "Yes. His friend decided to register as a conscientious objector and to serve his time in hospital duty."

When Lij closed the office door behind them, Jennifer had a sudden desire to run. Did wedding nerves extend to the bride's best person?

She elected to sit in an easy chair with her loafers kicked off and her feet tucked under her. She took a sip of hot coffee. Having delayed as long as she could, she asked, "What did you want to talk about?"

"Us."

Just as she'd thought. She'd make it easy. Tilting her head to one side, she asked, "Is this goodbye?"

He was taken aback. "I forgot your straightforward attack on the world," he said with a faint smile.

"Right. I believe in getting the bad stuff over."

His dark gaze probed hers for a minute. "Maybe it isn't so bad. I wanted to ask you to marry me."

The words fell into the silence like a rock into an abyss. There was no sound of its striking bottom.

Finally, "Are you asking?"

"Yes."

She shook her head. "I never planned on getting married."

"You did one time," he reminded her, his tone deep and quiet. He was being gentle with her.

"A long time ago, when I was young and foolish."

"Is it so hard to think of marrying me?"

She'd thought he was getting tired of sharing his life, but he wanted marriage. She thought of entanglements: Tissy and Bradford just starting their married life; Elaine and Mac just ending theirs.

"It wouldn't work." She rose and paced the room, flinging her hands wide at the books and papers that covered all surfaces. "My work, the way I live, they aren't conducive to marriage. I wouldn't be a traditional wife. You'd hate it."

He went to her and clasped his hands on her arms. "I don't expect you to keep house. We can afford a maid. And when Amy comes home, we'll have a full-time sitter. But I want a home, Jen. I want you."

His words sank into her whirling mind. "You have a home," she said. She stared up at him, aware of his hands on her shoulders, his fingers caressing her through her sweatshirt.

"It isn't enough, not the way we live now."

She twisted away, not wanting to hear. "Why can't we go on the way we are?" The status quo seemed safe to her. They were together, yet the very nature of an affair kept their emotions in check. This way, she wouldn't depend on him.

"I need a wife," he said simply. "My lawyer says that would look better than living together. For Amy's sake. In case there's a custody battle."

A glimmer of understanding dawned. "You need to get married because of your in-laws."

He nodded and rubbed a hand wearily over this face. Taking a seat on the sofa, he coaxed, "Sit down and let's talk."

Her emotions underwent several tumultuous shifts in about five seconds, from panic at the thought of marriage to fury at his reason. He wanted to marry her because of his lousy in-laws. "That isn't a good enough reason."

"Will you listen?" he demanded.

She nodded.

When she was seated, he told her about the pictures he'd received and of the threats. "Amy's doing so well. I can't risk tearing her apart in a custody fight. After the accident, she . . . retreated from the world. Do you know what autism is?"

Jennifer nodded. She gave him her rapt attention even though she knew she wasn't the one for him. He needed a traditional wife, one who would be home at the end of the day, one who could take care of his child. She loved Amy, but she didn't think she was the motherly type. She'd been on her own far too long.

"I nearly lost Amy once to death, then I nearly lost her due to the emotional trauma. I thought I'd lost part of her because of brain damage. Now she has a chance for a full life, perhaps not a full recovery, but fairly close. I mean to see that she gets it. Do you understand?"

"Yes, you need to get married for Amy's sake."

He reached over and removed the cup from her hands. "Quit hiding from me," he ordered. "I want to marry you. *You.* But if you won't . . . if you're too afraid—"

"I'm not afraid," she interrupted.

"I think you are. You're afraid of commitment, of getting trapped like your mother was trapped, always waiting, always on the edge of your husband's life. I understand that. You're afraid we'll end up like your friends in Texas, divorced and angry, because we're different. I think we can work it out."

"You intend to be an astronaut."

"Yes. It's something that interests me. 'To go where no man has gone before,' well, not very many." He smiled, enticing her with his humor, his challenge to life. "Say yes, Jen. I'll even make up my own vows if you'd like."

"Lij—"

"I, Elijah Basil Branigan, pledge my troth to you, Jennifer Wright," he said softly. "I promise to share life, to never shut you out . . . or if I do, you can kick me and remind me not to. We can work together. You'll be there, taking notes and writing your pamphlets on the space program. I'll be your favorite subject. We'll give Amy a home and have other children, if you want. We can visit Tissy and

Bradford and let our kids fight or marry or whatever they want. We can be happy."

She sighed and reached for her coffee cup. "You make it sound simple."

"It is simple. It's other things that are hard—like not being sure of where I stand with you." He paused and looked at the room, filled with her work and a life separate from his. "You brought all your stuff to Berkeley. Weren't you coming back?"

"I don't know," she said honestly. "I thought things were...cooling off between us."

"Not for me." He looked at her steadily.

She held his gaze. "Nor for me."

"Well, then?"

She couldn't say yes and she couldn't say no. She was thrilled at the thought of his wanting her like that, but... "There are so many complications," she finally said.

"I know."

"Am I selfish? I want to make my own choices and live my own life, not just be an extension of a man's. I like being able to take an interesting job when it comes along."

"You can do all that."

"How?" She shook her head. "You don't know. It's so hard for a woman."

"I do know. I don't expect you to do everything. I'll try to share life with you, the hard day-to-day grind of it as well as the fun parts."

She looked at him, really looked at him. He was everything she'd ever thought she wanted in a man—exciting and handsome, yes, but more than that. She'd seen so many facets of him. He was tender and patient. He'd try to understand her side and give her room to grow.

But life had a way of piling up. He might not expect it, but he would prefer a wife who stayed home with the kids while he went out and did great and wonderful things. It was so easy for both males and females to slip into the roles society dictated.

What of his work? Could she stand by and watch him rocket off into space, knowing that death, as much as glory, was part of the game? Would she grow to hate him for putting her through that? She looked at him helplessly, her doubts in her eyes.

"I won't beg," he said. "I need you, but I won't beg." He stood. "Think about it." He lifted her in his arms and placed her in his lap. "Think about us."

She saw the need in his eyes, the love he felt for her. It beat against her fears, but it didn't shatter them. She had a whole lifetime of experiences to go on.

"I love you," she whispered after he kissed her, "but I don't think I can marry you." Why did doing the right thing have to hurt so much? She knew she was acting in the best interests of Lij and Amy as well as herself, but . . . it hurt.

"Yes, you can."

They looked at each other. It was a standoff.

Chapter Thirteen

Wednesday, December 17, 1969

The clear waters of the Gulf of Mexico lapped against the boat. Lij and Bill sat at the back of the power craft, fishing rods in hand, each lost in his own thoughts. The two friends had decided to take the afternoon off after Bill brought an astronaut over from Edwards. Bill had to go back the next morning.

A strike interrupted the lull. Lij set the hook and reeled in the fish.

"Nice size," Bill commented as Lij lifted the flounder over the side and onto the deck.

"You're invited to dinner," Lij said. He deftly cleaned the fish, then put it in the ice locker.

"Will Jennifer be there?"

Lij baited his hook and dropped it over the side, going for the bottom where the flounder hid. "She's in Berkeley. Why? You got a date with Brenda? You can bring her for dinner."

"Nah. She's decided she doesn't like pilots, especially military ones. She's going with some fancy lawyer dude."

Lij had to chuckle at that. Bill was the oldest son of a well-established family, one of the wealthiest in the States. He could rival any "dude" when it came to money, education and social position. That he had chosen not to, indicated his waning interest in the pretty widow.

"So, how're things going on the home front? You and the flower child gonna raise some little petunias?" Bill asked.

Lij shook his head. Before he could explain, he had another strike. He pulled in the flounder before answering. "We're at a stalemate. I've asked her to marry me. She said no."

"Well, I'll be damned." Bill shook his head in disbelief. He'd always thought Lij could have any woman he wanted. Jennifer was a different kettle of fish. "So you've split?"

Lij grimaced at the thrashing flounder. "Not exactly. But we're not getting anywhere."

"Too bad," Bill sympathized. "What's happening with the kid and the grandparents? They know about her progress?"

"Yeah. I let their doctor see her. To show how reasonable I could be. Now that they know she's going to be all right, they're determined to have her." His expression hardened. "They didn't want her when she was hurt."

"Is that the reason you want to get married?" Bill raised a skeptical eyebrow. "Killer wouldn't take kindly to that."

Lij didn't react to Bill's nickname for Jennifer, although it irritated him. Was he jealous of the friendship between them? He heaved a deep breath and threw the cleaned fish into the locker. "No," he muttered, slamming the lid. He wanted Jennifer for one reason: he loved her. Life was lonely without her.

A noise below drew his attention.

"I'll get her," Bill said. He dropped into the hatch and reappeared in a minute, Amy in his arms. "Look who's here, Beeping Sleauty."

"I'm Amy," Amy told him. She frowned. "Da, pee-pee."

"Oh-oh, she's all yours," Bill said, handing her over.

Lij carried her down the steps and set her on the toilet, her legs dangling in midair. She chattered happily from that position, so natural and unconcerned, it squeezed his heart.

As she grew and learned, society's mores would take over, but for now . . . he loved her just the way she was.

After that, she had to see the fish, then have something to eat. He unwrapped a peanut-butter-and-jelly sandwich.

Scenes from Woodstock appeared in his mind—the children playing in the pond, the young people relaxing in the sun, the thousands of peanut-butter-and-jelly sandwiches being handed out, Jennifer writing it all down. He missed it suddenly. The joy. The freedom from worry and responsibility the weekend signified. Just living for the moment . . . and being with Jennifer.

He felt a twisting pain in his gut. He hadn't seen her since the hippie wedding of her friends. He'd asked her to go to Montana with him and Amy last weekend, but she'd had too much work. His family had asked cautious questions when Amy mentioned her new friend, Jen-fer. They hadn't liked his equally cautious answers.

His younger sister—twenty-three, working on her master's in sociology—considered herself wiser than he. She warned him about falling for another woman like Rona.

She should meet Jennifer, he thought moodily. Then his nosy little sis would really be worried. Jennifer was nothing like the dependent, fun-seeking child Rona had been.

"'Thoughts too deep to be expressed?'" Bill asked, quoting the Bard.

Lij realized he'd unconsciously sighed. "Yeah." He grinned. "There's something to be said for just dragging a woman to your cave by the hair. It gets too complicated when you have to ask."

Bill, in the act of taking a swig of Coke, choked on laughter. Amy patted him on the back. She laughed, too.

Christmas, Lij thought. He'd give Jennifer till then to decide. He felt the weight of the future press against his chest. What if she still refused? He gazed into the distance where the blue sea met the blue sky. Then he knew: he needed to get married for himself. He loved Jennifer Wright with all that was in him. And that was the truth.

DR. BENTON SMILED AT his star pupil. "Well, you made it into the program," he said.

The final cut had been made. Eight of them—Bobko, Crippen, Fullerton, Hartsfield, Overmyer, Peterson, Truly and Branigan—had been selected for the Air Force Manned Orbiting Laboratory project. They had been informed of the decision that morning.

"We're moving into a different phase of space exploration," the physicist continued. "We know humans can make it up and back. Now we can get on with scientific experiments."

Lij smiled. The professor was ever the scientist. Space was a vast new laboratory for him, the challenge of getting men up and back merely one of the steps in achieving his goal.

"You'll be going to Edwards to try out some preliminary simulators—"

"When?" Lij broke in.

"Tomorrow."

Lij wouldn't let himself think of Jennifer. Tomorrow was Friday, the nineteenth. He'd decided to fly up and see her over the weekend. That would be postponed. "Fine."

Dr. Benton smiled like a cherub. "She's already there."

"She?" His heart started pounding.

"Jennifer Wright." The doctor brought his hands in front of him and tapped his fingertips against each other.

A spider doing leaps on a mirror, Lij thought, watching Dr. Benton's hands. He didn't like it that Jennifer had the power to affect his body against his will. A man couldn't afford that kind of distraction in his type of work. When he saw her, he'd have it out. A clean break. That was the way to go.

THE CAFETERIA WAS ALMOST empty when Jennifer and Bill entered on Friday at nine o'clock. It was too early for mid-morning break for most people. They got coffee and settled at a table.

"Saw Lij on Wednesday," Bill drawled.

Jennifer was aware that Bill watched her as he said this. She blinked and looked away, more disturbed than she wanted to admit by the sound of Lij's name. Her gaze came back to Bill's unblinking stare. "How was he?"

"Lonely."

"With you around?" She shook her head and laughed. She felt the slight tremor on her lips and hoped he wouldn't notice.

"We took Amy and went fishing. The kid's a natural. She caught two fish, decided there was nothing to it and played with her doll the rest of the time. She asked about you."

Jennifer sipped the steaming coffee, which was too hot to drink. She held the cup in front of her and blew across its surface. "She's cute, isn't she?"

"Yeah." Bill spooned a couple of pieces of ice into his cup from the water glass. "What are you going to do about them?" he suddenly asked.

She set her cup down carefully. "I don't know."

"You have to decide. You can't treat a man—"

"Don't," she requested. Her voice was quietly desperate. "I didn't ask for this, any of this." She made a helpless gesture that took in the whole of her relationship with Lij.

"You have to decide," Bill repeated. "Lij is here."

"At the base?"

Bill nodded. "He landed an hour ago. He's going to check out some new equipment." He leaned forward and watched her closely as he added, "He made the team. He's officially an astronaut."

Jennifer bit her lip to stop the protest that rose to her throat. Instead, she nodded as if she wasn't in the least surprised at the news. She wasn't. There had been no question in her mind that he would be among the chosen.

"I thought you might like to think that over before you saw him." Bill smiled sympathetically. "He knows you're here. Benton told him."

She had to swallow before she could thank him for the warning. Bill, she realized, was a friend to her as well as Lij. "Dr. Benton is a strange cupid," she said, trying for a lighter tone.

"Isn't that the truth," Bill agreed. His grin was wry.

"Well, I have an appointment with Dr. Boone. He's going to fill me in on the Manned Orbital Laboratory plans. Thanks for the coffee . . . and the advice."

"Are you going to heed it?" he asked, openly curious.

She nodded. "When I see Lij, I'll tell him what I've decided." Her eyes met Bill's. He recognized the decision.

"So long, Killer," he murmured.

His words echoed with finality and played over and over in her head. Saying goodbye was the hardest thing to do.

She went to her meeting with the base historian, then to a general staff meeting of some air force officers and Pentagon VIPs. They discussed the future of the space program and the goals of the space lab. A new concept was a transport system that could be used over and over again, a sort of space ferry that would carry parts of the lab into orbit where astronauts would assemble it on the spot. It sounded exciting.

She knew Lij would love being a part of it. He'd probably volunteer to be the first astrophysicist in space. How long would he be in orbit? Months, most likely. And where would the little wife be? Back home minding the kids.

By midafternoon, her nerves were jangling from too much coffee and from waiting to see Lij. Every time she turned a corner, she expected to run into him. What would he say? How could she explain the fact that she hadn't returned to Houston? He knew she could write her brochures anywhere. In fact, it would be more convenient to be close to the Space Center in case she needed to check her information.

Coward.

You're right, she told her conscience.

"That should have given you a good idea of where we're heading," Dr. Boone said. His sad face crinkled into a sad smile. "Assuming Congress gives us the money."

"I don't think the space program is going to go away," she assured him. "It might proceed more slowly."

"I wish we would discover something new and important during my lifetime," he said.

Jennifer gave him a disbelieving glance. "Going to the moon wasn't important?"

The sloping lines of his face drooped even more. "Merely the opening act. Now it's time for the real thing."

Jennifer smiled and said goodbye at the corridor leading to the parking lot exit. *The real thing.* Was that what she and Lij had? Was that what she would be throwing away if she refused his proposal? She thought of Amy. The child was darling, one she'd be proud to claim as her own. Already her feelings for Lij's daughter were strong and growing deeper.

Bill was right. She should have made her decision and stuck with it right after the wedding. Why prolong the agony? That was the coward's way. She'd tell Lij tonight. She'd look him up and talk to him openly and honestly.

He'd find someone else....

Tears filmed her vision, blinding her for a second. She ran into an air force captain as she reached for the door.

"Sorry," he said, steadying her with a hand on her arm.

"My fault," she murmured, keeping her head down. As soon as she reached her car, she dug a tissue out of her purse and wiped her eyes. She hated not being in control.

She'd known the risks when she'd first met Lij Branigan. She should have heeded the warnings. The attraction had been there from the start. They had both recognized it; neither had wanted it. Tissy would have said they had been fated to meet, to love, but Tissy was an idealist.

Elaine was the one with logical advice. She had gone through with the divorce, selling the house and moving to an apartment until she found something she could afford. She and Jennifer often talked on the phone. Elaine thought Jennifer should maintain her independence and not let Lij's charm and looks cajole her into something she wasn't ready for.

Jennifer agreed. She had to look on the practical side of life, to face it the way Elaine had done.

But did it have to hurt so much?

JENNIFER SIGHED IN FRUSTRATION. Lij was as elusive as a rain storm in the desert. She had tried to call him through the base locator, but he wasn't in TDY quarters. Apparently he'd stayed at a motel in town. Or perhaps his trip had been postponed.

She tried Bill's place. No answer. The evening so far had been an exercise in futility.

She wrapped the towel more securely around her wet hair and sat at the small table in her room to give herself a pedicure and manicure. Anything to fill the time and occupy her mind.

Someone knocked on her door.

She glanced at the clock. Nine. Walking to the door in her bare feet, she peeked out.

Lij.

Her hand flew to the towel. She looked a mess.

"Jennifer, open up. I know you're in there," he said. He was tired and out of sorts. He'd been trying to run her to ground all afternoon, but she'd stayed just out of reach.

When he was free, she was in a meeting; when she was free, he was tied up. It had frustrated the hell out of him.

Everything had frustrated the hell out of him lately. Including her. No, especially her. It didn't take a genius to realize she was avoiding him. He'd had it with her evasions. He was going to know where he stood with her before this evening was over or by damn—

She opened the door and stared at him.

He looked her over, all the way from her turban-wrapped hair to her bare feet, her toes curling nervously in the carpet. His temper cooled as his gaze warmed. God, she was beautiful. The sudden flare of longing, fierce and primitive, caused him to reach for her, his resentments and grievances forgotten.

He had to touch her, just for a moment. The need was greater than his need for air.

Before Jennifer could protest or even think, she was enfolded in his arms and crushed against his chest. His lips nuzzled her neck and along her ear. His mouth found hers.

She could no more have turned away than she could have refused a glass of water after being lost in the desert for days. Her body had thirsted for his touch. Now she felt it bloom with desire until all the empty hollows were filled with the clamoring of her heart. "Lij," she whispered shakily when he released her lips.

"God, you taste good," he said. "I'd forgotten how good."

He kissed her again. With a tightening of his arms, he lifted her clear off the floor. She felt the bed touch the backs of her legs, then they were falling, tumbling from the sky, down and down and down, until they sank and bounced against the mattress. She felt as if they were on a cloud.

Gone were her good intentions. She forgot all the sensible arguments she'd marshalled that would show him how useless their affair was. She wanted only to lose herself in the drastic passion of their embrace and forget all else.

Lij's intentions evaporated in the heat of their kiss. As soon as he'd seen her, still damp from her shower, he had forgotten what he'd planned to say: the demands he had been going to make, the practical arguments that would have swayed her to see things his way. All he had known was the need.

It racked through him now, stronger than his good sense, stronger than his will to fight it. He had to have her, this one woman who tormented his sleep and invaded his every waking moment.

The towel fell from her head. He ran his fingers into the damp strands, holding her captive while he stared into her eyes.

They filled with tears.

"Don't," he said, as moved as she. "Don't cry."

He would love her until the pain was gone, until neither of them could think of the parting he knew was coming. But not now. Now was the time for them. He had to touch her and love her and *know* her.

Jennifer experienced a desperate urgency. With trembling hands, she unfastened her robe. His hands were there to do it for her. She reached for the buttons on his shirt. He helped her. The barriers melted, and there were only the two of them with no civilized obstacles between them. They came together, naked with their needs, their longing.

His hands were those of a poet. They created poems and rhymes wherever they touched. Her face. Her breasts. Her thighs.

She experienced him as a thing of wonder, a magnificent sculpture, the beauty of his form fascinating to her senses. She touched him everywhere. And deep inside, she felt the heat, the expanding of her body to accept his, the ache of a woman's desire for the man she craved.

They were together. Like the sea surging to shore, they moved toward each other, higher and higher, crested, reformed, rose again, crested. They lay panting, their energy spent.

It was only when they moved, when Lij pulled the passion-tossed covers over them, that they spoke.

"Hello. Nice evening," he said.

"Yes, isn't it?"

They started laughing for no good reason.

"WHATEVER YOU SAID TO HIM, it wasn't goodbye," Bill commented. He and Jennifer were in his office. He had already shown her the artist's conception of the space lab. Now he was supposed to be answering any questions she had.

Jennifer felt the heat rise in her neck. Bill seemed to think anything that touched his friend's life was also his business. He had such a concerned air that she couldn't rebuff him.

She and Lij hadn't talked at all. They had slept, awakened with the dawn, made love, then he'd left for an early briefing. She'd taken a shower, her body pleasantly tired from their morning exertions, and let her mind drift, holding recriminations at bay.

The insanity of the moment had overridden her common sense...no, it was the sheer joy of seeing him. Nothing could make her give up the memories of last night.

"Ah, hell," Bill said. He let out a disgusted breath. "I can see it's no use talking to you. You're as bad as he is. One look and you both fall apart."

She grimaced ruefully. "I think you're right."

His smile erased the frown. "So what happens now, Killer?"

"You tell me."

"You marry and live happily ever after with Amy and lots of other little petunias to keep you company."

"I've never been good at raising flowers."

"You'll learn." He leaned toward her, serious. "You can't back out now. You let him think things were okay between you."

"He didn't give me a chance to say otherwise," she muttered, remembering how he'd swept her into his arms before she'd even invited him in. Which she hadn't planned to do. Which he probably knew she had had no intention of doing. Which had probably been his plan in the first place.

Enough. Things were already too complicated. She didn't need to add more muddled thoughts to the stewpot in her mind.

"There's a briefing at 1300." Bill glanced at his watch. "Come on. We can make it."

Taking her arm, he ushered her along the hall and into a conference room. Lij was seated near the front. There were only a few other men and one female air force officer present. Jennifer and Bill joined Lij. His eyes sent a special message to her, but his face remained impassive. He nodded toward Bill.

Jennifer tried to concentrate on the discussion of the flight test of an experimental plane, planned for that afternoon. The engineers discussed the project with the pilot, going over the test procedures in detail. They were worried about a certain maneuver. She gathered two pilots had augered in performing the same test. The hair stood up on the back of her neck.

She glanced at Lij. His gaze met hers without flinching. This type of danger is part of my life, he seemed to be saying. Can you take it?

And if she couldn't?

The answer to that was easy. No matter what they had shared last night, they'd have to write off their relationship. It could never bear the weight of uncertainty between them.

When the session was over, Bill leaned near to say, "I'll take her to the lookout point."

"What's going on?" she asked, looking from Bill to Lij.

"Lij is flying chase for today's test. The pilot asked for him."

"The granting of a last request?" she asked, remembering the other two tests that had failed.

Lij touched her arm. "We don't talk like that." He seemed angry with her.

"Why?" But she knew. The subject of death was always skirted, kept disguised by humorous sayings. "Bought the farm." "Augered in." But a human life was gone, and a woman was left to mourn its loss.

"Because we know the risk. There's no use in talking about it," Lij said, his tone gentle.

She glanced at him in surprise. His eyes asked for understanding. She grudgingly gave it.

"Let's go," Bill said. "Thumbs up," he said to Lij.

Thumbs up, Jennifer thought, following Bill outside, the Roman sign to spare the life of a gladiator who had performed well in the arena.

She climbed into the standard army utility vehicle. Bill took off, careening over the unpaved track and leaving a flurry of dust behind them. When they arrived at the hillock about seven miles from the base, Bill stopped and killed the engine.

"Watch this and think of Lij being in a spacecraft. Ask yourself if you can take it," Bill advised.

"Is that why you brought me out here?"

He nodded. "You need to know." His smile was kind. "Then I think you'll know the answer to your future. And Lij's."

Tension crawled in waves like centipedes along her spine. She sat stiffly and waited for the test plane and the chase plane to come into sight. Fifteen minutes passed. Sweat gathered between her breasts and soaked into her bra.

She heard the sonic boom first, then she saw the planes. They zoomed across the desert, side by side, a few thousand feet up. Together they rolled out to the west, making a great circle. Jennifer pivoted, watching.

"They won't be going out of sight today. The trouble has been during low passes," Bill told her.

"What happens?"

"Something locks up and the pilot loses control."

She asked no more questions.

The planes performed a pas de deux of perfect symmetry. They climbed and dived like two eagles at play.

A deadly serious game, she thought. Her eyes followed every maneuver. From the ground, all seemed well. She imagined Lij off in space, his life dependent on his craft and skill just as it was now. It didn't seem as scary as it once had. She understood more about flying. She knew the risk. She had experienced the thrill.

"Hot damn," Bill muttered.

She looked at him with her heart in her eyes. "Is everything all right?"

"Yeah. Sorry. I was just admiring the way those two handle a plane." He was a Norman Rockwell sketch—red-gold hair, freckles and wide-mouthed grin. "Yanking and banking, turning and burning—that's what we call it when we fly test maneuvers. Or when we're just having fun," he added truthfully.

Bill hadn't been able to smuggle a receiver out of Spares this time, so they had to content themselves with watching the two planes perform their sky gymnastics. Jennifer relaxed and, under Bill's tutelage, began to appreciate the skill involved in the close-formation flying she was witnessing.

She tensed when one plane circled the other in a long, spiraling roll. Long, spiraling rolls still had the ability to frighten her.

"Lij is checking him out," Bill explained.

"For what?"

"Anything he can see that doesn't look right."

Some intuition warned her that the test was about to enter its dangerous phase. But Lij wasn't in the experimental plane. She felt relief, immediately followed by guilt for being glad the other pilot was the one at risk.

Life with Lij was apt to keep her emotions in turmoil, she surmised. So many complications. She wanted simple things, like a peaceful life and a tranquil mind. Was that too much to ask?

"Here comes the fatal moment," Bill said with macabre humor.

Jennifer pulled out of her musings and concentrated on the sky. She saw the test plane shoot up like a glider on a thermal. Lij was right beside him. They streaked almost out of sight, then fell over in a lazy dive.

"Now," Bill murmured, "now. Take it out. Pull up. Damn it, pull up."

Jennifer realized the "something" mentioned earlier must have locked up. "Is it out of control?"

Bill didn't respond.

His silence was answer enough. Jennifer watched as Lij flew around the test craft, obviously looking for flaws. She wondered if he spotted anything. "I wish we had a radio," she said.

"Yeah. I think he's got it," Bill said suddenly.

She saw the test plane level off, then turn. It was heading directly toward them. She saw Lij flip upside down and slide under the other plane's belly, lover-close, checking it out. He fell away, rose and stayed on the tail for a few seconds, then banked and came at it from the side in a screaming dive.

"What the hell?" Bill exclaimed. Then, "It's out of control."

At that moment, Jennifer realized one of three things was about to happen: Lij and the pilot were going to die; she and Bill were going to die; or all of them were going to die.

Chapter Fourteen

"Lij, she's locked up tighter'n a drum," the other pilot said.

"What did you do a minute ago to unlock it?"

"Hell, I don't know."

Lij ran through some possibilities. He suggested a couple of moves. Nothing worked.

"I'd hoped we could figure it out," the pilot complained.

"Me, too. You'd better bail out of there, old buddy. You're gonna buy the farm in another minute."

"Right. There's just one more thing I want to try...."

Lij opened to the left to give the man a clear space for ejection. The general was going to flip out when they lost another plane, but it couldn't be helped.

"Lij!" the pilot shouted. "There's a jeep on the floor!"

Lij rolled his wings and looked. Bill and Jennifer were on the little hill. The doomed plane would hit in that vicinity.

"Bill, if you can hear me, get the hell out of there," Lij said with calm intensity. "Cliborne is out of control and jumping ship. Get out."

He watched the sun glint off the jeep's windshield. He was too far away yet to see Bill and Jennifer, but the vehicle sat stubbornly on the crest of the hill with no sign of moving.

"He doesn't have a receiver," Lij concluded. "Get out, I'll take care of your plane."

"What are you going to do?"

"Go for the tail. I should be able to deflect it. You have ten seconds to eject."

"Right." The pilot called in a last set of instrument readings and hit the button. The canopy exploded and he shot into the air, free and clear.

Lij banked hard, the harness holding him against the G forces that grabbed at his body. Then he dived, pouring on all the power at his disposal. If he failed, Jennifer would most likely die. Bill, too. He didn't think of his own death. That was one of the normal risks. Jennifer's death wasn't.

Time slowed. Einstein had said it did if you accelerated at the speed of light. Lij found it happened at much less than that. Scenes, intimate and sweet, flashed through his mind. Jennifer, cool and elusive at the party where they had met. Jennifer, hot and welcoming at Woodstock. Jennifer, troubled and unsure after the wedding in Berkeley.

Had he ever told her he loved her?

Loving her was like flying. With her, new horizons opened before him. When they made love, he felt larger than life, the same way he felt when he broke through the atmosphere and found the stars shining right along with the sun. With her, he discovered a new universe where anything was possible.

Flying wasn't forever; Jenny was.

BILL REALIZED THE DANGER at the same moment he realized there was nothing he could do. There was no time to climb into the jeep and get the hell out of there. A new crater was going to be formed in the desert and he and Jennifer were going to be in the middle of it. He glanced at her and she met his eyes. She knew.

"What's he doing?" She motioned toward the sky.

Bill looked up. The pilot was safe. He swung gently to and fro under the canopy of his parachute. The test plane streaked toward them close to the speed of sound. Bill thought of the cone of shockwaves coming at them and what would follow.

For a second he felt sorry for Lij. His friend would live, but Jennifer would die. He glanced at her again. Killer. He smiled. If he had to leave this life, there wasn't anyone else he'd rather go out with. He froze. What the hell *was* Lij doing?

"He's going to ram it," Bill muttered, not believing his eyes. "My God, he's going to try to ram it."

Jennifer didn't speak. She'd realized that fact two seconds before Bill had. She watched the action, her heart in her throat. She was afraid... and so helpless. All she could do was stand there and watch the man she loved more than life itself try to save her life. She wanted to tell him not to. Her life wasn't worth his.

Lij, oh, love, don't. Please...

LIJ CAME SCREAMING OUT of the blue. At maximum speed, he leveled out, riding easy, feeling his plane respond, trembling, eager. Like Jennifer. "Come on, lady," he coaxed, taking everything she could give. He kept his eyes on the test plane, judging the distance as he closed on it.

"Five seconds," he counted, "...four...three... two...one...."

His wing struck the tail fin with a mighty *whack*. Metal flew like feathers around him, obscuring his vision. He strained back on the stick, reaching for sky, praying he'd clear the debris. He felt the insistent pull to the left and glanced out. Poor lady. Her wing was dinged up pretty bad at the tip.

He brought her up and under control. To the west of him, he saw the pilot's parachute collapsing as he touched down.

To the east, a huge fireball rose as the test plane crashed in one gigantic explosion. To the south, he saw the jeep, sitting on its little hill. Safe.

He banked into a turn and headed for the base. Dust rose as the ambulance and fire truck raced toward the site. Below, he saw the jeep bounce across the desert floor and pick up the jock.

JENNIFER CLENCHED HER HANDS as they headed back to the base. The pilot of the test plane sat in the front beside Bill. None of them had anything to say. The pilot looked exhausted.

Lij was waiting when they drove up, the ambulance right behind them.

"Hey," the medic yelled, jumping out. "That's our job. We're supposed to check him out before he's moved."

The test jock shook his head, but walked over and let them examine him.

Jennifer looked at Lij. She was aware of Bill quietly fading into the background, then disappearing inside the building. She couldn't stand it another second. She rushed to Lij and threw her arms around his broad, solid chest. She pressed her face into his neck.

"I thought you were going to die," she whispered, shaky with relief as well as fear.

"I thought you were," he said, burying his face in her hair.

For a long minute, they comforted each other. His hands caressed her back. Gentle hands, so gentle.

"I'll resign," he murmured against her hair. "I can work with Dr. Benton as a physicist."

She shook her head and held him tighter.

"We'd better talk," he said.

They went inside and found two chairs with a little table between them. There was a second of silence.

"Shall we draw straws?" he asked, lightening the solemnity of the moment. "I'll volunteer to go first." He reached across and trapped her nervous hands between his. "I love you. More than I love flying...." His voice thickened. "More than I love anything. *Anything.*"

She knew he was thinking of that moment on the desert when the plane streaked toward her, locked on a path of death. "I love you, too." She sighed, feeling the weight of her love and its demands. Did women always have to sacrifice their lives for it?

"Oh, hell," he said. "Come here."

He pushed his chair back and pulled her into his lap, cradling her against his chest.

"So where do we go from here?" he asked.

"Back to Houston. You go into intensive training and I write about it."

He shook his head. "I won't put you through that, Jen. I realized today, when I thought you would die, what you must go through—"

She laid a hand over his lips. "I *am* afraid of your dying. The pain would be terrible, but I'd survive, Lij. I have before. It's more than death, it's life that scares me."

With her fingertips, she explored his beloved face, the hard contours of his jaw, the softness of his mouth. Laying her hand on his chest, she felt his heartbeat, steady and strong. Like him.

"I'm afraid I'll get bogged down in the little, messy details of life that women seem to get stuck with. I'm afraid I'll grow to resent that . . . and you."

"We can hire people to handle those things," he promised. "We'll make our decisions together, as a team."

"Your career would take precedence over mine."

"No," he said. "I realize it takes two to keep the home-fires stoked up and burning. I'll do my part."

Looking into his eyes, she realized he would try. Would it be enough?

"I know you'll need to travel in order to do your research. If possible, I'll go with you. If not, I'll stay at home and wait. Amy and I." He gazed at her with all the longing in the world in his eyes. He waited.

The tenderness in his expression shredded her heart.

"Amy," she murmured, remembering responsibilities and other people's lives. A marriage didn't involve just two people.

"She's part of my life and always will be. I hope she'll come home to live with me soon. But she'll be my responsibility."

"Mine, too. I do love her, Lij."

"She's a lovable kid. Takes after her old man."

He slipped his hand behind her neck, pulling her to him. He kissed her, then drew back. "I'd like a chance at one space shot. At my age, that's probably all I'll get."

Jennifer realized what he was promising her. A full life. Freedom to do her own thing. All he was asking was the right to love her, to live with her and share as much of her life as she was willing to give.

She remembered Woodstock. Janis Joplin singing "Me and Bobby McGee" in her heart-catching, whiskey-rough voice. The loneliness of that song and the singer had touched all of them.

She thought about the past six years of her life. She'd lived it in perfect freedom, able to come and go as she pleased. There had been people who cared—her mother and grandparents, Tissy and Bradford—but she'd kept them on the periphery of her life. Elaine had been right. She'd lived in a vacuum where nothing could hurt.

She looked at Lij, who at Woodstock had been kind and patient and tolerant. Her friend. Her lover. Her love.

"If I don't get a flight within three years, I'll move on," he was saying. "I'll be home so much, you'll be wishing I was off to Mars."

"Can we find a world together?" she asked wistfully. "Mars is too far away."

He understood. His hand tightened briefly on her neck, then he pulled her to him, his mouth closing on hers with crushing force. She felt the hot, wild explosion within. Her need was greater than she knew.

"Marry me, Jen," he said shakily. "I want more than bits and pieces of your life. I need you too much."

"Yes, I will." She touched him, exploring the shape of his face, the strength of his shoulders and arms, the hardness of his rib cage where his heart beat with increasing rhythm.

"I've been practicing my vows. I've about got them down pat, so we can proceed with the ceremony whenever you're ready."

When he kissed her, Jennifer forgot about vows. It seemed they'd already said it all. "I've missed you," she said, "so much. Can we leave?"

"Let me change," Lij said. "Then we can go."

She nodded.

It took almost an hour for them to get away. Lij rushed the debriefing and hurried back to Jennifer.

They went to her motel.

Inside, Lij leaned against the door, just looking at her. Then he enfolded her in his arms.

With gentle hands, he undressed her and tucked her into bed. In a minute, he joined her. They turned to each other. She knew it was going to be different this time. Last night had been filled with the desperate uncertainty of goodbye; tonight was filled with the urgency of hello.

He came to her, his movements slow, savoring. She felt the power in his body, each movement controlled, her pleasure first in his mind. She relaxed and let the voyage begin.

"To the stars," he murmured.

"Together." This was one adventure neither of them could make alone.

Epilogue

Jennifer brought out a platter of sliced meat, artfully arranged like tiny cornucopias spilling over with a vegetable stuffing. Other dishes covered the red table cloth in a display of holiday opulence.

The rings on her finger glinted in the candlelight. Both wedding band and engagement ring were lavish with diamonds. She was a bride of one week.

She glanced around the living room of the Houston town house. They'd already decided to sell it and buy a larger home with a yard. Amy would need room for a swing set.

Their guests, she saw, were mingling easily. Her mother talked with Lij's mother, the two women sharing childhood memories of their newly married children. Jennifer's grandfather was talking politics with Lij's father while Lij's younger sister listened. Gram was sitting in front of the fire, knitting a gray sweater. Obviously the color of Lij's eyes. Jennifer smiled and went to hug the older woman.

"Happy, child?" Gram asked.

"More than I thought possible."

"You made a good choice."

"Thank you."

Looking into her grandmother's eyes, the color of her own, Jennifer felt the connection of generations running through her. The line ran back through time, unbroken, right to the very first instant of the very first spark of life. She liked the thought.

Across the room, Elaine and Bill were arguing about something with a great deal of good-natured wrangling. Jennifer wondered.... It was too soon, of course. Elaine's divorce wasn't even final and her friend would be wary of involvement for a long time, but still...

Elaine hadn't attended Tissy's or Jennifer's weddings. Jennifer had understood. Elaine couldn't bear to cry in front of people. That was okay. Bill was a super person. He'd be good for Elaine.

She laughed at herself. It was true. A happily married woman turned into a matchmaker. It seemed natural to want her friends to share the bliss.

Bradford chatted with Lij. The two men had started out teasing each other about being old married men and trying to decide whose wedding vows had promised the most to their women. After that, they'd gotten down to the real business of convincing each other the space program was either a boon to mankind with its spin-off technology—Lij's argument—or a waste of enormous resources better used for society's general benefit—Bradford's point of view.

Tissy, leaning against Bradford's arm, looked dreamy and content. She had organized a sit-in concerning women's rights on campus, to take place after the first of the year.

"Dinner," Jennifer called, drawing all eyes to her.

Lij turned his head. For a minute, he was outlined against the window, the moon shining over his right shoulder and forming a nimbus around his dark hair. Someday he'd probably be walking there, leaving his footprints in the six-inch layer of dust. She'd wait for him.

He grinned in that slow way he had, his eyes darkening with promises of good things to come. As soon as their guests left, his eyes seemed to say.

That happened about one o'clock in the morning, after they'd welcomed the New Year with laughter, kisses and a few tears. Then they'd said good-night to their guests and, arm in arm, watched them leave.

Lij locked the door against the December chill. Together they walked down the hall to the guest room and looked in on Amy. She slept like a cherub.

"She needs a brother or sister," Jennifer said, closing the door again.

He touched her under the chin, lifting her face to study it with undisguised love. "I had wondered if we'd have children. I was afraid to ask."

"I'd like to adopt Amy. If you wouldn't mind."

She felt him stop breathing for a long ten seconds before he answered. "That's a lot of commitment, lady. Like, forever."

"So is marriage." She was sure of herself now. She knew what she wanted, how much she could give, how much she could take.

"Then the answer is yes."

"I love you."

Lij held her close. "We're not so different, after all, are we?" he mused. "It's still love that makes the world go round."

"Roger that," she said with a catch in her throat.

Lij lifted her in his arms and carried her to their bedroom. It still amazed her that this man, this daredevil adventurer, could be so tender with her and Amy. Somewhere in his ancestry had been a caveman who had lifted his woman just like this and taken her to his cave—all tidied up to impress her, of course.

Jennifer smiled at the image. She did a lot of that lately, smiling and imagining things.

"Do you want to go to a demonstration?" she asked, toying with his hair.

Lij placed her on the bed and bent to take off her shoes. He lifted his eyebrows. "For peace?" He had never felt so content.

"For women's opportunities. Do you realize there are no women astronauts? What about female cadets at West Point?" Her grin was a challenge he couldn't ignore.

"I'll go."

He kissed her, unable to resist the sweetness of her lips. Her breasts were full and eager against his palms. He eased the sweater her grandmother had given her over her head and tossed it onto a chair.

She would never be a housewife in the traditional sense, which probably only existed in movies, anyway. She'd be off covering stories and joining sit-ins. He'd probably have to bail her out of jail someday.

She might worry him to death, but she'd also love him with every ounce of love she had in her. He'd take that. He'd have to. She was the love of his life.

And that's the way it is.

He wouldn't have it any other way.

H A R L E Q U I N
American Romance®

ABOUT THE AUTHOR

When Libby Hall was asked why she chose to write about the Sixties, she replied, ''The Sixties were, you know, like, wow, man!''

Libby entered the decade as a bride of less than six months, moving from a small Kentucky town to Cape Canaveral. She and her husband worked, went to college, had a daughter and bought their first house.

Libby witnessed each launch into space—Shepherd, Grissom, Glenn. Later as an engineer on the space program, she watched the last Apollo mission lift off. Before she left to write full-time, she received the NASA Outstanding Achievement Award for her work on the Apollo-Soyez mission.

''We came out of the Sixties less starry-eyed,'' Libby says, ''but when I look at my daughter just starting her family, I realize the age of Aquarius is still with us.''

The author of over a dozen novels written under her real name and the pseudonym Laurie Page, Libby Hall makes her home in the Bay Area.

Author's note: A controversy arose over Neil Armstrong's ''moon'' statement. The VOX transmission was: ''That's one small step for man; one giant leap for mankind.'' He meant to say: ''That's one small step for a man . . .'' After returning to Earth, Neil decided he really did leave the a out. Some history and quotation books have elected to use the corrected version, but I preferred to use the actual since I was writing in ''real'' time—LH

H A R L E Q U I N
American Romance®
RELIVE THE MEMORIES....

From New York's immigrant experience to San Francisco's Great Quake of '06. From the western front of World War I to the Roaring Twenties. From the indomitable spirit of the thirties to the home front of the Fabulous Forties to the baby-boom fifties... A CENTURY OF AMERICAN ROMANCE takes you on a nostalgic journey.

From the turn of the century to the dawn of the year 2000, you'll revel in the romance of a time gone by and sneak a peek at romance in an exciting future.

Watch for all the CENTURY OF AMERICAN ROMANCE titles coming to you one per month over the next four months in Harlequin American Romance.

Don't miss a day of A CENTURY OF AMERICAN ROMANCE.

A CENTURY OF
AMERICAN ROMANCE
1960s

The women... the men... the passions... the memories...

Coming soon
to an easy chair near you.

FIRST CLASS is Harlequin's armchair travel plan for the incurably romantic. You'll visit a different dreamy destination every month from January through December without ever packing a bag. No jet lag, no expensive air fares and *no* lost luggage. Just First Class Harlequin Romance reading, featuring exotic settings from Tasmania to Thailand, from Egypt to Australia, and more.

FIRST CLASS romantic excursions guaranteed! Start your world tour in January. Look for the special **FIRST CLASS** destination on selected Harlequin Romance titles—there's a new one every month.

NEXT DESTINATION:
THAILAND

 Harlequin Books

JTR2